About the au

John Fuller Ryan has a lifelong interest in World War II. He holds a Master's Degree with fifty additional credit hours in history.

John was fortunate, given his interests, to have been sent to Germany during military service in the early '60s. Among those Ryan met in Europe were *Wehrmacht* and *Luftwaffe* veterans, who he is afraid he hounded ceaselessly for details of their service. Many of the authentic 'soldier-slang' terms used in the novel, as well as the author's understanding of soldiers' attitudes as the war progressed, stem from this period.

Mr Ryan's interest in the period continued throughout his career as an educator and persists to this day. John has published articles based on veteran interviews for World War II-oriented publications, outlining the experiences of German, American and Soviet combatants. He has also written two commercially successful nonfiction books dealing with transportation logistics during the war.

THE MAN WHO FLEW
THE AMERIKA BOMBER

A NOVEL BASED ON THE HISTORY OF WORLD WAR II

JOHN FULLER RYAN

THE MAN WHO FLEW
THE AMERIKA BOMBER

A NOVEL BASED ON THE HISTORY OF WORLD
WAR II

Vanguard Press

A CIP catalogue record for this title is
available from the British Library.

ISBN 978 1 80016 186 3

*Vanguard Press is an imprint of
Pegasus Elliot MacKenzie Publishers Ltd.*
www.pegasuspublishers.com

First Published in 2021

**Vanguard Press
Sheraton House Castle Park
Cambridge England**

Printed & Bound in Great Britain

Dedication

The author wishes to dedicate this book to
veterans of all nations who helped him to
better understand the Great Conflict
of 1939–1945.

Acknowledgements

The author wishes to thank all of the people who helped with the creation of this book: All of the members of the Writer's Café sponsored by the Osher Lifelong Learning Institute at the University of Illinois, especially Frank Chadwick, under whose guidance the Café continues to encourage novices like me. Professor Emeritus Dick Figge, whose deep knowledge of German was of great value. Editors Elizabeth Piva and Phil Clinker who corrected my many errors with patience and understanding. Thanks to all of those in the reenacting community, whose insights were invaluable. Finally, I wish to thank my beloved wife Susan, without whose continual support none of this would have happened.

CHAPTER 1

"In German there is an expression, and even though I am Austrian, the expression is relevant: 'To live like God in France', meaning to live a perfect life and that is how we lived for a few years."

His accent was very mild, just a little softening of the "f" and a slight "v" sound to his "w", but it was distinctly German.

"So he probably is Germanic," she thought. *"He certainly looks like one, and he'd be about the right age — late 60s or early 70s."*

He did indeed look like a stereotypical German or ski-poster Austrian: a mane of white hair that she could tell had once been blond, large blocky head, eyes so blue they looked artificial.

He was a small, compact man, a physique she had learned was common among Europeans of his age. He was tanned and weathered, walked with a slight limp, and he coughed a lot, though she saw no evidence he was a smoker.

"*Ja*, we 'young eagles' lived well in the early days, forty-one or forty-two years ago, 1940, 1941 — after that it became not so good."

She nodded, sipped her coffee and he continued, "If you'd like to see what it was like, watch the first part of that old movie, *The Battle of Britain*. The film was made by United Artists in 1969, and it has all sorts of stars like Laurence Olivier and the young Michael Caine. You might want to look at it — it's on video; I have a copy if you'd like." He began to rise, but she waved him to sit again.

"Maybe later. Please, go on."

"Well, the first part of that movie shows what a German airstrip in France looked like, and all the pomp and ceremony that came with an inspection; but it also shows how we young pilots lived at the time. Like I said, *'Wie Gott in Frankreich'*."

"Yes, like God in France," she replied, and then, "So you flew for the *Luftwaffe* during the Battle of Britain?"

"*Ja*, and I flew in Spain before the big war, then in Poland, and I flew in Russia, and, believe it or not, I flew here."

"Here?" she asked, puzzled. "You mean you flew off the coast, or flew here in the US after the war?"

"No," he chuckled, with a slight cough. "I flew here to Maine, to Owl's Head, in 1944."

"Hold on, Mr Wald, are you trying to tell me that you flew a piston-engine airplane from Germany to the US forty years ago, in 1944?"

"No," he smiled, showing very white teeth, and laughed a bit again. "That would be a lie. I flew from Bergen, Norway, to Detroit, and then here to Owl's Head in 1944."

"That's pretty hard to believe, given the technology of the time; and I have some modest understanding of that technology."

"I know. That is one of the reasons I called you to tell my story. You see, I read your book."

"Oh, so *you're* the one," she replied, trotting out her standard answer.

She had worked hard on that book for four years, a story of France during the war based on a fragment of a memoir written by her mother and half-remembered second-hand stories told by her adoptive mother, Celine. Celine had known Peggy's biological mother well. They met after the war, before her biological mother died right after she, Peggy, was born.

Peggy had spent every spare hour writing, fact-checking, prying still-classified information out of archives. She had nearly gone broke travelling to England and France three times, tracking down old *resistants* and British SOE operators.

She had lost a first-rate reporting job and sacrificed a deep, promising long-term romantic relationship for that book. When it was finally finished, she pounded the word processor again, and again, pestering publishers and agents, earning a sore ear from telephoning her publishing contacts for another year. She built a fine pile of rejection letters, until she found a small publisher who took a chance on the book.

She had been so proud when it finally came out in print, a fine-looking little book with a nice slick cover that showed the Resistance Medal in blue, white and red. The book had gotten good reviews, and sold nearly a thousand copies. Then it had simply stalled. Now, four years later, it was sold on remainder tables, only a few copies each year, and some years none at all.

Now and then, though, some World War II buff would write to say that they had enjoyed it, or she would very occasionally meet someone who had read it. She had never made a dime, and, in fact, lost thousands travelling and paying for photocopies and old photographs; and now here was this old aviator, if that is what he was, saying he had read and admired it. *But what did that have to do with airplanes or a flight to the US?*

Sensing her confusion, he told her, "Your data on the performance of planes like the Wellington, the Lysander and the C47 are striking. That, and your stories about the crews of the Allied bombers, what they experienced before being shot down, those things made me think you might understand my story. Also," he added, "your papa and mama were very kind to me when I came here."

"You knew Pete?" she asked, eager to hear more; but his eyes were suddenly shiny, and he excused himself abruptly for a trip to the bathroom. She could hear him blowing his nose and clearing his throat, and when he returned his eyes were red and he was dabbing them with a tissue.

"Allergies," he muttered. "Bad this time of year." She nodded again, hoping to hear more about her adoptive father, her papa Pete, but he suddenly stood. "You have a car, yes?"

"Of course," she answered, rather briskly. *"Hell, did he think I hiked up here into the middle of the woods, five miles from town, in heels?"* Peggy thought.

"Oh, indeed, of course," he responded, grasping the situation. "Sometimes I forget how remote it is here. Could we take a short drive?"

Under different circumstances, she would have declined, but her mama Celine had sent her to see him, telling her he was someone she should meet, and Celine knew where she was, so she assumed she was safe. Moreover, there was a certain frailty about the man. She had at least twenty pounds and three inches on him, so she didn't have any worries about her safety. She had not worried about that from the moment she met him, because of that frailty and the inherent old-world courtesy she sensed from him. So, she decided to do what he asked.

Her little Toyota bumped down the rutted trail onto the blacktop, and he pointed right. "Please, the lighthouse." He indicated. Peggy knew what he meant, but wondered why he wanted to go there.

They drove in silence for a few minutes and then pulled up in the parking lot near the Owl's Head lighthouse.

She knew the place, of course. She had grown up in Owl's Head, and like every local schoolchild, she had been thoroughly indoctrinated about one of the town's primary tourist sites, the picturesque Owl's Head

Lighthouse. She'd had to visit Owl's Head Lighthouse on field trips every year until she had become entirely sick of the place. She hadn't been there in years, and now, as an adult, she saw it with new eyes.

In the summer light of late afternoon, the old building damn near glowed, sitting up on its little hill, a squat, white-painted tower, beautiful almost beyond belief. Peggy resisted the urge to cry out, utterly gob smacked, as her Brit friends used to say, at the unexpected effect it had on her. An overwhelming flood of memories and a sense of *belonging* stopped her where she stood.

"Maybe this is where I need to be right now," Peggy thought. She felt a little dizzy, but recovered quickly, shaking off the emotions, dismissing her feelings as mere nostalgia. "Built around 1824," she told him as she followed him up the steps to the overlook. He was panting and his limp seemed worse. When he got to the top, he paused to catch his breath. Then he straightened abruptly, wiped his mouth with a tissue and pointed out to sea. The ocean was spectacular from here, the shrieking white seabirds and dark sea contrasting sharply. A stiff onshore breeze was blowing, and he had to raise his voice to be heard.

"Out there, maybe a couple of miles from here, at the bottom of the sea, is an experimental German aircraft, a Junkers 390 six-engine airplane designed for long-range bombing, cargo-carrying and ocean patrol. Last machine I ever flew. It was put together from another, more famous long-range aircraft, the JU 290."

"The 290s are the aircraft that shadowed the North Atlantic convoys, right?"

"The very same."

"They replaced the Condor?"

"See, I knew I picked the right person for this story."

She felt a completely unaccustomed surge of pride, but immediately reined herself in. *"Who is this old guy anyway, that I should care what he thinks?"* Though she was pleased that he had recognized her hard work. After all, he was, or at least claimed to be, an expert. "What happened to the others — there must have been others, no?"

"All dead, I'm afraid. Two washed up on the beach around the end of September 1944, though I didn't know that at the time."

"But how…?"

He raised his hand. "That's enough for today. I don't have the stamina I once did, and I'm now tired. Would you mind driving me back?"

"Certainly," she said, and as they walked back to her battered little station wagon, she caught him looking at her closely, and then he looked away, blinking.

She dropped him at his remote cabin as it became twilight, and he told her he would contact her again for another chat, if that was all right. She agreed, though she had her reservations about his tale, and then pulled away down the trail as he waved goodbye. She got to the blacktop and headed for town, but suddenly, unaccountably, she was utterly overcome with grief, as if something had broken inside her.

Peggy hadn't cried much when Ian, her long-term boyfriend, moved out, nor when her papa Pete died. She hadn't cried much when her book went under, either. She was not, after all, some pampered princess. She grew up in the deep woods. She had chopped wood, tracked animals and hunted and fished with her papa Pete, who some said was the toughest game warden in the state of Maine.

Peggy had had a difficult time in high school; after the other kids found out she was adopted, they started calling her a "war bastard" a "D.P.", and other unkind things. She hadn't shed tears then; instead, it had resulted in some difficulties related to fighting until the taunting stopped.

Accepted by a demanding Journalism school, she received a small stipend, but to make ends meet waitressed in busy, sometimes unruly Boston bars and restaurants. Attractive, statuesque and tall, with black hair and striking hazel eyes, Peggy was always the target of whistles, suggestions and occasionally crude overt propositions.

She'd handled all of it with skill and charm, tucking better-than-average tips into her pocket, chaffing the would-be Romeos, and sometimes physically facing down potentially challenging drunks she'd had to deal with.

Peggy had graduated near the top of her class. She had landed a good job on a prominent Boston paper, at a time when women were unusual in the city rooms of major newspapers.

She was, or had been, a competent reporter in a difficult environment, and wasn't prone to sentiment, or so she thought. She had gained a reputation for single-mindedness when pursuing a story, and some of her colleagues found her lack of empathy and intensity off-putting. Much of the time she was sociable and a willing participant in office chat and the shenanigans that went on in a busy urban news organisation, but when she was immersed in a task, her colleagues discovered it was best to leave her alone.

It was understood that Peggy Pederson was often what they called "a serious person", not given to emotion when pursuing a story.

But today, she pulled onto the shoulder and cried — bawled, really — mourning her lost, valiant mother, and Pete, her often-silent, tough but beloved papa. She cried because she felt she had driven away Ian, her now-ex-boyfriend, while working so hard and concentrating so much on her writing.

She wept over the shitty outcome of the book she had worked so hard on, and the sacrifices she had made for it. She even mourned those poor lost German boys, washed up on a cold, stony autumn beach ever so many years ago.

She cried and sobbed and couldn't stop until a logging truck blew past, the blast of its bow wave rocking her car, its horn blaring, and startled her. Then she snuffled, straightened up, poked around for the hanky she knew she didn't have, wiped her eyes with the palms of her hands and drove on home.

CHAPTER 2

Peggy Pederson had returned to Owl's Head from Boston after Pete died in 1983.

With Pete's death, his widow, Celine, could no longer stay at the forest service cabin she and Pete had called home. So, with Pete's life insurance and assisted by her widow's pension, Celine purchased a little building in the settlement of Owl's Head. It was a storefront on the ground floor, with two nice one-bedroom apartments upstairs. The place, once equipped, was perfect for Celine's expanding catered baked goods business.

Celine now had two helpers, young girls from town, but she found she couldn't talk to them much, and she had become lonely. Celine asked Peggy to come home, at least for a while.

Peggy, recovering from the collapse of her book, the heartbreaking failure of an intense relationship, stuck in the unrewarding dead-end editing job she'd ended up with after getting fired from the newspaper, was tired of big city life. She was almost relieved to come back to Owl's Head.

Now thirty-six, Peggy worked part-time at the newspaper in nearby Rockland, editing, writing copy, doing a little reporting. She helped her mama with the baking, ordering supplies and making deliveries, living with Celine "over the store", as Peggy put it.

It comforted Peggy a great deal that she could justify the move as helping her mama — rather than just being another loser who hadn't made it in Boston.

The day after her visit with "the pilot in the woods", as she had started to think of him, she took a break from her work at the Rockland *Courier* and went to the basement archive, rolling through the microfiche until she came to September of 1944. There were a couple of items, neither of which were on the front page. The first said that a Coast Guard patrol craft had engaged a German submarine in Penobscot Bay off Vinalhaven Island on 18th of September.

The article stated that the Coast Guard had depth-charged the sub, and that bodies in German uniforms had later washed up near Owl's Head light. Also, according to the article, the FBI had taken charge of the investigation, the site where the bodies were found was cordoned off, and the corpses were removed to Boston "for further investigation".

The bodies had been found by a nineteen-year-old, walking on the beach, but the young man's name was given only as "Bill, a local lobsterman". A picture of the Coast Guard cutter was featured, along with a stock photo of a German submarine. The article was dated 28th of September 1944.

The second article was just a paragraph which noted that strange lights had been spotted by townspeople off the coast near Owl's Head on the night of 18 September. Authorities had investigated, and were unable to find any cause. "It may have been a trick of the moonlight," an FBI agent named Kelly was quoted as saying. That article was dated the 28th as well.

That afternoon, Peggy did a little more digging in the paper's research files, coming up with a Coast Guard chart that showed the area around Vinalhaven Island in Penobscot Bay. The waters in that area were not very deep, and the bay there was studded with small islands.

"Why would a submarine be in such shallow, crowded waters?" Peggy wondered. *"Hell, the U-boat I saw in Chicago looked pretty big and would be hard to hide, let alone navigate in such an area,"* she thought. She'd made a mental note to look into it further.

Peggy felt an excitement she hadn't experienced for a while. This was turning out to be something of a mystery, maybe even a story.

Later that day she had a talk with her editor, and asked him about the discrepancies she had noticed in the story.

He looked briefly at her copy of the articles, and said, "Of course, I wasn't here during the war, I was overseas, but this sort of article might just be a government plant."

"Could you explain that?" she asked, opening her notebook.

"Well, during the war the press was pretty tightly controlled, and harnessed to the war effort. That's why, for instance, people almost never saw a picture of

Franklin Roosevelt in his wheelchair, or anything else that authorities felt might adversely affect morale.

"Another example is when the Japanese fire-bombed the forests in the Pacific Northwest."

"You mean the balloon-bomb attack?"

"Nah," he replied. "They sent a couple of float planes to drop incendiary bombs and started some fires, which were quickly extinguished. The Japanese had these big subs that had a watertight compartment on the hull big enough to carry a small seaplane. The newspapers were told to report that the fires were started by lightning, lest people panic at the thought their cities might be bombed, and the newspapers obeyed. This might be that kind of story.

"You ought to see Ed Williams — he's the go-to guy for information on wrecks and so forth. He's given us a lot of good information over the years, but lately, since his wife died, he's been sort of a recluse. Lives outside of Owl's Head. Number's in the book. Now, how about that story on the testing problem at the high school?"

"Oh, that's finished and being checked by the feature editor. You should have it by this afternoon."

"Good," he said, and turned back to the papers on his desk.

After work, she went back to the microfiche and checked the articles again. *"Odd,"* she thought, *"the name of the patrol craft isn't given, no bow number is visible in the photo, and the crew aren't listed. Wouldn't they have wanted to give the local Coast Guard credit for sinking a submarine?"* All this information made Peggy wonder if this really might be a plant. *"Well, it will have to wait until tomorrow,"* Peggy said to herself. *"We've got the DeMarsh wedding cake and three dozen other orders to finish, and then there's always uncle's gateau."*

CHAPTER 3

After two weeks, Peggy finally made contact with Ed Williams. She had called his number twice, with no answer, not even an answering machine — so late one afternoon she drove out to his little cottage on the outskirts of Owl's Head. As she pulled up on the gravel driveway, she was greeted by three yelping hound-looking dogs, throwing themselves against a rickety picket fence.

The screen door of the small run-down house banged open and a bearded man appeared, yelling at the dogs. When he saw her, he called out, "I don't want whatever yer sellin', and I don't need no help, so just be on your way."

"Mr Williams, just give me a minute. My name is Peggy Pederson and I'm a reporter for the Rockland *Courier-Gazette*. I want to ask you a few questions about a submarine the Coast Guard depth-charged in 1944. My editor said you've been helpful in the past."

He raised his voice to be heard over the dogs' yelping. "Submarine? I don't know nothing about that, so you're barking up the wrong tree, young lady."

He turned and was stepping back into the house as she said, "OK, I'm sorry to have troubled you, but I brought this cake from my mama, who told me to say 'hi' when I saw you."

The bearded man paused, then asked, "So who's yer mama, then?"

"Celine Pederson."

"Shut the hell up," he bellowed, and Peggy took a step back, before she realized he was yelling at the dogs. "Are you Pete Pederson's girl?"

"That I am."

"Well, I'll be dipped," he drawled. "I can't turn down a cake from Celine, that's for damned sure, and Pete did me a couple of good turns over the years, so I guess I can give you a minute."

After she negotiated the overgrown yard and the attentions of the three suddenly affectionate hounds, she found herself seated in a surprisingly tidy kitchen with a hot cup of coffee, while he carefully carved a slice of the beautifully decorated cake, she had asked her mother to make.

The cake was a trick she learned from a crusty old crime reporter on her first newspaper job. He told her if she wanted co-operation, there was nothing like pastry to smooth the way, and she found it to be true. Firemen, policemen, taxi drivers, maintenance workers, hotel staff... Everybody, it seemed, appreciated a little treat to brighten their day, and became more willing to give her the few minutes she needed to nail down a story.

"Doughnut diplomacy, kid," the reporter had growled at her, "works every time, and if doughnuts don't work, try whiskey."

She hid a smile at the memory, declined Williams' offer of a slice of cake. "Do you mind telling me how you knew Pete?"

"Oh, hell, Pete was the best," Williams laughed. "You know, during the war, Pete was kind of the law hereabouts, at least for the things the sheriff in Rockland couldn't handle, and in those days, before I married my Bessie and settled down, you might say I was sort of rough. One night I was up at the tavern —drunk, I suppose — and got in a fight with some loudmouthed canuck logger. Well, he pulled a knife and I broke a beer bottle and we was just about to go at it, when Pete walked in. Like I said, I was a rough one in those days, and I had a terrible temper — I had murder in my heart, and God knows what woulda happened if the bartender hadn't called Pete.

"Pete looked at us and just hollered, 'What do you two assholes mean, wakin' me up at two a.m. and makin' me leave my sweet little wife and warm bed? Now you two stop all this damned nonsense and get on home before somebody gets hurt.'" Williams chuckled at the memory.

"Well," Williams continued after a sip of coffee and a bite of cake, "that logger looked Pete up and down and saw he didn't have a gun or nothin', so he starts advancing on Pete with that knife and says, 'Why, you goddamn one-legged no-good herring-choking Swede, get outta here or I'll cut your damn throat!' And he looked like he meant it. But old Pete, he just got in that logger's face and bellered, 'I ain't no goddamn one-

28

legged no-good herring-choking Swede, damn you, I'm a goddamn one-legged no-good herring-choking *Norwegian*, and don't you forget it!' And Pete's accent got so rich and comical that everybody in the place just started laughing, laughing till our sides hurt, and the logger, he just started laughing, too.

"Then everybody calmed down, and Pete, he bought us a beer and left."

"What a great story," Peggy said, pleased, as always, to have heard more about her papa.

"Pete used to handle stuff like that all the time," Williams said. "People still tell that story and they mimic Pete's accent. Heck, it still gets a laugh." He went on, "I was only nineteen then; I got drafted a month later. I was sent to the Pacific, and when I came back my Bessie and I got married, I bought my boat, and the rest, like they say, is history."

"Do you remember anything about September of 1944?"

"Sure, I do. I'm old, but I'm not senile yet. But the FBI told everybody not to say anything—" He scrunched his eyebrows and gently rubbed the top of his head. "Ah, hell, that don't matter no more, does it?"

"Unless you signed something, you don't have to worry about telling me. I've checked on that for some other work I've done. You can tell what happened or what you know."

"Okay," Williams answered, "but I don't want my name in the paper. Can you promise me that?"

"Yes, I can. It's what we call 'on background', and if I ever did want to use your name, I would have to have your permission."

"All right, then, on background, like you say."

Williams stood and poured more coffee for both of them, got another slice of cake and started in: "I was the one who found them bodies on the beach."

Her hair stood on end. *"What unbelievable luck!"* she thought.

He continued, "I was walkin' the beach, lookin' for some lobster pots I'd lost, and come across the bodies. There was two of them, been in the water a while, and they were dressed like pilots or such-like."

"But the paper said they were from a submarine the Coast Guard sank off Vinalhaven Island."

Williams snorted and, after a sip of coffee, said, "There wasn't no sub anywhere near Vinalhaven, and no sub would ever go there. I lobstered those waters for years, and it's too shallow for a sub. There's no wrecks out there, either. And if them Coasties from Rockland had sunk a U-boat, they'd *still* be braggin' about it! No, these boys came from an airplane, but Kelly, he was the one who made up the submarine story and gave it to the paper."

"Who is Kelly?" she asked, as if she didn't already know.

"Kelly was the FBI guy they flew out from Boston after Pete called the sheriff. He was kinda a loudmouth, and he kept callin' me 'Bill', 'cause my last name is Williams, even though I told him my right name. I didn't like him much, but he seemed to know his job. As soon as he got to the beach, he got the Coast Guard guys to keep people away, and he had a photographer from the Navy base come and take pictures before they moved the bodies."

"Pictures? He got pictures?" Peggy thought, already mentally framing the Freedom of Information Act request she would file. "OK, let's go back a bit. How do you know they came from a plane?"

"Oh, well," Williams answered, "when I was in the Pacific during the war, I was a mate on a search and rescue craft that operated near our carriers, and we pulled out a half-dozen airmen that had ended up in the water. They were not German, of course, but they all had pretty much the same gear: you know, leather jackets, throat mikes, headphones, oxygen masks — and these bodies on the beach, they were dressed like that. Plus, I got the hat."

"H-h-h?" Peggy stuttered. "Hat, what hat?"

"Wait a minute," Williams answered, and left the room. She could hear him muttering to himself and fumbling around. Then he returned with a blue military cap, which he handed her.

"You got this where?"

"I got it on the beach, next to one of them bodies. It's a German air force cap. I checked."

She looked at the blue cloth in her hand, mothed a bit, faded; the silver trim around the edge was green and corroded. There was an eagle on the front, clutching a swastika, and some kind of cording forming a triangle.

"Look inside," Williams told her.

Peggy looked, and almost jumped out of her chair. There was faint writing on the leather sweatband. *"Was it a name?"* Peggy wondered.

"Did you ever show this to anyone?"

"Only Pete, 'cause he was the first one to come to the beach after I sent the kid to get him."

"Kid?"

"Yeah, a kid came by, walkin' his dog, and I told him to go fast and get Pete, and Pete come down in his Jeep. I showed him the cap and he told me to hang on to it, not to lose it, in case anybody asked about it. We dragged the bodies up above the high-tide line. Then the sheriff came, and the Coast Guard, the FBI guy, and half of Owl's Head, so I sort of forgot it was in my jacket pocket.

"I forgot all about it until I got home, then stuck it in a drawer. Nobody ever asked about it, and then when I found it again years later, I thought I might get in trouble 'cause I didn't turn it in right away, so I just put it back in the drawer — haven't thought about it much over the years, except I looked it up once in a book to be sure what it was."

Later, when Peggy said goodbye, she asked permission to borrow the cap, and asked if she could return to talk again.

"Oh, sure. Especially if you bring some more of that cake." He shooed the dogs away as he walked her to the gate.

"I always kinda wondered what the dickens that was all about, so would you let me know what you find out?"

"Of course."

"Oh, and you might want to have a talk with Cap Roberts, who fishes outta Rockland. He's told me some stories about somethin' snaggin' fishing gear out past Owl's Head light."

"I certainly will do that," she replied, as he turned back to the house, roaring at the dogs; and, raising her voice, she called after him, "Thank you!"

"Say hi to Celine," he answered, as the screen door banged shut.

CHAPTER 4

The next time Peggy made her way to see the "pilot in the woods", she had some information of her own. But first, she told him, she wanted to hear his story from the beginning.

"OK, well, my name is—"

"I already know that, I think," she said, flipping to a page in her notebook. "You are Maximillian Hans-Georg, Hereditary Baron von Waldberg, born Kufstein, Austria, in 1911, am I right?"

"*Ja*, but how—?"

"I searched records held in the Bundesarchiv in Koblenz, and a *Luftwaffe* history. After all, there weren't all that many Austrian aviators, and you are listed as 'missing, presumed dead' in 1944. And the name you are using — 'Wald' — was a bit of a giveaway once I got into the records.

"I also followed up with some local people. One told me about some bodies washed up on the beach in fall of '44, and another who told me that since the war, scallop fishermen have avoided an area about two-and-a-half miles off Owl's Head Light, because something was damaging their dredges in that area. I've also filed a Freedom of Information Act request with the FBI for photographs, but I doubt they will comply.

"I am convinced that if you are some sort of crackpot, you are a very clever one and I am prepared to proceed with your story as genuine until proven otherwise."

"How complimentary," he remarked archly, but she held up her hand.

"I mean no disrespect, but I am trained as a journalist, and we were taught to start at the beginning, and, if you are unhappy about my scepticism, we were also taught that: 'If your mother says she loves you, check it out.'"

They both laughed and the mood in the room was noticeably lighter. "I want to hear about you, about flying, about your family."

"OK, miss reporter lady, let's start at the beginning."

Peggy turned on her recorder and nodded at Max to begin.

Later, when she played back the recordings, this is what she typed up for her notes:

Maximillian, Baron von Waldberg, born 1911, Kufstein, Austria, to Hauptmann Otto von Waldberg and Maria *née* Kesselstein von Waldberg. Max hardly knew his father, who left for the war in 1915 and was killed in 1917 in France. Otto was an aviator, flying with the famous von Richtofen squadron, which was at that time commanded by Hermann Goering, later head of Hitler's *Luftwaffe* and until 1945, Hitler's designated successor. Otto was born German, thus he flew for the

Imperial German air force, rather than that of Austria. He was shot down and killed while flying a reconnaissance mission over British lines.

After his father's death, Max and his mother Maria moved in with Maria's mother, Margarethe, Gräfin von Kesselstein, who was also a widow. The two women were a formidable pair. Maria was well educated, trained as a linguist and translator, while her mother Margarethe had been thoroughly tutored at home, as was the custom for aristocratic women at the time. Together, the two managed the von Kesselstein estate, a few miles from Kufstein, supervising agricultural and artisan operations with great skill.

Maria's portion of the Von Waldberg family holdings was sold for cash, allowing Maria and Max considerable security, as the funds were managed by an astute English banker. Maria also made a fair sum doing translation and multilingual correspondence for publishing houses, and this increased her sense of independence.

Despite her elegant upbringing, grandmother Margarethe had served as a nurse in German army hospitals during the World War I, and had developed a pragmatic, even cynical view of her aristocratic countrymen, who constantly bemoaned their financial losses after 1918.

Her feeling was that if she had seen the chaos coming, so should they. She was also convinced that the hereditary aristocracy was an anachronism that neither Germany nor Austria would long continue to tolerate.

So, she secured her property from roving bands of communists and "other bandits", as she called them, by hiring guards from the local shooting club. Such organizations, called *Schützenverein*, had a long tradition of being ceremonial bodyguards for the aristocracy, and this particular group was fiercely loyal to the family.

The women safeguarded their funds by getting most of the family money out of the country (using totally illegal couriers) before ruinous inflation took hold. After a period of disruption, things calmed down and the two women settled into a comfortable existence, living well but not in luxury, both knowing that they had a considerable financial cushion salted away in a number of foreign currencies, gold, diamonds and trustworthy foreign banks, should bad times recur.

The women shared an unusually liberal philosophy about child-rearing, and after initially being privately tutored, Max attended a local Catholic school for boys. The headmaster was cautioned by Maria not to treat Max differently than other students. This, along with a substantial donation, assured that Max was taught and disciplined as all of the other boys, and referred to as "Master Waldberg" rather than by his title.

Max indicates he was also allowed considerable freedom when away from his lessons. He roamed about the Austrian countryside on his bicycle, and became familiar with many of the local farmers and craftsmen, whose sons he already knew from school. Max was very interested in the blacksmithing and woodworking trades, and hung about those shops when he got a chance. Like many young Austrians, he developed an interest in skiing, and also had a few other hobbies. Like many boys his age, he liked mechanical gadgets, and tinkered with intricate clocks, mechanical toys and locks. But above all else, Max says, he became utterly fascinated by aircraft and aviation.

At age fourteen, Max wangled a ride in an airplane piloted by the same Hermann Goering who had commanded his father's unit during the war — though he didn't immediately know that. Goering had been making barnstorming tours of Germany and Austria, eking out a living by performing aerial shows and collecting fees for rides in his open-cockpit plane. He was also accepting charters to fly wealthy people about, and had just completed one such flight to Kufstein. When Max learned there was an actual airplane nearby, and that the pilot would be staying in the town's hotel overnight, he emptied his little savings box and leapt on his bike, pedalling the distance to the village in record time.

Goering was tired, but tempted by a gold coin the boy offered, a keepsake given to Max by his uncle, he and Max were soon aloft. Max recounts he felt he was going mad with happiness during the short flight, even standing upright in the back seat until ordered to sit and buckle his seatbelt. Even a few stunts and rolls did not alter his enthusiasm, and he begged for another ride the next day. Goering asked his name, and when told, he confirmed the boy's father's name and gave him his coin back, telling him his own name, and praising the boy's father. Unfortunately, Goering said he had to return with his aircraft to Denmark the next day. Max remembers Goering saying he believed some day, Max might fly his own airplane, and gave Max his address.

The next day, Goering's Curtiss Jenny circled Schloss Kesselstein, waggled its wings and flew off. Max shouted himself hoarse, running and waving until the plane was out of sight. After that, Max says he took greater interest in his studies, especially in mathematics and physics, and was constantly tinkering with flying gadgets.

He started with kites and then moved on to elaborate model airplanes, all the while reading every book on aviation in the local library and sending for others from booksellers. Since he had learned excellent English from his British tutor and his mother, he even ordered books from overseas, and managed to struggle through many unfamiliar technical terms. He learned more English in the process, as well as a little French.

At first, Maria and Margarethe indulged the boy's obsession, thinking it a harmless phase, but in 1927, when sixteen-year-old Max tried to make his bicycle fly, and was injured in the process, they knew something had to be done.

Max says he had done the mathematics, and wheedled his friend's woodworker father into making an impressive pair of wings. He got metal attachments made by a blacksmith and assembled the whole apparatus secretly. Then, cheered on by a crowd of his schoolmates and barking dogs, he raced the contraption down a steep hill, and, for a brief but glorious moment, actually became airborne.

Then the whole thing went "ass over teakettle", and he crashed awkwardly, breaking his right ankle in a cloud of dust. "I must have miscalculated the centre of gravity," Max recalls muttering. The local doctor treated his painful injury.

Thereafter, a furious and badly frightened Maria simply forbade Max from "messing with flying machines", and that was that! Airplanes had killed his father, she told him, and she'd be damned if they were going to kill him as well.

Max was miserable, moping about on crutches, eating little, and he became disinterested in schoolwork. His grades suffered and he was sulky and irritable, snapping at his mother and barking at the staff. Worst of all, he wasn't doing the exercises needed to properly rehabilitate his broken ankle, and Maria and Margerethe both feared he would end up with a disabling limp.

After a month of this, the headmaster, who was also troubled by Max's decline, showed up with an idea. He told Maria that a local youth organisation had established a glider club, training boys to fly in safe, well-built, unpowered aircraft that were towed aloft by trucks or other aircraft. The group was supervised by skilled pilots, the teacher said, who carefully instructed the boys before they flew. He also informed Maria that there was a drawback — that the gliding club was sponsored by the local Nazi party branch, of which neither of them approved.

The teacher told Maria that his understanding was that they were training young men in gliders to circumvent the restrictions of the postwar Versailles Treaty, which limited pilot training in Germany and Austria.

That night, Max learned later, Maria sat down with Margerethe and they discussed the problem. Margerethe finally concluded that the sponsors might be Nazis, but they were *Austrian* Nazis, not the *saupreussen* (Prussian swine) and other oafs that were causing so much trouble in Germany. Margarethe felt that between her, Maria, the schoolmaster and the parish priest, they could probably handle any political nonsense they might try to put into the boy's head. All of them knew Max was desperately unhappy, so after a lecture it was agreed that when his ankle was properly healed and his grades and behavior improved, he could apply for the glider club.

Five months later, Max, whose grades and gait were much better, was delighted to be accepted by the Austrian National Socialist Flying Corps youth glider program, and within another six months he was soaring above the gorgeous Austrian countryside. He even got a few brief clandestine lessons from the pilot of the tow plane — a badly banged-about surplus Fokker that, as the pilot put it, "flew like a wounded omnibus".

That notwithstanding, Max says he truly excelled at flying. Instructors noted he flew with great joy and skill, but he was also conscious of the limitations of the old aircraft, and flew safely. He was also patient, sitting calmly through lectures on Aryan superiority and other "Nazi Claptrap", as he thought of it.

Max's family had dealt with Jewish merchants and tenants for centuries, and there was a well-established Jewish aristocracy in Austria, so Max discounted most of what the instructors called "Racial Theory" as political pandering to lure ultra-nationalists and racists to the Nazi cause. However, Max *was* excited, as many young men were, about the enormous changes sweeping Germany.

He liked the camaraderie with boys who shared his interests, and he enjoyed the marching and group singing, and the swagger of the smart uniform the glider club wore. He could not help but admire the efficiency of the new German regime, as they reduced unemployment, stabilized the economy, rebuilt the army, and "Made Germany Awake".

Essentially, he didn't care who was in charge, as long as they let him fly.

Max's enthusiasm and discipline were recognized by staff, and with their recommendations, his family contacts and his excellent grades, Max was accepted at age eighteen to the tiny Austrian air force as an aviation cadet.

The Austrian air force was a paramilitary organisation, secretly supported by the small *Bundesheer* (Austrian army), flying surplus American, British and Italian aircraft. In eighteen months, Max was rated a competent pilot, within the limitations of the meagre resources of the post-Versailles Austrian air force. He was commissioned as a Junior Lieutenant.

Max was assigned as an instructor first to one of the glider programs, and then to another of Austria's clandestine pilot-training programs, an ostensibly civilian flying club, operating from an unobtrusive grass airstrip. The club was training future military pilots with obsolete World War I aircraft and a few newer machines purchased from Italy and the US.

Max says he loved the work, though it was slightly routine, and he felt he was doing it well, when he was summoned to a nearby commercial airport to meet with the airport manager. Max worried about what might have prompted this summons. Had one of his trainees buzzed the place, flown too low or done stunts over the field? He parked at the administration building and was directed to the office of the manager, a man he immediately recognized.

The airport manager was Benno von Fernbrugg, a highly-decorated leading flyer of the First War Austrian air force. Max felt stunned. He had long admired Von Fernbrugg — not only as a great pilot, but as an innovator. Trained as a mechanical engineer, Fernbrugg was among the first to experiment with aircraft-mounted machine guns, airborne radio and other technical breakthroughs, meanwhile shooting down something like twenty-eight enemy aircraft.

Max had Fernbrugg's photo on the wall of his room at home, and sincerely hoped that he hadn't been summoned for some disciplinary reason.

Max asked what he could do for Von Fernbrugg. To his great relief, the famous flyer offered him a drink, clapped him on the back, asked after his family, and then jovially got down to business, asking Max if he was interested in flying for an airline. Fernbrugg told Max that he and other senior figures were aware of what Max had done for the fledgling Austrian air force and his country, at low pay and with no public appreciation, but that the country needed Max to move along so that they could open his position to another potential pilot.

Given the severe financial limitations of the army under the Versailles restrictions, the older man continued, some of the men already trained must leave so others could be accepted into training. In order to do that, Fernbrugg explained, he was encouraging Max to take a position with Austria's new commercial airline, the *Österreichische Luftverkehrs AG*, and learn to fly heavier aircraft.

The pay would be higher, the work interesting, he would still be flying and he would be granted a reserve commission as a captain. This way, Austria would retain his skill as a pilot while opening a position for a new trainee, and what did Max think?

Max was floored, confused, and then intrigued. He really didn't want to fly transports, but it was certainly better than wet-nursing cadets and flying alone only once a week. Within a few minutes, he agreed, and within a week he was at flight school near Vienna — a benefit in itself — doing classroom work which amounted to an extremely intense course in aeronautical engineering, fulfilling his ambition for a better understanding of the physics of flight.

After four months, he was introduced to the transport workhouse of European commercial aviation in the '30s, the iconic Junkers JU 52 Trimotor. The JU 52 was not a beautiful aircraft. It was boxy and constructed of corrugated metal, which made it resemble a farm building, but it handled well in the air unless there was a strong crosswind. Landing was difficult, but once that was mastered, the aircraft was astonishingly versatile.

The JU could take off and land using short, primitive grass runways, could accommodate 4,000lb of cargo or eighteen passengers, and in military service it could carry bombs, torpedoes or twelve fully-loaded troops. Max was not thrilled to be flying such a lumbering airplane, but flying was flying, and he learned quickly. By 1937, he was rated as a qualified transport pilot, and was working a regular route between Vienna and Munich, carrying passengers and mail.

It was in Munich that Max learned of Hitler's plan to annex Austria into the *Reich*.

CHAPTER 5

At this point, Peggy added a personal *aide memoire* to keep historical events straight for later reference: **Members of Adolf Hitler's Nazi Party were elected to the German parliament by a slim margin in 1932, and then a powerful coalition of business and financial interests coalesced to promote Hitler's rise to *Reichskanzler*, or prime minister. These influential men thought that by promoting Hitler, they could control the unruly masses of his party, dismantle a perceived Communist menace, and "buy Hitler off" with a certain degree of respectability, while limiting his power. They had underestimated Hitler and his henchmen.**

Almost immediately upon Hitler's assumption of office in 1933, the German parliament building was set afire and destroyed. Hitler blamed the Communists, and panicked legislators with the threat that a nationwide Communist uprising was in progress, stoking their fear with hysterical articles in his tame newspapers. Hitler demanded and was granted sweeping emergency powers to control the (largely exaggerated) "Red Menace".

Thereafter, Germany was ruled as a dictatorship by Hitler and his cronies.

Between 1933 and 1938, Hitler consolidated his grip on power in Germany. He jailed or murdered political opponents, and cowed any resistance with brutally applied force. In 1936, Hitler marched troops into the Allied-controlled Rhineland in violation of the Versailles Treaty, and France and England did nothing. He announced the re-establishment of military conscription, and again, the victorious powers did not act.

Then, in 1938, Hitler was poised to occupy Austria, which occurred on 12th March. Thereafter, the Austrian Army was absorbed into the German *Wehrmacht*, so the Austrian air force became part of the *Luftwaffe*.

Peggy's transcript of Max's narrative continues:

Since Max was an officer in the Austrian reserves, he was encouraged to "volunteer" for special duty, and advised that refusal was not a viable option. There were many fine positions available in the infantry, Max remembers the selection officer saying, should Max choose not to use his aviation skills to serve the New Greater Germany. So, shortly thereafter, in May of 1938, Max found himself flying transports in Spain.

His flights were in service of the Nationalist faction in a civil war, a faction supported by Hitler and Mussolini, against the Republican forces supported by Moscow and left-leaning international groups.

Germany established a bogus airline in Spain to avoid direct involvement, and the aircraft were painted up in those colors, but were still the same old trustworthy JU 52s.

Meanwhile, turmoil disrupted Austrian civil life, mostly in Vienna, as anti-Nazi leaders were carted off to prison, Jews were beaten in the streets and Nazi-inspired mobs burned synagogues. Police arrested dissidents and prominent Roman Catholics.

In Kufstein, Maria and Margerethe helped those they could, and found that the Nazis, try though they might, could not penetrate the circles of intense clan, religious and family loyalty which characterized their remote and mountainous region. Maria and Margerethe maintained contact with local Austrian authorities and rural police, making sure they received ample warning of any raids or searches.

After all, Margerethe had done her duty nursing in World War I, and Maria was the widow of a decorated soldier, whose only son was serving Germany as a distinguished flier. Were not such women above suspicion?

They managed to get word to Max that they were all right through the Austrian old boy network, and Max was relieved that they were safe.

The Von Waldbergs and Von Kesselsteins had produced military officers, diplomats and government officials since the days of Frederick the Great and Empress Maria Theresa respectively, so both Austrian and German roots ran deep. The two women had an immense network of resources to mobilize if needed, so

Max was confident they could weather any political storms.

Max was not aware at the time of the virulence of Hitler's campaign against the Jews. Max says, "No one believed the threats the Nazis made. In certain nationalist right-wing political circles in Germany and Austria, phrases like 'corrupt influence of world Jewry' and calls to eliminate 'the stranglehold of Jewish bankers' and other such slanders were routine. Such rantings were considered *de rigueur* for these parties, like 'America First', 'Tough on Communism' and 'Tough on Crime' have been in American politics — just a means of appealing to a certain sort of voter."

At this point, Max broke off his narrative and began to tell Peggy about a video of a play called *The Wannsee Conference* that she might want to see. It is a German film with English subtitles, and Max offered it as a way of explaining some of Hitler's campaign against the Jews. Peggy encouraged Max to return to his narrative, promising to watch the video if she could, and Max began again.

Max dutifully drove his "flying truck", ferrying supplies to the Nationalist forces, until one day he got sloppy, flew a bit too low, and had half of his tailplane sawn off by a Republican machine gunner. That damage caused Max and his co-pilot to crash just inside Nationalist lines, and while both men were unhurt, the aircraft was a total loss. The incident was a wake-up call for Max that this was war, not training.

That was at the end of September, 1938, and Max was grateful for the respite, though he regretted the loss of the aircraft. He and his co-pilot had been flying nearly non-stop since May, shuttling troops (mostly Moroccan Moors under Spanish officers), ammunition, food and once a cargo of six mules. The mules hadn't liked flying at all, and had made an unholy mess of the plane. He and his co-pilot became the butt of a thousand muleskinner jokes, and they were greeted by their comrades with braying for months.

It took them a week to get back to their unit, shuttled from village to village by cheerful North African Nationalist soldiers in a series of wheezing trucks. One of Hitler's first acts in support of Franco had been to provide a fleet of transports to fly thirteen thousand of these soldiers — the bulk of Franco's army — from Africa to Spain. Without these troops, Franco would have gotten nowhere. It was no wonder that Hitler was furious when Franco insisted that Spain remain neutral during the subsequent world war.

By the time they got back, things had changed, and what had been a sleepy rear-area supply base, now was swarming with soldiers, trucks and airplanes.

A surprise Republican offensive on the Ebro River had begun, and all aircraft were required to support the beleaguered Nationalists. So, the very next day, Max and his co-pilot were assigned a new aircraft, another JU 52. Instead of the usual supplies — food, fuel and so forth — it was loaded with bombs: small bombs from the First War, stored upright in wooden frames, in groups of twelve. And they had two men added to their crew, a couple of very young *Luftwaffe* mechanics.

Max's unit commander, an elderly major, told Max, "I am delighted you are back, and just in the nick of time. We are short of pilots for an unusual operation. Nationalist forces are held up by Basque fighters in this area" — he showed the two pilots a spot on his map — "and we must assist them; so today, my fine young gentlemen, you will be flying a bomber, not a cargo plane." At least, Max says, that's how he remembers it.

"Just follow me, like everyone else, and your crew will know what to do." Before either Max or his co-pilot, a young Berliner named Alfons Dietrich, could ask a question or get any details, they were airborne, following ten other JUs in a loose formation. After a few minutes they were joined by a group of JU 87 dive bombers, and then four Bf 109 fighters as an escort, and finally the whole group of aircraft droned along together, the nimble 109s weaving around the slower planes so as not to leave them behind.

Max eyed the fighters enviously as the shark-like, yellow-nosed planes sped by, gaining altitude in case any Republican fighters showed up. "Damn, *Herr Hauptmann*, this is more like it," crowed Dietrich — he had often complained of the dullness of their mundane transport tasks. "This is the sort of thing which can bring Iron Crosses, no?" the younger man shouted over the engine noise and the wind blowing in through the open rear cargo door.

"You pay attention, or you'll end up with a wooden cross," an irritated Max says he barked as he saw the squadron leader's wings waggle, and objects start falling from the side of his aircraft. *"Jesus, are they just going to chuck them out the door?"* He turned to see that this was precisely what the two, ground crew were doing, one turning a wrench on each bomb's fuse, the other kicking them out of the cargo door, still in their wooden cases.

Max looked down and saw a small village, perched on the side of a mountain above a winding road, looking much like villages in Austria, except hotter and drier. He saw a crowd on the road, and another in the village square, all the people looking up, dressed in bright clothing, some even waving; and then everything disappeared in a gigantic cloud of dust and smoke.

The squadron commander waggled his wings again, and the formation followed him, circling to return to the rising pillar of smoke and dust, to make another pass over the carnage, pitching the rest of their bombs into the seething mass below. Then, as Max pulled away, he saw the dive bombers in line astern dropping one by one to add their bombs to the inferno. Max felt ill. The crew in the back closed the cargo door and sat back on the bench along the side of the aircraft, lighting cigarettes and punching each other, signaling thumbs-up and making explosion motions.

Max shot a glance at Dietrich as he fought the air currents created by the blasts, and was gratified that the younger man seemed subdued. Both men realized that not a single shot had been fired from the ground, that no military vehicles or fortifications had been spotted, and not a single enemy aircraft had shown up.

"What have we done, *Herr Hauptmann*?" asked Dietrich.

"I don't know," Max says he answered, "*but I don't want to do it again.*"

CHAPTER 6

After completing her notes, Peggy spent every spare minute verifying everything she could, following up with a large newspaper collection in Boston, and trying to confirm dates and other data with public library computers and phone calls to other archives.

She also watched the two movies Max mentioned. The first, about the Battle of Britain, was as good a war movie as she had ever seen, and did indeed capture something of the lifestyle of German pilots in France.

The second was far more difficult to find, and, once she found it, even more difficult to watch. The filmed drama was based on a single surviving transcript of meeting minutes from an elegant conference centre outside Berlin in January 1942, during which the German leadership discussed the mechanics of the extermination of European Jewry. Present at this meeting were officials of the Nazi party, functionaries of the SS, some civilians representing industry, economic planning, the legal system, and administrators of conquered Eastern territories.

The pivotal point of the film was, at least to Peggy, the slowly-dawning realisation, especially among the civilian lawyers present, that the Nazi leadership was actually planning — indeed, beginning to carry out —

the systematic murder of millions of people. Not only did these men begin to comprehend the horrible reality of the Nazis' goal, but she could watch them as they started to understand that they, themselves, would be inescapably complicit in one of history's greatest crimes.

As Peggy turned off the VHS machine, an old proverb came to her: *"He who sups with the devil had best bring a long spoon."*

These bureaucrats had spouted Nazi rhetoric, gone along with the program for personal gain and career advancement, and now they found themselves aghast, staring into the abyss, unable to escape responsibility. They had dined with the devil, and now the devil had them by the throat. Their spoons had not been long enough.

"Not long enough indeed," Max mused, as she quoted him the proverb at their next meeting, after tea and some questions from Max about her childhood and career.

"How about *your* spoon, *Herr* Baron?" she asked. "I've read about some of the bombing in Spain, the killing of civilians with no cause or warning. In fact," she went on, "some of the sources state, that it was done for *practice*, to test how well the bombs and aircraft worked. So how long was *your* spoon?" She was calm, but she was angry.

"I see what you mean — and please call me Max," he replied. "Maybe that raid was some sort of test, but I never found out, because two months later, I left."

"You mean you left the service?"

"*Ach, nein*, one didn't leave the service in Germany unless it was feet first. No, I left Spain and went back to Germany to train as a fighter pilot."

"How did you pull that off?"

"Remember I told you that I met Goering when I was a kid?" She nodded. "Well, I wrote to him, reminded him of our meeting and my father's connection, and begged for a transfer to fighters. By some miracle, he saw my letter, remembered me, and approved my reassignment."

"How did that help? You were still flying for the same regime."

"*Ja*, that is so, but at least in fighters, I thought, if I had to kill somebody, it would be somebody that was trying to kill me."

Peggy remained impassive. "Then what?"

"Well, then it was back to school for me. I was twenty-seven by then, a little old for fighter training, but the younger students couldn't tease me because I was, after all, a captain, while they were still lieutenants. Even still, there was a certain amount of snickering. Anyway, a lot of the theoretical stuff could be waived because of my earlier training and experience.

"So, after I successfully flew some of the older models, I finally got permission to fly the Bf 109, which later became famous as the Messerschmidt, at that time considered one of the greatest fighter aircraft ever designed."

"That must have been quite a change from transports."

"It was indeed. The 109 was hard to taxi, as the pilot could not see over the nose until the plane rotated to take off, and one had to turn this way and that…"

"Zig-zag?"

"*Ja*, like you say, 'zig-zag' while taxiing until the speed was high enough to rotate the airplane and take off. In the air the thing was so damn *fast* that at first, I had trouble keeping up with it, and gunnery was something entirely new to me, so that took a lot of practice. Landing was hard, too, because the 109 had a very narrow landing gear and was hard to control, especially on grass runways.

"Later in the war, a lot of young pilots and airplanes were lost because they crashed on landing, but I got good enough within six months to fly and shoot without embarrassing myself, and was assigned to a squadron near Berlin for further experience. Then, after five months or so of flying routine patrols, practising formation flying and mock dogfighting, I was finally qualified in fighters."

"Then came the invasion of Poland?" Peggy asked.

"Well, before that something surprising happened; Hitler signed a non-aggression treaty with the USSR, which stunned everyone."

"Why was that?" she asked.

"Well, to many people it revealed the cynicism of the regime. The Nazis had campaigned on a strong anti-communist program, stressing the terrible menace that

Stalin's USSR posed to Europe. They had jailed or murdered thousands of socialists and communists, shut down their newspapers and forbidden their associations, and now here they were, snuggling up to the Reds.

"Then came Poland. Once Hitler and Stalin signed their treaty, Poland was doomed. Our army crossed the border on 1 September 1939, and about two weeks later the Red Army invaded from the East. The Poles never had a chance."

"Did you see action in Poland?"

"Oh, *ja*, I flew a 109 in Poland. We shot up some of their air force on the ground, but they fought back. They sent up fighters, if you can call them that; old-fashioned high-wing monoplanes — P11Cs, they were called. The Poles fought hard, flying very bravely in those outdated aircraft, and they destroyed a lot of our airplanes. But we had them heavily outnumbered and shot many of them down. It was all over before the end of September, when the German and Soviet armies overran the country, and six months later my unit was ordered back to Germany."

"But you scored two victories, correct?"

"*Ja*, I got two." He fell silent, grim.

"What?" she asked.

"Well, there were some things I saw in Poland that should have made me realize more clearly what was going on. Our base was near a railroad, and we saw locked cattle cars sitting there on the tracks, with strange noises coming from them; moaning, not like cattle, but like humans. We walked over to see what was happening, but SS guards with submachine guns rudely ordered us away.

"Since I was the most senior officer present, I puffed myself up and 'pulled rank' — barking at one of the guards to ask if there were people in those cars. 'People, *Herr Hauptmann*?' I remember him sneering and saying something like, 'These are not people, they are subhumans, *Untermensch*! We are taking them to Lodz, to a place where they will not infect the rest of the population. Now get back and mind your airplanes, *ja*?' I was about to dress him down for insolence and take his name, when the train started to move, and he jumped aboard, laughing at me; and then he was gone."

"So," Peggy asked, "you still didn't figure out what was going on?"

"Not entirely," Max answered. "After all, the SS were always arrogant, and I still had no real idea of what was happening to people in Eastern Europe." He hesitated. "Maybe... Let's talk more about that later."

Peggy nodded, reluctant to abandon that topic, but wanting to hear the rest of his story. "So then you went back to Germany?"

"*Ja*, back to Germany, for more training, then to France during the invasion. I didn't see much action in France, because my unit spent most of its time escorting dive bombers, though I did get one French plane, a poorly-flown Dewoitine that I shot out of the sky in seconds. The pilots I knew who did come up against the British felt their planes were rather sluggish, and their pilot performance substandard."

"Were those Spitfires?" Peggy asked.

"*Ach, nein*, these were Hurricanes. It turned out that the British didn't commit many Spitfires to the defence of France and saved them for the Battle of Britain that came later, but I'm afraid that's a story for another day. Is that okay? I'm worn out and it's almost dark."

Peggy packed up her things, and Max watched her tail-lights recede, then made a cup of tea and sat in front of his VHS player.

Selecting the *Battle of Britain* tape, Waldberg popped it in, leaned back and was soon lost in memory.

"They had indeed lived well," he thought, *"driving fast cars, drinking the finest French vintages from bottles marked 'Only For German Armed Forces', eating the very best food the rich agriculture and cuisine of France had to offer, items hard to obtain in Germany."*

Occupation authorities had valued the Deutschmark much higher than its actual value compared to the franc, so soldiers in France could buy luxury items like perfume, lovely dresses, stockings and such to send back to their women in the Reich. German soldiers going on leave back to Germany were burdened like pack mules, toting wonderful things back to Germany.

Many thousands of French PoWs, about ten percent of the male population, were kept in captivity in Germany, contributing to a severe manpower shortage in France; thus, some French women flocked to the glamorous young German pilots.

Some sought romance, and others likely looked for security or perhaps only for access to the luxuries these handsome young men could provide. But the young aviators didn't care what their motives were.

He'd been one of them — the Young Eagles — the victors, the men who had succeeded where their fathers had failed. They felt they had earned their good life, flying triumphantly over Spain, Poland, the Netherlands and France. *"Of course, there was always the chance you could get bumped off the next day,"* he mused. *"But when you are young and strong, you think you are immortal. It's always the other guy that's going to get it, never you."*

And then came England.

Flying over England, they had been shocked by the skill of the English pilots, their increasing aggressiveness, and the improved performance of their Hurricanes. In addition, there was the Spitfire, which the Germans had rarely encountered in France. Now, the British always seemed to be above them, swooping down on their fighters as they escorted lumbering bombers, killing bomber crews and fighter pilots at a pace the *Luftwaffe* could not afford.

Of course, now he knew why; why the English had done so much better over England than over France. As he thought about that, he began to doze, so he shuffled off to bed.

CHAPTER 7

"Radar," Max told her at their next meeting, "that's why they were always waiting above, with the sun behind them. The radar gave the British warning of our flights, allowing their pilots to gain altitude and loiter, then pounce. They didn't dogfight unless they had to, simply diving through German bomber formations and picking somebody off, then roaring off at high speed, appearing again from altitude later. We chased them, but our 109s only had about twelve minutes of flying time over England, as we were nearly at the limit of our range if the target was inland from the coast."

"Didn't your high command realize any of these things? Didn't they try to do something to make things more effective?"

"Actually, no, because on top of everything else, Goering ordered us — the fighters — to stay close to the bombers, because there had been too many casualties among bomber crews. These orders robbed us of many of our advantages, like speed and surprise. We had to slog along with the bombers and just wait for the *Tommies* to hit us.

"It was maddening. It was also true that whenever an Englishman was shot up, if he wasn't killed outright or seriously wounded, he had a good chance of returning to the fight. An English pilot either bailed out or crash-landed in his own country, but German pilots in disabled aircraft were lost for good if they couldn't get back across the Channel. Also, we were stunned by the performance of the RAF over England compared to their actions over France."

"Why was that?"

"Part of it was the Spitfire, a superb aircraft that hadn't been employed much over France, but even the 'Hurrys'... er, Hurricanes, seemed to be better. The pilots were much more aggressive, and quite skillful. They used innovative formations and always seemed to be one step ahead of us. I got two of them, the 'Spits', after I learned that if they dived quickly or flew inverted, their carburetors would malfunction and the engine sputter momentarily, giving me the few seconds, I needed. But then they got me," he told her, tapping his chest.

"The British Spitfires were just a bit faster than the 109 because, we discovered after the war, they were burning 100-octane fuel provided by America, while our aircraft used 87-octane gasoline. That also tended to explain why the RAF was so much better over England than France.

"That, and the fact they were defending their homeland, which always counts a lot. They also turned tighter, and one of them got inside me, and shot up my engine."

She noted he was using his hands to illustrate the maneuvers, in the manner of pilots all over the world, and she smiled. He noticed. "*Ja*, all pilots speak with their hands" — and he smiled as well.

"Anyway, the scrap from the bullets and pieces of the engine hit me here, in the breast, and in my arm, and it suddenly became hard to breathe, and the plane lost power, sputtering and smoking, with oil streaming up onto the windshield. The Tommy pilot must have thought I was done for, because he broke off and went after someone else, while I tried to gain altitude."

She interrupted. "Were you trying to get high enough to use your parachute?"

"Well, that's another part of the story. You see, a lot of us used to break the rules, and sit on our parachutes so we could be a little higher in the cockpit, and with the injury that I had, I couldn't get the straps over my shoulders. So, no, I was trying to get altitude so that I could glide if I had to, to help get back to our side of the Channel; but believe me, I never sat on my 'chute again!"

He started coughing, and made an excuse to get them both some tea; then, when the coughing stopped, he asked, "What is it you Americans say about 'close'?"

"Oh, 'Close only counts in horseshoes and hand grenades'?"

"*Ja*, that's it. I came *close* to getting back to France, but had to ditch in the Channel, about eight hundred meters from shore. I was doing well, keeping the nose up, dragging my tail to slow the plane down, as I'd been taught, but then I caught a wingtip and slammed into the water, bashing my head on the edge of the cockpit, knocking myself silly.

"I was pulled out by some Navy boys who were practising in the area, and taken to the big German hospital in Paris after I was patched up in a field hospital in Normandy. They fixed up my injuries in Paris, and I was given leave." He drew breath to continue, but Peggy stopped him.

"Please tell me about Paris. I'm told my mother lived there."

"Did she indeed?" he answered. "Well, I had a month's medical leave because my injuries were not completely healed, and I had to check in to the hospital every two weeks; so, after a week at home, I went back to Paris. How can I describe it? There I was, a fine-looking young pilot officer with a brand-new uniform, a shiny wound badge in silver, and an Iron Cross First Class they gave me for trying to get back despite being injured.

"I received the Iron Cross Second Class after my 'scores' in England, France and Poland, so they gave me the First Class for getting back to France even while wounded, since I could have crash-landed in England or ditched off the Dover coast. I also had some other decorations from Spain and Poland. Oh, I was a thing of beauty, I can assure you." He chuckled. "All the girls swooned, and since it was France, so did some of the men!" They both laughed.

"Do you have any photographs?" she asked.

"Well, let me see." He walked to a desk in the corner and sorted through some papers. "Well, here's one taken later," he said, and handed her a black-and-white 4 x 6 photo on very stiff paper, with the stamp of a German photographer on the back, dated 1942. It showed a handsome young Waldberg, with a number of medals and an Iron Cross pinned to his chest.

"Wow, Paris?" she said.

"No, that was in Berlin. Paris was wonderful. I was billeted at a very nice hotel reserved for German military, and went out every night to wonderful restaurants, shows and art exhibitions. It was an experience I shall never forget. After all, we Germans were on top of the world. We had done what our fathers could not do. I met very sophisticated people. Coco Chanel had a German boyfriend, and I dined with the couple one night. I met many distinguished German officers, including the German writer Ernst Jünger. Have you ever heard of him?"

"Jünger? Oh, yes, I read *Storm of Steel* in college. It was presented as pro-war propaganda."

"Well, that's what it was. After the war, Jünger became famous as a philosopher and entomologist, and more or less backed down from his position that war was necessary and cleansing for a society. In 1941, he was like a god to us young officers. Jünger carried the 'Pour le Merite' — the famous Blue Max — for his heroism in the First War, and he had an Iron Cross for his work in France in 1940. He was a terrific infantry officer. In fact, he saved my life."

"He did? How?"

"I met Jünger at Café du Dôme, introduced by an officer we both knew. The Dôme was well-known as a literary hang-out, and I used to notice a few people sitting there, writing away. One was a nice-looking woman that Jünger said came in every day, who turned out to be Simone de Beauvoir, the novelist. Little did I know she would turn out to be active in the Resistance, along with her lover Jean-Paul Sartre. She came into the cafe to keep warm, since shipments of coal and other fuel had been diverted to the German armed forces, so we stayed warm while Parisians shivered, that early spring of 1941.

"Jünger had heard of my family, and took an interest in me. He asked me to dine with him, and told me about some of the lesser-known points of interest in the city, places that weren't thronged with vacationing soldiers. He showed me the Roman ruins under Notre Dame, and introduced me to some prominent French artists and writers, performers and notables like Edith Piaf. One evening, he asked me if I wanted to meet Picasso, and I said of course I would. He told me I would have to wear civilian clothes because Picasso, like many people in France, did not like being seen with Germans.

"I met Jünger the next day, in civvies, and we started out for Picasso's studio in a velocab. A velocab is a small-wheeled compartment attached to the back of a tandem bicycle, which two muscular young cyclists pedaled through the streets. They were common in Paris because fuel for vehicles was in very short supply, and severely rationed.

"On the way, we had a small accident with an army truck; nothing major, but I hit my chest against the front of the compartment and suddenly I could barely breathe. We were near the famous American hospital in Paris, and Jünger knew the man who was one of the more important doctors there, a First War American surgeon. The American doctor and his French wife more or less ran the hospital, which, being an American institution, was still neutral.

"Jünger ordered the velocab to take us there, half-dragged me into the emergency surgery and threw me up on a gurney while he yelled in English for help. Some nurses responded, but they didn't know what to do, and they said there was no doctor about. It was getting progressively harder for me to breathe and I couldn't speak, and then a woman in a white coat appeared next to me, with a stethoscope. She produced a pair of scissors and cut open my shirt, then she listened, tapped my chest, poked my neck hard, mumbled something in what sounded like German, then asked again for a doctor.

"When the nurses said there was no doctor in the building, she picked up an enormous steel needle and drove it straight into my chest. Then, while I writhed on the table, she told me — no, *ordered* me, now in very terse German — to hold the needle while she secured it in place!"

"Yikes!" Peggy exclaimed, wincing.

"I am afraid I said something stronger than 'yikes'," Max chuckled.

"She turned to the group of nurses and spoke in French too rapid for me to understand, and while she spoke, I noted, despite my pain, that she was unusually attractive, dark-haired and tall, with a very lively demeanor. She seemed to be very much in charge, barking instructions to three or four nurses who fluttered about, apparently doing what she told them.

"I was able to breathe much easier, although I did have pain, of course. I asked her how she knew I was a German. She spoke to me in my native tongue and said, 'You're with *him*' — indicating Jünger, who bowed and clicked his heels — 'and everybody knows *he* is German. That, and the fact that you curse in German. And,' she added, patting my cheek, 'you look like a recruiting poster. But let's keep that to ourselves for now, and get you out of here, as soon as I set up a drainage bottle.'

"Jünger got on the phone and arranged transport to the Air Force hospital, while the mysterious woman set up the now-familiar bubbling bottle, which I had seen in my earlier treatment, and secured the needle in my chest with many layers of adhesive tape.

"'What happened?' I begged her as she worked.

"She told me that the wound in my lung had reopened, so air could get out of my lung but not out of my chest, because the wound in my chest wall had healed. What she had done was release the air trapped in my chest, which was pushing against my heart and other lung. 'Your friend was right to bring you here, because you would have died before you got to the German hospital. We cannot keep you here; you are German military and we represent a neutral nation, so off you go.'

"German medics soon showed up and loaded me into an ambulance. Jünger shook my hand and said goodbye, and the young woman patted my shoulder and said, 'Let's forget this ever happened. Good luck, *Herr Hauptmann*,' then she turned on her heel and walked briskly away.

"Forget that? Forget her? Not bloody likely, I told myself. She reminded me of my grandmother — absolutely no-nonsense, but strikingly feminine at the same time.

"Please don't be offended," he continued, catching her look. "Today there are many such women, but in Paris in May of 1941, such ladies were rare indeed — or at least I had never met any other than my grandmother and, to a certain extent, my mother."

"What happened after that?" asked Peggy.

"I was taken to the *Luftwaffe* hospital in Clichy, an industrial suburb of Paris, and spent ten miserable days in bed, bubbling away, until the quacks came up with something. Finally, they used a chemical to roughen the inside of my chest, so that my lung would stick to it after the scars healed and not collapse again, and then they told me I couldn't fly any more.

"They gave me another two weeks of convalescent leave and told me to report to *Luftwaffe* headquarters in

Paris for an administrative assignment. I was *zerstört* — destroyed," he muttered, grimacing.

"Well, Paris was not the worst place to be a German soldier in 1941," she teased.

"*Ach*, no," he answered, "but I had joined the military to fly, not sit at a desk and process paperwork about absent *Luftwaffe* personnel, which was what I was assigned to do. No matter how beautiful the city, regardless of its many diversions, I was miserable. There was one bright spot, though."

"And that was?"

"I met that woman again."

"Ah, *cherchez la femme*, no?" Peggy teased again.

"It was by chance. I was at a cafe with Jünger again, complaining about my lot in life, and he spotted her across the room. 'Don't look now,' Jünger murmured, 'but your angel of mercy with the big needle is here.'

"She was sitting with two other women, one of whom I recognized as one of the nurses from the American hospital. I was reluctant to approach her, even though I was in civilian clothes, because I knew, as I told you, that some French people did not like being seen associating with Germans; but she noticed me, and, excusing herself, made her way to our table.

"She declined to sit when invited by Jünger, who, though we both stood as she approached, mercifully did not click his heels, and she addressed me and asked, 'So, *Herr Hauptmann*, how is your chest these days?'

"I could not tell if her interest was professional or out of courtesy, so I stammered out an answer about feeling well enough, but being most disappointed at not being able to fly any more. She asked a few questions about the technicalities occurring at Clichy, then nodded and made to leave.

"'Please, *mademoiselle*,' I said, using my very best schoolboy French, 'may I express my thanks for your excellent and timely care, and may I know your name?' 'My name?' she asked, and looking me straight in the eye she told me, in Berlin-accented German, 'My name is Rachel, Rachel Liebeskind.' I think she meant for me to wince, or blink, or express some distaste at the Jewish surname, but I simply shook her hand, thanked her again, and wished her a good evening, since she obviously wished to return to her table.

"'So, my friend,' Jünger said gently, 'from the look in your eyes, you have been pierced again, not by a needle, but by Cupid's arrow. Be very careful, young man; the regime does not look kindly on young captains who chase Jewish women.'

"'Chasing? Who's chasing?' I answered. 'I merely wished to thank her,' I told him. I'll never forget his answer.

"'Ah, yes,' chortled Jünger, 'tell that to your face!'"

CHAPTER 8

"The next morning, I spent two hours at the office of the French police, the *gendarmerie*, where I often went to collect information about my air force deserters, or, with some guards, physically collect them if they had been apprehended by the French. I was known there, and had become familiar, if not yet friendly, with one of their inspectors, a man named Rion. Rion had been a prisoner in Germany during the First War and had learned passable German, so he was assigned as my liaison with the French police.

"Rion was a clever and crafty fellow. He had been an ordinary *flic*, as the French call their beat cops, until he worked his way up to detective status. He was a master of the monstrous index file the police kept of all the people and events in the city. He knew all the alleys and byways, the secrets of underworld Paris, and he was a typical tough, mildly corrupt French policeman.

"It was rumored he dabbled tentatively in the black market, and that he was not averse to the occasional five-*franc* note or nice cut of meat as an incentive to look the other way, or do an extra favor.

"Thus, it was that a few bottles marked 'German Armed Forces Only' found their way into Rion's cellar, and the complete file on Rachel Liebeskind found its way to my briefcase. 'You may read this, *Herr Hauptmann*, but I must have it back tomorrow morning,' Rion told me.

"Later, in the privacy of my own office, I went through the file. Rachel Liebeskind had been born in Berlin in an affluent suburb in 1912. Her father was an apothecary, her mother taught French in a private academy for women. Her father had served with some distinction as an artillery officer in World War I.

"Rachel entered medical school in Berlin in 1930, at the unusually young age of eighteen. More unusual still, she had been accepted into the surgery program, not paediatrics or obstetrics, where the few women admitted to medical studies in those days were encouraged to train.

"According to a document in support of her subsequent application for the Sorbonne, she had good reviews from her professors and excellent grades, but was dismissed from physician's training after Nazi exclusion laws began to be enforced. Her parents left Berlin and moved to Eastern Poland, where her mother had relatives.

"Rachel was determined to continue her studies; thus, she had travelled to France, and by 1936 was petitioning the Sorbonne medical faculty for admission. Her petition was denied because she was not a French citizen. It was also possibly denied because of growing anti-Semitic sentiment in France.

"French politics were characterized by many groups who were sympathetic to the Nazis' persecution of Jews, groups that wanted to exclude Jews from professions and do other things the Nazis had done. The French don't like to talk about that today."

"What is this all about?" thought Peggy, and asked Max to perhaps move on with the story.

Max paused momentarily, shook his head and said, "This is part of the story; please let me go on."

Peggy stifled a sigh, hoping this part of the story wouldn't take too much time, and nodded.

"Well, Rachel found work as an instructor in surgical nursing at the American Hospital in Paris in 1937, and obtained French citizenship in 1938. Since Rachel worked for an American institution, she was not subject to French anti-Jewish legislation which was enacted after the French defeat. However, as a 'Foreign Jew', she merited special entries in her file. There were notations accompanied by German signatures and stamps. One of those notations was a reference to a list maintained by the RSHA, the Reichs Security Agency and Gestapo, and I asked Rion about that the next day when I returned the file.

"He was not entirely sure, but he thought it was a list of those whom the Gestapo believed merited watching. He said Rachel had been active in Jewish refugee affairs upon her arrival in France in '35, and that may have drawn the attention of the Gestapo.

"I experienced a mixed feeling of fear and relief," Max continued to Peggy; "fear because the Gestapo were known to be dangerous, and relief that Rachel was under American protection."

Peggy noticed he seemed fatigued, had gone a bit pale. She asked if he was tired, and when he nodded, she packed her things and prepared to leave.

"Will you be all right?" she queried, her hand on his arm.

"*Ach*, a bit of schnapps and a nap, and I will be, as you Americans say, 'right as rain'. Good night, and say hello to your mama for me. One of these days I'll come into town and see her."

CHAPTER 9

Two weeks later, they met again at Max's little cabin. After a conversation about weather, how each was feeling and what Celine had been doing, Max began. "After what I saw in Spain and Poland, plus the things I learned on leave in Kufstein after I was wounded…"

"Wait, in Kufstein, what things? When?"

"After I was shot down over England, and got out of the hospital the first time, I was given home leave, remember?" Peggy nodded. "Well, when I arrived at my grandmother's estate, I was surprised by the number of people working there. Where there had only been five or six employees when I left, now there were dozens of men and women around, and there were a number of children noisily running about."

"Were they local children? Did your family know them?"

"No, they looked like city kids, but I will explain. My mother and grandmother were overjoyed to see me — my mother was particularly pleased when I told her I was no longer flying — and they both fussed over me terribly. Then, at supper the first night, I asked my grandmother why she had so many people around the place.

"Grandmother rose from the table and closed the dining room doors before she answered. 'Those people,' she told me, 'are what the Nazis call *undesirables*. They are Socialists, prominent Catholics, Jews, even a couple of fundamentalist Christians — all of whom the Nazis would like to put in camps.' She and my mother had decided to do what they could for them. They told me it was hard for everyone, but they were getting by. 'The children are quite noisy,' my grandmother told me, frowning, 'and there were challenges with food, some folks having to sleep in the barn, but everyone helped out, and they took things day by day.'

"'But why?' I asked her," Max continued. "I knew they could both get into a lot of trouble, and at that time I thought surely the camps could not be so bad. My mother got up at that point and moved her chair next to mine. I still remember her telling me. 'You have no idea,' she almost whispered. 'People are beaten and starved. If their children look "Aryan", they are given to German families. Those that don't are simply left to beg in the streets. Many people just disappear into the camps and are never heard from again.'

"A tear appeared on my mother's cheek, and she dabbed at it with her napkin. She said, 'We are Christian people, and if we can help, we must do so,' at which her voice broke.

"My grandmother took my hand at that point, and, also in a low voice, said to me, 'Look at me, Max, and listen. Hitler and his thugs are going to lose this war, and there will be a reckoning. I know this from my military and diplomatic contacts, who have never misled me, and they all say the same thing. Hitler's Reich survives by looting.

"'The Nazi economy is like a shark,' she murmured, 'which must keep swimming to survive. They have looted every country they have occupied. They are looting the synagogues and homes of deported Jews and other so-called "enemies of the people". They are confiscating art, gold reserves and individual holdings in banks, and this is just the beginning. They are running out of loot, so they must find another country to pillage, and my friends tell me Hitler will soon invade Russia.

"'That will mean a two-front war, because England will never surrender, and that will be Germany's downfall, mark my words.' I remember this clearly, because I had never heard my grandmother speak with such emotion.

"I did not believe it all at the time, but later, back in Paris, things started to happen and I began to understand more," Max told Peggy.

"So, OK," Peggy began, as Max paused. "We got a little out of order here. Am I understanding this correctly? First Spain, then Poland, then back to Germany, then to France, then over England, wounded, briefly home to Kufstein, then Paris, and then things started to happen in Paris?"

"*Ja*."

"You mean that your wound reopened?"

"*Ja*, that. But other things as well — frightening things."

"Will you tell me about that while I make some tea?"

"*Ja*, with a bit of schnapps, if you don't mind."

She nodded and puttered about while he talked, knowing the recorder was picking up his story.

"First, Rion the policeman came to me about the American Hospital. He said the hospital badly needed food, that it was becoming overloaded with sick expatriate Americans and other foreign nationals, and needed help.

"The American Hospital had been allowed to continue to operate, and indeed operated even after America entered the war, because it was cheaper to have ex-pat Americans and other foreigners treated there, rather than in French institutions. I was puzzled by his interest in this situation. I asked him, 'What has that to do with me, or you, for that matter, *M'sieur l'inspecteur*?' He said he thought I might be able to help. 'Almost every time we pick up one of your deserters, they are carrying food of some kind, usually that canned meat, a sort of *pâté*.'

"Of course he meant *eiserne Ration* — so-called iron rations. They were issued to combat troops as an emergency ration should they be caught somewhere without supplies, and they were part of *Luftwaffe* survival packs, so there were lots of them around every airbase. Rion told me those little tins of meat had become a very desirable source of protein, and mentioned that a young lady at the American Hospital had asked if I might be able to acquire some of them to help with the food shortage there. He told me this young lady was a Mademoiselle Liebeskind, the woman whose file he had loaned me.

"The effect on me was like an electric shock, and Rion noticed my reaction. He was kind enough to hide his smile.

"I responded — rather gruffly, I'm afraid — that I still didn't understand my involvement in the matter. Rion answered, asking me what happened to those *eiserne Ration* cans when a deserter was arrested. I said I hadn't thought about it before, and Rion continued, a crafty glint in his eye, 'If our cops catch them, they "confiscate" whatever of value the man is carrying — your military police do the same. Regardless of whoever makes the arrest, the items simply disappear. Would it not be more efficient if an order went out under your authority that such items should be turned in for, shall we say, redistribution?'

"I almost laughed, but stifled it, as I asked, 'Pray tell, *Monsieur* Rion, who would manage such redistribution?' To which Rion said, 'Ah, *Herr Hauptmann*, may I offer the services of my humble self?'

"And then he thrust out one leg, spread his arms and gave a courtly old-fashioned bow, at which point I did actually laugh, and so did he.

"I said, 'I presume, *Monsieur l'Inspecteur*, there would be an appropriate, shall we say, carrying charge?'

And he replied, 'Ah, *oui, le prix pour livraison,* er, charge for delivery? But of course, *Herr Hauptmann*; after all, one must get by as well, *n'est ce pas*?'

"Well, I knew he was up to no good, but I had begun to like the man, and he was a very valuable asset to me — for information, among other things — so, as you say here in America, I went along with the… the… 'plan', is it?"

"Program," Peggy responded, setting down the teacups and the schnapps bottle.

"*Ja*, that's it — I 'went along with the program'."

He added a splash of schnapps to his cup and held up the bottle to Peggy. She nodded, so he poured a small amount into her tea as well. They sipped in silence for a moment, before Max continued.

"Within a couple of weeks, a twelve-year-old kid was riding a delivery bike from the *gendarmerie* to the American Hospital every week or so, with a basket full of meat tins and cigarettes, and I, a decorated German officer, became an agent of the '*marché noir*', the black market."

"The black market? Why?"

"There were far too many items for them all to have been taken from German military personnel. Rion was obviously buying things up on the black market, or getting people to steal them, and sending them to the American Hospital, in addition to what was grabbed from our absconders, and both of us knew it. And, I noticed, Rion seemed not to be taking a cut."

"What was he up to?" Peggy mused, as she sipped her tea.

"That is a story for another day, I am afraid. I am tired again. Can you come next week?" Peggy looked disappointed, so he said, "Sorry, I tire so easily these days, but all of this memory, it is a bit overwhelming for me."

"Sure," she said, noting the moisture in his eyes, and, glancing out of the window, that dusk was coming on. "See you Wednesday next week. In the morning?"

"Bob brings my groceries in the morning, so afternoon is better for me — say one p.m.?"

"I'll be here." She finished her tea and snapped off the little recorder, making a mental note to talk to 'Bob-who-brought-the-groceries', whoever the hell *he* was.

CHAPTER 10

Finding Bob turned out to be easy. All she had to do was ask Celine who it was that delivered things to the 'pilot in the woods'. "You mean Max?" Celine queried.

"Yes."

"What do you think of him? Pete and I became very good friends with Max during the war."

"He's got an interesting story. How did you meet him?"

Celine laughed. "Pete catched — I mean caught — him up in the woods and we locked him up in the cellar until the sheriff came to get him, and that took a while, because the sheriff had to wait for the FBI to come from Boston, and there was a storm. We had to feed him, so he had meals with us — and we talked, and we both got to know him. He jumped out of an airplane with a *parapluie*, I mean parachute, and landed in the woods with his leg hurt. He got lost, but Pete, he found him."

"Why did you tell me to go and see him?" Peggy asked.

"Max has a great story to tell, if you will listen, and I thought that it might maybe be a book for you, no?"

"Maybe, mama, maybe not. Anyway, who is this Bob who brings the groceries?"

"Oh, *oui*, Bob — he works for his papa David at the Grocery King in Rockland. You know, where we sell the lemon cookies?"

"Oh, *that* Bob. What is his story? He seems a bit slow, and his speech is very — well, you know."

"Bobby was a fine boy, smart and good-looking, but then he went to Vietnam and he got his head hurt, so now he works for his papa and helps in the store and delivers things."

"Can I ask him about Max?"

"*Oui, certainment*," Celine responded, "but if you are going to Rockland, can you take the lemon cookies? That way they will be nice and fresh, because Bob, he comes on..."

"I know, mama, Wednesday morning next week."

During the drive to Rockland with boxes of cookies on the back seat, Peggy started to think about Pete, her beloved papa. Most of what she knew came from talks she and Pete had when they went fishing together, and from what Celine had told her over the years, and she knew a little from what neighbors told her growing up. She mused over these memories as she drove.

Piet "Pete" Pederson was nobody's fool, and everybody in that area of Maine, the area around Rockland, knew it. Maybe the kids made fun of his rolling gait, and maybe a few careless adults snickered about his accent, but the people who lived and worked the woods and ocean thereabouts, and the people of the smaller settlements, knew him to be tough, steady and honest, traits "Down Easters" rank next to Godliness.

Pete had been a scallop dredger, as his immigrant father had been. He had left his father's boat at nineteen, when the old man retired. His father's boat wasn't in good enough shape to continue working, and Pete didn't have enough money to buy his own boat or repair his old man's, so Pete had signed on with others.

"Just until we get enough money to buy our own," he had told Celine, his girlfriend, a French-Canadian girl he had started dating during their sophomore year of high school, and whom he loved "something awful", as he put it to Peggy years later. Even at nineteen, Pete was as hardened and experienced a hand as anyone on the coast, and by twenty-one he was considered one of the best and toughest workers around, well on his way to being captain of his own craft in a couple of years.

And then, one rainy Wednesday, as he was hauling in gear, his life changed. The four-hundred-pound steel dredge he was winching in broke loose, skidded across the slippery steel deck and caught his left leg between its steel reinforcements and an open companionway door, smashing — near pulverizing — both bones in his lower leg and almost amputating his foot at the ankle.

"I'm afraid I'm done for," he told Celine from his hospital bed. "I can't fish no more. I'm gonna have to have a wooden leg, because they had to cut mine off. I can't be on deck, the doc says. I'm pretty much useless. Can't balance right any more, so you're gonna have to let me go and find somebody else."

The next half hour was not pleasant for Pete, as Celine tore him up one side and then the other, half in

English, half in explosive French — which, outside of a few words, he was glad he didn't understand, the English being quite caustic enough.

In essence, she told him to get up off his sorry butt, though the word she used was "*derriére*", which he understood just fine, that scallop fishing was not the only way in the world to make a living and that she'd be damned if she settled for any of "these sorry shriveled specimens hereabout", when Pete, leg or no leg, "could still whip the *merde* [another word he understood] out of any of them, and outwork them to boot." She kissed him on the mouth, hard, and flounced out of the room, leaving him slack-jawed and speechless.

"That," said the nursing sister who had witnessed her outburst, "is, if you and the Lord will forgive the expression, one hell of a young woman, and you'd better pay heed, young man." Then, red-faced and shaking her wimple, she left the room with a singularly un-nun-like guffaw, leaving him to ponder his fate. And while he pondered, Celine was off to see her uncle.

The extensive Bourque clan, from which Celine descended, had French roots, but they were as much a part of Maine as the pine trees. Bourques had been in Maine since the Great Expulsion of 1755, when the English deported French settlers from the territory they controlled in New France, French Canada. Bourque ancestors had been shipped to Maine — then part of the Massachusetts colony — rather than suffering the fate of those shipped south, as in the epic poem *Evangeline*.

By the 1820s, French-Canadian culture had become commonplace in the now-independent American state of Maine. Some Bourques fought with Washington in the Revolution, and had been granted land. Building upon that and other political power, the Bourques and other French-speaking families had gained considerable financial and political influence in the state.

Among these influential Francophones was the man all of them called Uncle Toussaint, a well-connected political fixer in Augusta, who spent summers near his boyhood home in the heart of his legislative district, in a well-appointed house in Rockland, Maine, where Celine found him sitting on the wraparound veranda, sipping an *aperitif*.

Within an hour all had been settled. It turned out that Uncle Toussaint owed Celine's father a big debt, having to do with Toussaint's extrication from a painful youthful indiscretion, and, moreover, young Pete's plight offered Uncle Toussaint a possible solution to a thorny problem.

Uncle Toussaint was charged with making appointments to certain offices within his district, and one of those positions had just become available. The current incumbent had become unable to serve on account of advancing age and an incurable fondness for "*le vin rouge*".

Celine's uncle faced a dilemma: none of his French protégés were up to the job, as this office required a man with considerable energy, strength and stamina, yet he was reluctant to confer such an appointment on any of the other possible candidates, lest his constituents accuse him of favoring the hated *Anglais*.

The other two significant segments of his constituency, the Portuguese and the Irish, were either apolitical or voted almost exclusively for their own candidates, and wouldn't vote for Uncle Toussaint no matter who he appointed. Therefore, young Pete represented a near-perfect appointment.

Pete was not French, but he wasn't *Anglais* either, and this appointment would cement Toussaint's standing with Celine's branch of the Bourques. Also, this dispensation of patronage had the advantage of beneficence, in that he was helping an injured young citizen, and might even endear Toussaint to the maritime Norwegians.

Thus it was, that Pete Pederson was appointed Assistant Game Warden for Knox County, Maine, pending — of course — his recovery, on this day of Our Lord, 20 March 1934.

Pete healed quickly with Celine's ferocious encouragement, and was soon fitted with a prosthetic limb, which worked well, though it conferred a distinct swinging gait as Pete had to take the weight off his left side and swing the new leg forward from his knee with each step.

At first, he used a cane, but within two weeks he was walking unassisted, ambulating well enough to walk down the aisle and be married to Celine — the happiest day of his life so far, he had told Peggy. Within a month, his stump had toughened up enough that he was able to report for duty at the county forestry office.

He was assigned to an experienced warden in a neighboring county, and his evaluation, written by the district superintendent a year later, cited him as "an exceptionally fast learner who has quickly developed a rapport with both the public and his fellow officers. I can recommend him without reservation for independent duty."

Pete was pleased to have his own assignment, and Celine was simply delighted that they could move from her parents' home to their own snug quarters, the forestry department's housing for his district. Celine had begun a small business providing French-style baked goods for weddings and other family events, and was overjoyed to find that their comfortable cabin, on the edge of the settlement at Owl's Head, was equipped with a modern gas oven.

Pete soon settled in to his new routine, patrolling his beat conscientiously, and collaring the occasional poacher, writing citations for out-of-season hunting, and keeping track of the plant and animal population of his area.

He had a small truck for official use, a Ford Model A. Driving was a challenge for Pete at first, as his prosthetic tended to slip off the clutch pedal, and the unaccustomed angle of pressure hurt his stump; but after the forestry mechanic had reduced the tension required for shifting a bit, Pete was whizzing about the area, delighted with his new mobility and independence.

Celine never did master driving, and hired a local man to deliver her goods to customers, and once each month, without fail, she "bribed" the postman (another of the endless supply of cousins of the Bourque clan) with her locally famous *mille crêpe* cakes, and in return, he conveyed a couple of freshly-baked *Gateaux Breton* to her beloved uncle upon the postman's return to the main Post Office in Rockland.

Pete soon learned the ways of the animals in his district, the types and growth patterns of the forest plants and the wily ways of the poachers, smugglers, moonshiners and other malefactors who roamed his beat in the Maine woods, as should be expected of an experienced warden. He had also become something of an expert in forest search techniques, often consulted by agencies from neighboring districts for help and advice in locating missing people.

After December 1941, Pete had also learned a great deal about what went on in the small towns and villages that bordered his usual area of responsibility. With so many young men away at the war, and many other potential police recruits working for terrific wages at defence plants like the shipyards at Bath, the sheriff's office based in Rockland had become short-handed, and the dispatchers tended to call on Pete from time to time for assistance.

Pete got permission from the county forest office to respond to events he thought he could handle, and became something of a back-up peace officer. So Pete soon learned who was beating his wife, who was dangerous when drunk, and who just might be breaking into other people's houses, along with a few darker neighborhood secrets.

Pete handled these situations with such a combination of charm, humor, discretion, and, when necessary, rapidly and efficiently applied force, that he soon became widely respected both as a lawman and peacemaker.

People noticed that when Pete got involved in a dispute, his Norwegian accent got thicker and more comical and with that alone folks started laughing and the situation was defused. Everybody wondered whether that was just natural or if it was part of Pete's bag of tricks, but it worked, and Pete was widely well-liked and respected. As Ed had told Peggy, people still told Pete Pederson stories in the local bars and barber shops.

That notwithstanding, after one close call with a crazed, knife-wielding fisherman, Pete had taken to wearing a military sidearm on police calls, "just in case", instead of always carrying a heavy state-issued hunting rifle.

Celine was worried about this aspect of his job, and the need for a handgun, but when she mentioned it, Pete just laughed and said, "Ah, Celine honey, that's just for show; usually I just tease 'em until the whole fracas blows over."

"Well," she countered, "when we have a baby, you're going to have to lock that thing up"; and then they both got quiet for a while, because there didn't seem to be any baby in their future, though God knows they tried. They were truly happy together, though they got lonely in their cabin on the edge of the forest sometimes.

Pete was by nature somewhat solitary, but Celine truly yearned for a baby, as did Celine's mother, who mentioned the absence frequently. "I want to be *grandmere* Bourque," the old lady would mutter when Celine visited, and it became an unspoken burden for Celine and Pete, a shadow over an otherwise happy life.

"So," Celine frequently told Peggy when she was a child, "I prayed to our Blessed Holy Virgin *Notre Dame* every day, and after a while, you came to us." Peggy had been told of her adoption many times, the story becoming a bedtime ritual. "Your mother was a poor Catholic war refugee girl from France, who was brought to Boston during the war by a French Catholic aid agency run by the Church.

"She had been living in the woods in France for years because the Germans were chasing her, and she was in very poor shape when she came over in the winter of 1944. She was in a hospital for a while, then the Boston priests got hold of us, because I spoke French and we were Catholic. They asked if we could help her, so Pete and I took her in and fed her good food until she got stronger.

"She was a very smart and hard-working girl, and she helped with the baking. She even learned to ride one of those three-wheeled motorcycles the army sold off after the war, and did deliveries, but then she left."

93

"Why did she leave, Mama?" little Peggy would then ask.

"Why else?" Celine would chirp. "For a man, *pour l'amour*, of course — she met a man and she was gone. We never knew who he was, but she came back five months later, and she was pregnant. She stayed with us, and we loved her very much and took care of her because she was so terribly sick.

"She had been treated so badly during the war, underfed and overworked with too much worry, bad food and water, that she died right after the baby — that's you, Peggy — was born, and we took you home."

"What did she die of, Mama?" was always Peggy's next question.

"She died of what the doctor said was an aneurysm, a broken artery, because of what happened overseas; but you were fine and healthy, and we've loved you ever since."

Again, for the second time since the "pilot in the woods" showed up, present-day Peggy had to pull over to the side of the road and cry for half an hour. Then she went on to Rockland to see "Bob-who-delivered-the-groceries".

CHAPTER 11

"Let's see, we left off in spring of 1941. You and Rion were sending food to the American Hospital. Then what happened after that?"

Although Peggy had many more questions for Max, she tried to remain patient. She wanted to let him finish his story in his own way. So she wrote down her questions so she wouldn't forget them, and let each session run its course.

"That's when everything started going to hell," Max answered. "As you know, in June Hitler invaded the USSR, and grandmother's words clanged in my head, *'two-front war, downfall of Germany'*. The leaders argued that 'all one needs to do is kick in the front door and the whole rotten structure will collapse'. But I looked at a map and I wasn't so sure. The Soviet Union is like a giant triangle, with the narrow part near Germany, and it gets wider and wider the further you go east.

"Anyway, Paris started to empty out; younger troops were leaving, often being replaced by older, and less motivated, soldiers. The wounded and sick crowding the military hospitals in Paris came from the East, apparently sent to France to hide them from the

German public, or maybe because the German hospitals were getting crowded, too.

"Many of the wounded were thoroughly demoralized. Here they were, wounded or ill, many with stomach ailments from poor food, and injuries like trench foot, chilblains or frostbite, and they couldn't see their families.

"Food and fuel were getting even scarcer for the French as supplies were sent to the East. Rationing became terribly restrictive, and French resentment began to increase. Many of our soldiers did not want to serve in the East, so more of them began to desert, sometimes with weapons, sometimes living as criminals.

"I was very busy, cataloguing missing — or as you say, AWOL —troops, deluged with paperwork. The two young, efficient military clerks I had become accustomed to were replaced by older soldiers —— First War veterans who resented being away from their families and were not very hardworking. I worried about Rion getting caught in whatever he was up to and implicating me, and I noticed he was distracted when we had meetings."

"Did you have any idea what was wrong with him?" Peggy asked.

"I wasn't sure, but I got the impression Rion was worried, as I was, about being caught in something. He sometimes seemed insecure, even furtive. Not his usual outgoing self."

"Well, as I recall, things were getting a bit turbulent in those days."

"Indeed, lots going on. Some of the French began to resist our administration with violence. The Communists, who had been forced to lie low while the Nazi-Soviet Pact was in force, now became aggressive and started blowing things up and killing individual German soldiers on the streets of Paris. We started to have to carry sidearms wherever we went, and German police agencies, like the Gestapo and the SD, started to be more assertive.

"This caused conflicts with other military and civil authorities. It was chaotic! The regimes, both Vichy and Nazi, could not understand that resistance calibrates itself to repression, and the tougher they became, the more people flocked to aid what the French had begun to call *'La Résistance'*.

"Then, near the end of November of '41, during one of the Paris police's routine sweeps of the seedier bars, they came upon a German pilot officer whose papers were not in order, and who began to wave a pistol around when confronted. The French police called the German Military Police, the Military Police disarmed and detained him, then called me, not quite knowing how to handle the situation. 'If it had been any ordinary soldier,' the MP Sergeant told me, 'that would not have been an issue; but this officer was very drunk and armed.'

"More significant, he had several decorations, and was asking for me by name. For me? I was mystified. I asked for the officer's name and was told, 'His name is Alfons Dietrich, says he flew with you in Spain.'

"I was, to say the least, unhappy, and decided to take Rion with me to handle the French police in case some report needed to be made, and because he had access to an unobtrusive civilian vehicle. Rion used a discreet automobile, an old Peugeot, instead of one of the flashier black Citroens favored by most police and German officials.

"He told me, 'If you drive about in one of those you might as well fire a rocket to announce your arrival, and these days that might get us both bumped off.' Rion was referring to the increasingly violent attacks on German soldiers and those the *resistants* considered collaborators.

"Well, Alfons had passed out in one of the cells, and he was a pitiful sight. He had thrown up on his uniform, and he had a swollen lip because there had been a bit of a tussle when the Military Police disarmed him. When I asked if anyone had been seriously injured, the sergeant said no, explaining that Dietrich had been pretty drunk. He also noted that he didn't think he was used to handling a pistol with his left hand.

"'His left hand; why his left hand? Alfons is right-handed,' I replied.

"The sergeant said, 'Not any more. He had lost three fingers of his right hand, among other wounds. That's why he was there in Paris. He was in hospital for injuries that he suffered in a plane crash in the East. He's been discharged from the hospital and had been posted back to the East as an administrator of some sort, but he missed his train three days prior, so he was technically absent without leave, which put him in my jurisdiction.' After telling me this, the sergeant asked me, 'What shall I do with him, *Herr Hauptmann*?'

"'Is it possible for you to turn him over to me?' I asked. 'Indeed, sir, I would be most happy to,' the sergeant responded briskly. 'We've got plenty of work to do without worrying about crazy-drunk *Luftwaffe* officers; but you'll have to sign for him.'

"I replied that that was fine, and went outside to tell Rion what was happening while the sergeant's clerk got the paperwork together. Rion immediately got out of the car and opened the trunk. He removed a burlap bag and a bottle of something, then said, 'Follow me, *Herr Hauptmann*, and see how an old copper, handles this.' A minute later, Rion was whispering to the MP NCO, and the bottle disappeared into a drawer of the sergeant's desk.

"The sergeant barked orders to a couple of enlisted men, handed one of them the bag, and within a very short time Alfons Dietrich stood woozily in the office, wrapped in a jail-issued blanket, with his uniform blouse and shirt in a sack at his feet.

"'Never put a pukey drunk in your car without cleaning him up a bit,' Rion said to me, smiling, as we manoeuvred Dietrich into the back seat. 'Your car will stink for a month if you don't.'

"'Words to live by,' I answered, as I got into the car.

"Dietrich, snoring on the back seat, suddenly roused himself, sat straight up, and bellowed, 'And never put mules on an airplane!' Then promptly passed out again."

"Gee," Peggy said, "that's damned funny."

"*Ja*, though, of course, Rion didn't understand it right away, but after I told him about Spain, about the mules, he understood and laughed as loudly as I did.

"But what Dietrich told me the next morning wasn't funny at all. I had taken him to my place, held him up in the shower and given the concierge a huge tip to clean up his uniform. I tucked him in on my big armchair, and he slept till ten a.m.

"Thankfully, it was a Sunday, so I had no duty, and when Dietrich woke '*mit Katzenjammer*', or, as you say in English, a hangover, he was terribly ashamed. I had coffee, a light omelet, aspirin and seltzer water waiting. I asked him what was going on with him, because he had always been conscientious, and other than his adolescent desire for military glory and medals, had been an ideal young German aviator.

"Alfons poured out his heart to me, telling me what was going on in the East, about the vicious SS *Einsatzgruppen* or special duty units that operated in the rear areas, about the relocation of thousands of people, about what was being said about killings, that people were being exterminated in huge numbers. I asked him how he knew all these things. 'I have seen it, with my own eyes, my friend, because some of these things happened near our aerodrome, and some of us were

100

curious about the truck traffic and the sound of shooting, so we went to see what was going on.

"'The SS men in charge waved us off, but we could see beyond them, see the lines of naked people, hear the screams and the shooting. I cannot go back there. I will desert or kill myself before I go back to the East.' He asked if there was any way I could help him.

"'Maybe,' I said, as Alfons wept. 'But you need to pull yourself together, go back to the hospital and tell them you have had a terrible case of dysentery, and you couldn't travel. Then go back to your quarters, make excuses, pretend to be sick, sit tight a week or so, and I'll see what I can do.' As I brought out his freshly-pressed uniform, I said to him, 'I see you got your Iron Cross.' 'Oh, yes,' he said, 'and I also got the Wound Badge in black; but as the soldiers say, they would rather have some clean underwear.'

"'What do you mean?' I asked. He responded by saying that the supply situation for our people in the East was terrible. 'In autumn, the roads turn to swamps, nothing gets through, and our troops are hungry and threadbare. They are cold, wet and miserable, and we don't have enough aircraft to supply them.'

"I didn't understand why we were using our precious airplanes to supply our army — why not trains or trucks?

"Dietrich explained that the Soviet railroad gauge was different from ours, and the Bolsheviks had destroyed or evacuated all of their locomotives and boxcars as they retreated. Even if we had laid new tracks, our locomotives couldn't burn Russian brown coal. Our trucks were made for European paved roads. They were breaking down under the rough conditions of Russia, and we were running out of gasoline. Our big European horses were dying of the cold and wet, so we couldn't even use horse carts to move supplies. The Red Army was getting stronger every day and their tanks were much better than ours.

"It wasn't even really winter, but our people were suffering from cold and wet all the time. I can still hear Dietrich saying to me, 'My good old friend, we are going to lose this war!' My grandmother's words echoed loudly in my head once again: *Two-front war, downfall of Germany*. I remembered what I had seen in Poland, and some of the things our recovered AWOL soldiers told me.

"I had thought these stories were exaggerations or misunderstandings, tales of misery intended to evoke pity for the culprits, but I had heard quite a few such tales, and they tallied with what Alfons told me. I decided that Alfons was telling the truth, so I pulled a few of my family's Austrian military strings and got Alfons Dietrich assigned to the *Luftwaffe* quartermaster's office in Paris."

"What became of him?" Peggy straightened up. She had become so engrossed in the story, she hadn't realized she had been leaning forward in her chair.

"After the war, his mother contacted my mother. Alfons' mother had found our address in his papers, and she was hoping I could tell her something about her son, but I was listed as 'missing/presumed dead', and that was what my mother told her. Alfons, his mother said, had been transferred to Berlin in 1944, and ended up dying in the last-ditch defence ordered by Hitler in April-May 1945."

"Oh, what a shame."

"He was one of thousands, a needless tragedy. Everyone knew by then that the war was lost, so all of these people died for nothing. Alfons' mother found out that Alfons was put in command of a bunch of kids with *Panzerfausts*, a primitive sort of bazooka. One crippled pilot and a bunch of twelve-year-olds, were supposed to hold off a swarm of T-34 tanks. His mother said he sent the kids home, told them to get lost. Someone denounced him and a few SS diehards strung him up from a lamp post.

There was a silence, and Peggy could hear a clock ticking somewhere in the little cabin, and birds chirping outside.

She waited a minute, looking around the cabin, to let Max recover a bit. Then she said, "Do you want to go on?"

"Yes, I will continue for a while." He cleared his throat again. "Two weeks later, on a chilly morning as I left my hotel, I noticed Rion across the street, leaning against his beat-up black Peugeot. He motioned to me, and as I approached, I could see that there was someone in the back seat, and a woman's bicycle leaning against the trunk. *"Now what?"* I thought, and my hand drifted towards the little pistol at my waist."

"What were you afraid of?"

"Well, Peggy, as I have told you, at this time of the war, German soldiers were being shot down in the streets of Paris, and we were all warned to be alert."

"But this was Rion. You knew him; didn't you trust him?"

"Yes, I had come to like him a great deal, but Rion was, after all, French. And this looked like an ambush. Someone lurking in the back seat, a bicycle available for a quick getaway. But Rion immediately tried to ease my anxiety by saying, 'Do not be alarmed, sir,' as he approached me. 'It is only a lady who wishes to speak with you.'

"Still, I was wary. I told him the last time I trusted him, I got myself mixed up in the black market — something I'd regretted. But he said, 'Believe me, *mon capitaine*, you will not regret this brief meeting. I will leave the two of you in privacy'; whereupon he walked away with the bicycle and sat on a bench down the street, out of earshot. He took a newspaper from his pocket and opened it, all the while watching, in the manner of veteran policemen worldwide, whatever moved on the street.

"Looking up the narrow street in the other direction, I saw a uniformed gendarme loitering at the corner, who gave me a nod. I realized then that Rion had gone to some trouble to provide security, for better or worse. The back door of the car opened, and it was her, Rachel, beckoning me and sliding over as I got in and closed the door."

"Goodness," Peggy said, "what a surprise."

"I was astonished. I was flummoxed. I was also very pleased to see her. She said she wanted to thank me for what I had done, for sending food to the hospital. I was waiting 'for the other shoe to drop', as you Americans say, and I think she sensed my wariness, because then she told me that she wanted nothing else, only to see me again some time, if I felt that was possible; somewhere private. I was stunned, and simply could not formulate a response. I sat there like an idiot, my mouth hanging open, and she continued, telling me she had thought of me since our first encounter, and then she took my hand."

Max faltered, and Peggy, in a small burst of impatience, asked, "Well, what happened?"

"Nothing, I am afraid. I just sat there like a fool, babbling something about my being a German officer, and she, ah, a refugee, and when I said that, I saw her face go slack, losing all expression. Her entire demeanor changed, and when she looked directly at me again, it was with something very much like contempt."

"But you *were* attracted to her, no?"

Max thought to himself, *"How can I answer that? How much can I say? I was madly attracted to this woman, had thought of her daily, hourly, since I met her, and here she was, telling me she wanted to be alone with me. Here she was, touching my hand, her scent, her gorgeous dark hair and eyes, her entirely beautiful and desirable self, and here was I, a person sworn to be on 'the other side', and worried about where any relationship would lead. Was she trying to seduce me from my duty? Was she trying to gain an advantage? And what about me? How could I have an honest relationship with a woman I genuinely respected for her abilities, when I possessed so much more power than she in this situation?"* Finally, Max told Peggy, "I was very attracted to her, but I could not say so, because of the situation we were in."

"I understand a little of that, given the circumstances, but then what happened?"

"As I sat there trying to think of something to say, Rachel got out of the car, slammed the door hard, walked back to Rion on his bench and mounted her bike to ride away, presumably back to the American Hospital."

"And that was it? That's all?" a disappointed Peggy asked.

"Ja, that is all," said Max, but his mind raced on. *"All? Not at all! I'm not telling everything, I just can't."* After Rachel left the car and mounted her bike, displaying a tantalising hint of thigh, he had started to get out of the back seat, and suddenly there she was, wrenching the curbside door open, dropping her bike on the cobbles. She had jumped into the car and for a moment he was frightened by her intensity. Then she grabbed him by the lapels and kissed him deeply, hungrily, pushing him back on the seat, clutching the back of his neck. He tasted her lipstick, and the slight hint of tobacco, her scent making him dizzy, and he kissed her back as deeply as she kissed him, and they

stayed that way for what seemed like forever. But then she broke off and slapped him, hard on the cheek. "Wake up!" she had told him. "I care for you, you Aryan-poster chump, so call me whenever you get your misguided Austrian-Catholic, quasi-Nazi conscience straightened out."

Peggy could see that Max was moved, and he excused himself for a few minutes, going to the small bedroom at the rear of the cabin and closing the door. Peggy took the opportunity to step outside and look around the area. The little cabin was quite small: just a couple of rooms with a tiny kitchen and bathroom. It looked improvised, like it had been built a little at a time, over many years. There were different materials making up the exterior, part aluminium siding, part weathered clapboard, some old-fashioned log construction at the rear. A sagging, unpainted shed stood behind the place, difficult to see well as evening approached. Peggy walked about a bit, noticing the chill in the air, fallen leaves crunching underfoot. Fall was fading, and the Maine winter was around the corner. *"How will I get up here in winter?"* she wondered. Her poor little wagon was no match for such a rutted, unplowed dirt road.

She had not seen a telephone inside, but the cabin had electricity, gas heat and running water. Peggy wondered how all of that was financed. Then, after a while, she heard him moving about in the kitchen and let herself back in, taking her usual seat at the table. "How did you come to live here, in this little house?"

Peggy asked. "I've spent a lot of time in these woods and never noticed this building." She felt Max looked haggard, and there was alcohol on his breath, but she could not control her curiosity.

"Well, the cabin was much smaller, dilapidated and overgrown when Pete bought it at a county auction after the war, so you probably couldn't see it. This was the shelter for a Fire Watcher station, and if you walk a bit out back, you'll see the foundations for the tower and some of the old ironwork. It was abandoned, like most of the Fire Watcher towers, in the late 40s. Pete bought it, then gave me a simple lease, and we fixed it up together with a few folks from town that Pete knew. You were probably a little girl when we were doing the work. Celine still holds the official deed and pays the taxes for me. I pay her back. That way, much paperwork is avoided. I do not care for paperwork."

"Well, speaking of paperwork," Peggy responded, "how do you get your money for groceries and so forth? How do you pay for your gas and electric bills?" Peggy sensed that Max needed a longer respite before returning to his memories of the war, so she hoped this was a good time to pose some of the questions she had written down. The grocery guy had told her Max always paid in cash. *"Where did the money come from?"* Peggy wondered.

"You forget, Peggy, I am Baron von Waldberg, heir to the Von Kesselstein estate. I still derive considerable income from our property and other holdings."

"Is your mother still alive in Austria?"

"No, she died years ago, but not in Austria. She lived quietly in Provence, since she could not stand to live in a German-speaking country after the war. I used to see her from time to time when she came to the US. Grandmother died near the end of the war, so I am the sole heir, and our English and Swiss bankers provide for me, and a professional manages what is left of the estate."

"But what about income tax, Social Security, all of that?"

"Peggy, I am not a US citizen. I have no passport, and my status here is a trifle, well, ambiguous. Let me just say that Swiss currency transfers and discreet bankers can accomplish a great deal in terms of avoiding unnecessary complications. But may we continue?"

She nodded. Max cleared his throat and took up the story.

"On top of all of our other difficulties, in December of '41 the idiots in Berlin declared war on the United States. I had fears that Germany was done for, and that there would be terrible retribution for the Reich's aggression, but what was I to do? There was no way out. If I deserted, my family would suffer. I just had to get through it as best I could, and await the inevitable, unless some opportunity arose, so I plodded on. I went to my duty grudgingly throughout the winter. I was gloomy and irritable. And I was sorry about my treatment of Rachel. I had dealt with that situation poorly, had deep regrets, but had no idea how to correct my error."

"Why not just call her, as she asked?"

"It wasn't that simple. I was complicit in illegal shipments to the hospital. If I called her there, and the call was monitored — well, it could endanger her. Any contact with her was extremely complicated, since I knew she had been marked by German security agencies, and they had become much more aggressive since the Communists began to resist. There had always been tension between the army and agencies like the Gestapo and SS about just who was in charge, and since these agencies were being given more authority by Berlin, they were more dangerous than ever.

"Anyway, in early summer of 1942," Max continued, "things seemed to get better. We had held on over the Russian winter and as the weather improved, we began an offensive that, at first, seemed to succeed. The *Wochenschau* newsreels were full of pictures of our troops cheerfully advancing, and masses of grim Soviet POWs. But I'd like to skip forward a bit, because things really started to happen to me that summer."

"Please do," said Peggy, already a little overwhelmed and rapidly scribbling supplementary notes, even though her little recorder was picking up the conversation.

CHAPTER 12

"In July of 1942, Rion came to my office, and he was a wreck. I had never seen him in such a state. First, he was wearing his full dress *gendarme* inspector's uniform, medals and all, but he was unshaven, red-eyed and dishevelled. He looked like he had been up all night, and had been drinking, from the smell of him. As we say in German, 'he was waving a brandy flag before him'. I told him he looked terrible and offered him a seat. I had become rather fond of Rion, and could not imagine why such a suave and clever fellow would be in such a state. I asked him what the matter was and he seemed surprised that I had not heard what happened that week with 'the Great Round-up'.

"I had heard of some disturbances, but nothing specific, so he enlightened me. Three days prior, the French police were ordered to round up all of the Jews in certain districts of the city, mostly the areas where recent Jewish immigrants lived, and take them to the big bicycle stadium, the *Velodrome d'Hiver*. Around four a.m., the first day, Rion was ordered to report in uniform to supervise the round-up in his old district, where he had been a beat cop, the 18th *arrondissement*. He knew most of the police there. He knew many of the people as well. 'These were poor, hardworking people, no danger to anyone,' Rion said to me. Rene Bosquet, the secretary-general of the police under the Vichy government, ordered this round-up at the insistence of SS officials, and had also lined up a bunch of young paramilitary thugs, a group of anti-Semitic toughs loyal to the Vichy government called *miliciens*, to 'assist' the police.

"'When I got to the area around five a.m.,' Rion continued, pausing occasionally to blow his nose or wipe his eyes, 'all hell had broken loose.' He described how people were running this way and that, and that buses were being loaded with confused, crying people, many of whom did not speak very good French. Mothers were being separated from children, if you can imagine that, and mothers and children were all crying. 'What kind of government tears babies from their mommas?' Rion asked me, pausing to blow his nose. These unfortunate people were refugees who had fled to France from Germany, or German satellite countries, seeking protection in France, the land of 'liberty, fraternity and equality'. Many of them were naturalized French citizens. Rion described it as pathetic to see them pleading with the arresting officers, clutching their identity cards or citizenship papers and being told that their citizenship had simply been revoked by the Vichy government just days before this mass arrest.

"'The damned *miliciens* were running amok,' Max said, quoting Rion, 'looting, breaking up furniture, beating people and throwing things out of windows.' He was appalled, and ordered this wanton violence to stop at once. He was challenged by one of their leaders, a twenty-or-so-year-old self-styled tough guy from the countryside, but one of my old police buddies took him aside, put a truncheon under his nose and told him a few basic facts about life in Paris. Then the thug calmed down and got his people mostly in order. Rion was able to let a few of the local coppers he knew take off and warn those they could, and he managed to get a man to the American Hospital to warn a certain young woman to lie low until she heard from Rion.

"'And then,' Rion went on, 'I rode one of the buses to the *velodrome*, to see what was happening—'

"It was at this point," Max told Peggy, "that Rion completely broke down. It was awful to see this tough, cynical policeman sobbing, tears coursing down his stubbly cheeks, covering his face finally with his ornate kepi; and then, after deep sobs, sniffling and apologizing, he was able to go on. He told me that when he got to the *velodrome*, it was a scene of utter chaos. No provisions had been made for food or water, and elderly people and kids were collapsing from the heat inside the building. All of the toilets were overflowing and the stench inside was unbearable. More people kept arriving, but there was no place for them to sit, and the few medical volunteers were simply overwhelmed.

"Rion told me that thousands of people were jammed into the place for two days in the summer heat, with no food and almost no water, then shipped off to a miserable camp at Drancy, outside the city.

"Rion also told me that he soon found himself to be the ranking *gendarme* present at one point, all of his superiors having disappeared once they saw what was happening, and that he had been able to get the Fire Department to open some hydrants in the place to provide some water for cleaning and to flush the toilets. The firemen were mobbed with people slipping them notes for friends and relatives.

"The fire brigadier, an old friend of Rion's, told some of his men to leave, taking the slips of paper with them. He even gave them bus fares so that they could deliver these pathetic messages. Rion also told me that he was able to get a back door open, telling the young *gendarme* on guard there to make himself scarce, and that he thought several hundred people, mostly children, had escaped. Then Rion took a flask out of his pocket, took a deep pull from it, and asked me to listen carefully to him. 'I can no longer remain in Paris, my friend; I was too overt in my actions at the *velodrome*,' he said. 'I must go away and become a "submarine".'

"This was a term we had both come to understand, which meant he intended to go underground and hide until the war was over; but, Rion added, there was one more important thing he wanted me to do. 'Max, if I may call you that,' Rion said, almost in a whisper.

"I nodded, and Rion went on, 'I have arranged to get Rachel Liebeskind out of the American Hospital. They were coming for her — not the French, but the Gestapo. We got her out with minutes to spare, and I am hiding her at my place.'

"We? I asked. 'Who is we?' Rion blushed, realising he had said too much, and continued, 'I have some friends, my dear Max, whom it is best you don't know about. I cannot keep Rachel any longer at my place, as my female companion and I are both going to "submerge", and I must find a place where Rachel can hide for a few days until my friends and I make some permanent arrangement for her. I am pleading with you to help her.'

"My God," Peggy said. "What did you do?"

Max didn't answer. Peggy could see from his appearance that he was far away, as wet-eyed as he had described Rion to be. Her own eyes were stinging, and there was a lump in her throat.

"Peggy, it is getting quite dark, and you must go. The track can be treacherous and slippery at night, and Celine would never forgive me if you were injured. Please come again tomorrow if you can, and we will talk more."

"Damn," Peggy thought to herself, *"just when things were getting interesting."* But looking out of the small back window, she could see he was right. It was getting dark and rain *was* on the way, so she agreed.

CHAPTER 13

The next day, Peggy showed up right on time. She was mindful that the subject of Rachel was sensitive to Max, so she asked him if it was too painful to tell her what happened after Rion asked him to shelter Rachel.

"*Ach*, yes," Max said. "It is hard to talk about, but it is an important part of the story, so I will go on."

Peggy was relieved that he could continue. At first, she had thought the story about Rachel was a distraction, but as Max kept returning to it, she had become very curious about his relationship with Rachel.

"As you can imagine, Rion's plea posed an immense problem for me, and I wasn't sure how to respond. My mind raced. I asked Rion if my help was the only possible alternative. Rion answered that he had exhausted all of his contacts. He said that since the Round-up, people were in hiding all over Paris — not only Jews, but everyone who feared the government, because they believed the Round-up was the signal for other mass arrests. Known dissidents, suspected *resistants*, anyone who had clashed with Vichy authorities felt they were at risk. He also told me that all of his safe houses were occupied, so there was no place for Rachel, and he could not get her out of the city until things calmed down.

"I felt trapped. I asked Rion what would happen to Rachel if they caught her. He said, 'If they catch her, she will be shipped immediately to a camp in the east, because her French citizenship was rescinded with all the rest, and she will be treated as a German Jew.' From what his group had learned, he told me she would then be mistreated and starved until she eventually died or was murdered.

"I remembered what I had seen in Poland, what Alfons had told me and things I had learned from our AWOL soldiers.

"All of that information, along with what Rion had just told me, convinced me that Rachel was in mortal danger. But all over Paris there were blood-red Vichy government posters warning of the consequences of aiding 'enemies of the government or the Occupation authorities'. The posters threatened imprisonment, even execution, and referred to anyone helping such 'enemies' as traitors. I knew the military had similar regulations, so how could I become involved? What would happen to my mother and grandmother if I was caught?

"Rion noticed my hesitation, approached me and grasped my arm tightly. He looked me directly in the eye and shook me. 'They will kill her, Max,' he said with a hiss. 'They will kill her as sure as we stand here, unless you help her. I am begging you. It will only be for a few days and we will get her out of the city, I promise you.'

"'Why does this one woman mean so much to you?' I demanded, pulling my arm loose. I will never forget what he said. 'I cannot save everyone, but maybe I can save a few. And maybe I can save this one remarkable young woman. Could you ever forgive yourself if you didn't help when you could? Could you forgive yourself if they killed her?'

"That was it. I was finished; he was right. Of course, I would never forgive myself if Rachel was harmed and I hadn't acted. 'What must I do?' I groaned, sinking into my chair. 'Just behave normally,' Rion said. 'Take your lunch as always, go home at the regular time, don't change your routine. You will hear from us.' He squeezed my hand and left, a little unsteady."

Peggy exhaled. She felt as if she had been holding her breath forever. "Wow, Max. What did you do?"

"I did what Rion said. I got through the morning, went to lunch, worked mechanically for the rest of the day, then went back to my hotel, worried sick the whole time. The concierge smiled at me as I passed her perch by the door, which was unusual.

"I took the creaky lift to my floor, opened the door to my suite, and immediately knew something was different. There was a faint but unmistakable odor — like food gone bad. I looked around my small sitting room and tiny kitchen and did not see anyone, so I opened the bedroom door and there was Rachel asleep, curled up on my bed, covered only with a thin overcoat. Curiously, there were wisps of straw in her hair.

"She looked worried, even while sleeping, and as I stood in the doorway she mumbled and jerked in her sleep. I tiptoed to the closet and pulled out a thick woolen army blanket, placing it over her and tucking it under her feet. She had kicked off her shoes. I picked them up and found they were wet and cold, and smelled bad, so I covered her with another blanket and put the shoes on the heating vent.

"Then I sat down in my armchair and waited for her to wake up. Three hours later, I heard her moving around in the bedroom. I got up to greet her, but then I heard the toilet flush and the bed springs creak. In the moment it took me to get to the bedroom door, she was asleep again, burrowed into the blankets, looking much more peaceful. I went back to my chair, covered myself with my greatcoat, and dropped off myself, exhausted by the tension of the day."

"I can imagine," said Peggy. "You must have been at your wit's end."

"Mostly, I was tired. Stress affects me that way. When I woke, it was near midnight and Rachel was peeking around the door of the bedroom. 'Well, hello, sleepyhead. Are you feeling better?' I asked.

"'What I really feel is hungry,' she said. 'Do you have anything to eat?' I yawned, stretched and tried to work the crick out of my neck from sleeping in the chair, and said, 'It's late, but I'll see what the concierge can pull together.'

"I went down and knocked gently on her door, which to my surprise was opened immediately.

Ordinarily, she was very reluctant to be disturbed after ten p.m. and grumpy if she *was* bothered, but that night she opened the door at once and greeted me warmly. 'Ah, *bon soir, mon capitaine*, I thought you might come down. You and your sister are hungry, perhaps?' she said.

"'My... ah, yes, yes, my sister. Indeed, she is hungry,' I answered weakly. 'I thought she might be,' she said, and handed me a large shopping bag, which smelled marvellous and clinked when I lifted it.

"Astonishingly, she declined the large tip I offered her, and patted me on the cheek with a twinkle in her eye. 'Inspector Rion is an old friend of mine, and a patriot. He takes care of things like this. You and your sister enjoy your meal, and I will send something up in the morning.' I returned to my flat, impressed once again with Rion's attention to detail.

"For the next hour, I watched Rachel, wolf down half of a roast chicken, four slices of buttered bread, a large sweet roll, and drink three glasses of very good red wine. I sipped some of the wine and ate a couple of crackers. Finally, she wiped her hands on a napkin and told me she had been hiding in the attic of the hospital for three days, and would I mind if she took a bath?

"I gathered a couple of towels, one of my long nightshirts, handed them to her, and she kissed me lightly on the cheek and disappeared into the bath off the bedroom. When she kissed me, I caught that odor again, stronger than before. An hour later, wondering if she was all right, I peeked into the bedroom and found her snoring lightly, once again deeply asleep on my bed, my hair brush lying unused next to her hand.

"I sighed, went back to my chair, pulled up the hassock, and drifted off."

CHAPTER 14

"When I woke, it was a sunny early morning in Paris. I could hear pigeons cooing outside my window. I was stiff and my feet were cold and cramped because of my contorted position on the chair. I heard crockery clinking and smelled coffee, and when I looked about, I saw Rachel in my kitchenette, working with the coffee press. She was fully dressed in a clean white blouse and a dark skirt, and I could not imagine where the clothes had come from.

"As far as I knew, when Rachel arrived the day before, she had nothing with her but the clothes on her back, and they were damp, smudged, smelly and wrinkled.

"She turned, saw me sprawled in the chair, and smiled brightly. Her dark hair was freshly brushed, neatly tied back, and her eyes were clear. She looked pert, rested and utterly, crushingly, beautiful. My heart leapt, and it was a joy to see her, despite the gravity of our situation.

"She crossed to my chair, handed me a cup of steaming coffee, and sat on the hassock facing me, holding a cup of her own. I noticed that her fresh blouse was a bit too big for her and realized it must have belonged to the concierge, a woman slightly larger than Rachel.

"'Good morning, Max,' she said. 'How did you sleep?' I laughed and told her, then asked her to please tell me what had happened, how she had come to my building, and how we were to proceed from now on.

"Rachel got up and returned with a croissant for me, and then began telling me what had happened. Four days previously, she said, she had been working at the hospital as usual, when a messenger arrived from Rion, warning her that a great dragnet had descended on Paris. The man told Rachel that while French police conducted a massive round-up of recent Jewish immigrants, the SS and Gestapo intended to arrest German refugees they had been watching for a while. He told Rachel she was on that list.

"Rachel said she asked the man — one of Rion's plainclothes policemen — why this was happening now and why her name was on the list. The man told her that the Nazis had been pressuring the French to turn over more Jews. They had set quotas for France, and France was falling behind. The Vichy regime was reluctant at this point to deport French Jews for fear of public unrest, so they had cynically offered up foreign Jews living in France to fill the requisite numbers. As for Rachel, the man told her that the Gestapo had been watching her for years due to her Jewish Aid activities in 1935 and 1936. He warned her not to leave the hospital, and that she should hide immediately. He said some of Rion's people would contact her as soon as possible. They would use the word 'elephant' to identify themselves."

Max interrupted his narrative to comment, "Imagine, Peggy, the Nazis had *quotas* established for human beings to be rounded up and deported. I found it hard to believe when Rachel told me that, but, of course, now I know it was true."

"True?" Peggy answered. "Indeed, it *was* true. At least once the French insisted that the Germans count Jewish *babies* to help make up their quota. I learned that during research for my book. But please go on. What did Rachel do?"

"Rachel said she acted quickly, snatching up a bit of food and a blanket, and taking refuge in a disused elevator equipment space in the attic of the hospital. She said she told only two of her most trusted colleagues where she would be, gave them the 'elephant' password, and asked them to watch for Rion's friends.

"The space in the attic was dark, stiflingly hot, not to mention musty, dirty and inhabited by a healthy population of mice and rats. Rachel said she quickly realized she had forgotten to bring any water, and cursed herself for her stupidity. She had been about to return to the lower floors to get some, when she heard heavy truck engines and orders being shouted in German. There was yelling, women crying and the sound of splintering wood as doors were broken down. Rachel was terrified.

"Eventually, everything became quiet again. After a while, one of the nurses stuck her head into the attic trapdoor. She told Rachel that the Germans had taken two of the staff, and warned her to stay put because she didn't know if they might return, then disappeared as quickly as she had come. Rachel was stuck in the attic for three days, because she didn't know if the Germans had left sentries or informants behind, or whether they would suddenly return. She survived on canned sardines, crackers and, ironically, one of the *eisern Ration* cans that Rion and I had arranged. She managed to lick a little water from condensation on water pipes running through the space, and on the second day she caught a little rainwater that leaked through the roof.

"Finally, at the end of the third day, well after dark, she was near-delirious when she was prodded awake by a man who said he was sent by the elephant. He helped her stagger down to the back courtyard and into a butcher's van, then quickly covered her with dirty, smelly straw. She was taken to Rion's apartment building and hidden overnight in an uncomfortable potato bin in the basement. The next afternoon, she was again loaded into the reeking van and driven to my hotel.

"Rachel said she was not totally conscious of her surroundings during the trip. She was disoriented, sleep-deprived and still terribly dehydrated. She remembered being greeted tenderly by the concierge, and drinking cup after cup of cool water from the tap in my kitchen, before she collapsed on my bed.

"When Rachel finished her story, she was shaking as if having a seizure, and sobbing into the front of my shirt. I put my arms around her and rocked her until she calmed a bit. Then she looked up and kissed me, hard, like she had in Rion's car. I gently pushed her away.

"'Rachel,' I said, 'we mustn't, it wouldn't be right. I don't want you to do anything just from gratitude.' She stood up in front of me. 'Oh, you are so right, my virtuous little captain,' she said, her eyes, flashing, locked on mine. 'Of course you are right, we must not,' she said again, and began to unbutton her blouse, smiling broadly. 'Of course, of course, we must not,' she repeated, removing the blouse and dropping it behind her. Apparently, the concierge hadn't had a spare brassiere. Oh! I'm so sorry."

"Oh, my," said Peggy, pretending to fan herself.

Max blushed until even his ears were red, having blurted out more than he had meant to, and lowered his eyes. "Let us just say, Peggy, we — we… became intimate."

Peggy realized he was going to go no further, and she was actually grateful, because she appreciated that he was quite embarrassed, as was she.

"So how long were you together?"

"Three days, and we never left my flat."

"Didn't you have to report for work?"

"Well, that's quite a tale. Because of my job, I had one of the few telephones assigned to a private room, and Rachel used it to pull off one of the greatest performances I have ever seen."

"Really? Tell me about that," said Peggy, pouring both of them a little more hot coffee, and settling in for a good story.

"Well, later that first morning, while I was preparing to go to work, Rachel asked me for the official German designation for my office. I told her, and then she picked up the phone, cranking to contact the switchboard. When the switchboard answered, she became an entirely different character, the very personification of an efficient, dispassionate military functionary. She put on a very severe face and sat primly erect, a striking effect, since she was wearing only my nightshirt.

"She reached my senior clerk and in rapid-fire bureaucratic military-style German, announced that she was *Unteroffizier des Medizinamts Fräulein* Niemand calling from the office of one *Professor Doktor Major* Falsch, of the *Luftwaffe Krankenklinik* in Clichy, to inform the office that *Hauptmann* von Waldberg had suffered a relapse.

"She said, that I was suffering pleurisy as a result of my previous chest injury and would be unavailable for a few days while undergoing treatment. She informed the clerk she would contact him when I was available for duty. She then demanded the clerk's name, had him spell it, gave a non-existent and garbled extension for a return call and promptly hung up with an abrupt *'Heil Hitler'*, well before the clerk had time to take notes.

"We dissolved with laughter when she hung up the phone, then she pulled that same severe face and ordered me back to the bedroom, using similar abrupt terminology."

He blushed again, then he and Peggy both laughed.

"As I said, we were together for three days and nights, some of the most joyous time I have ever spent. We learned about each other, sometimes talking through the night. Rachel developed a strong relationship with our concierge — who picked up her freshly-laundered clothes and arranged for groceries, when we did think to eat.

"Then, on the morning of the fourth day, my telephone jingled. I answered it and an official-sounding voice informed me that I was 'strongly requested' to report as soon as possible to the office of the *Luftwaffe* Inspector General at the Hotel Meurice to 'assist in some inquiries'. The speaker identified himself as a lieutenant in the general's office, and told me that if I was still unwell, he would arrange for medical transport for me, but otherwise an ordinary car would arrive to pick me up within the hour.

"I sat down suddenly and told Rachel that I thought the jig was up. I was sure they had found out about my participation in sending food to the American Hospital and faking illness. I knew I was doomed and I was cold all over, wondering what happened to an officer caught doing such things.

"Many of the AWOL soldiers we caught were sent to punishment battalions, which were always given the most dangerous assignments. They cleared mines and were put in the first wave of assaults. I was told they didn't last long. I wondered if there were similar formations for *Luftwaffe* officers.

"I told Rachel what was going on and she asked if I thought they knew about her. I told her that if they had known about her, there would be Gestapo thugs kicking down the door, not the military calling politely on the phone. I also told her she had to leave for her own safety, in case there was a search of my place during my meeting at headquarters. I asked her if she could contact Rion's friends and arrange to be moved, though it broke my heart to do so.

"Rachel blushed and hung her head. 'I heard from Rion two days ago through Madame Marchand, our concierge, but I asked to stay. I can be away in an hour or two, and I will wait at her place. I am sorry I didn't tell you, but I didn't want to leave.' She looked so contrite, what you Americans call 'hangdog', that I had to smile, and I gathered her in my arms. We stayed that way for a long time, but then I had to get ready to leave and she had to make her way downstairs and get a message to Rion.

"As I left the building dressed in my best uniform, Rachel and Madame Marchand peeked out of her door. Madame Marchand whispered '*courage*', while Rachel waved a sad goodbye, tears on her cheeks. I hoped that my medals and injuries would bring me some sympathy, but I expected the worst."

CHAPTER 15

"The legal department colonel, who was the Inspector General's deputy, and two other officers had been seated behind a long table, in a setting that looked like a court-martial, which was quite intimidating. I was asked to sit in a single chair facing them, then the colonel asked me if I knew a French policeman named Jean Rion.

"I told them that he had been assigned as my liaison with the French police, and one of the officers made a notation. Then I was asked to tell them about his visit to me just after the events of 16-17 July. I told them almost everything, including Rion's dishevelled state and that I thought he had been drinking. I also told them that Rion was very disturbed by what had happened in his old district. Then they changed the subject.

"They asked me if I knew anything about the names 'Goelette' or 'Prosper', which they said were networks of the French resistance, which were helping downed pilots to escape to neutral Spain. They said the Goelette network was thought to be associated with the American Hospital. I told them I knew nothing about that, and they asked me if I knew that Rion had disappeared.

"I told them that I was not surprised, given his demeanor after the Round-up and the events at the *velodrome.* Then one of them asked me what I had had to do with the American Hospital. I explained the entire incident of my re-injury, and another officer asked me how I had happened to go there, instead of a German facility. As soon as I mentioned Jünger's name, they all relaxed and I had the sense that I was no longer of interest to them. I had the impression they had already interviewed Jünger, and they were therefore satisfied with my explanation.

"That was when the colonel told me that Rion had stolen a truck, many sets of blank identity documents and a number of weapons from the *gendarmerie.* He told me Rion had almost certainly made his way to a resistance group in Brittany. They also told me that a search of Rion's residence had turned up a great many survival rations and German-issued cigarettes, which they assumed he had bought on the black market.

"I responded that I was shocked — shocked that Rion had turned out to be such a rogue — but assured them I had had no inkling of what he had been up to. I was then dismissed with handshakes all round, thanks for my co-operation and best wishes for a quick recovery from my pleurisy.

"I remembered to wince and hold my side as I rose from the chair, and walked out of the place in high spirits, until I realized that Rachel might not have left my place yet. I raced back to the hotel, and Madame Marchand met me at the door to tell me Rachel had been picked up by Rion's people half an hour earlier. I made my way to my room and found the nightshirt Rachel had worn draped over my armchair. I sat there clutching the soft material, desolate and missing her terribly." His face was red and he shuddered, fighting to hold off tears.

"Oh, my poor Max," Peggy said, touching his arm. "Why don't you come and stay with Celine and me tonight? We have plenty of room and a comfortable pull-out couch. Celine will be delighted to see you. I'll bring you back in the morning before I go to work."

To her surprise, Max agreed, gathered a small bag of his things, and spent the evening in quiet conversation with Celine, while Peggy worked on her notes. She left them alone, sensing they wanted privacy. Max slept well, ate a hearty breakfast and was in much better spirits when Peggy brought him back to the cabin the next morning.

Celine had provided him with a large supply of baked goods, which he stowed away quickly, joking that he would soon look like Father Christmas if he ate all of those things.

Peggy had become convinced that Max's history was a worthwhile subject for a book, and she was determined to complete his story for publication. She noted that snow was forecast, so she briefed Max on the use of her recorder. Her plan was for Grocery Bob to pick up the cassettes Max had narrated when he delivered Max's needs with his rugged four-wheel-drive vehicle. He would bring them to Peggy and return with fresh cassettes on the next trip if needed. That way, Peggy would not have to drive her little wagon to Max's place in the deep Maine winter, but she could continue to work on the project.

When she left, Max puttered with the recorder a bit, then he sat quietly watching the snow fall and thinking about Rachel.

"Of course, there had been other women; quite a few, in fact," he remembered. There had been the lusty village lass who taught him the first time, schoolgirls on ski trips when he was young, and flight attendants with the airline. There was even an aristocratic woman that he briefly thought he might marry, but she turned out to be promiscuous, incurably greedy and an enthusiastic Nazi. None of those women had been like Rachel, a person who was his intellectual equal, who was beautiful, brave and honest, a person he missed every day of his life.

Max got up from his chair and took a square of soft cloth from his desk. He settled back into his chair, put the material next to his cheek, and held it there, thinking about when it was part of his nightshirt, imagining some of her essence still clinging to it after all these years, and fell asleep.

CHAPTER 16

When Grocery Bob brought Peggy the first few tapes, she didn't think the recorder had been working properly. She heard a lot of clicking and other noises, rustling, thumping, and then, after about thirty seconds, a low mutter and what sounded like an expletive in German, "donner"-something. Then she heard throat-clearing, and Max's voice, faint at first and then stronger, as if he had moved closer to the mike or turned up the recording volume.

"OK," she heard Max say, then, "I'm glad you gave me this device, Peggy; you never would have gotten here in your little car. Bob said he had trouble even with his big truck. Also, since I'm talking about what happened after November of 1942, I'll need to pause from time to time. This is hard for me to talk about, so I may have to stop now and then, and I must look up a few things to be sure I am correct. I am glad I can stop the tape now and then and have no time limit — that is very helpful. I hope all of this makes sense to you.

"The fall of 1942 was a miserable time for me. I was lonely and felt isolated from my comrades, the other officers. I was beginning to believe these men were delusional, or deliberately misleading themselves. Our gains in the summer, when things looked so rosy for us, seemed to be resulting in a stalemate, just like the previous year before Moscow. Of course, the newspapers and newsreels were predicting total victory over the USSR at any moment, but by then I had learned to read between the lines, as you say here.

"When the newsreels trumpeted the accomplishments of our allies — the Rumanians, Hungarians and Italians — they showed pictures of happy, smiling soldiers. But if one looked closely, one could see the autumn rains had started and the roads were muddy again — not a good sign, as I had learned from Dietrich. Also, no matter how the propaganda company photographers tried, they could not make the Italian troops look cheery for very long, and they sometimes failed to switch off their cameras before grim looks appeared on the faces of our southern friends. This wasn't their war, and it certainly wasn't their climate.

"My brother officers, though, comfortable in Paris, seemed to have no doubt all was going well. 'You are too gloomy, Von Waldberg,' my colleagues would shout, clapping me on the back. 'Have faith in our leadership,' they boomed; 'they've done well so far.' But I noticed that alcohol consumption was increasing, some of the more senior officers seemed jittery, and many of the young officers were being reassigned to the East.

"Of course, I was missing Rachel, desperate for news of her since she had left Paris. I even missed Rion, who had been so candid with me at such great risk to himself. I hoped he was able to look after Rachel, because as the resistance got stronger, the security agencies grew bolder, and their reprisals increasingly violent. I had heard of atrocities in the countryside, and..." Waldberg's voice broke, and Peggy could tell he had turned the recorder off.

When the tape resumed, Waldberg's voice was strong but husky. "My work in Paris was repetitive. I was hauling in young deserters, documenting their sins on endless forms, and turning them over to military courts for trials, most of which resulted in prison terms, assignment to nearly certain death in punishment battalions or absolutely certain death before a firing squad.

"These were frightened kids mostly, many of whom had recently recovered from serious wounds, who only wanted to go home. To say I was depressed would have been a massive understatement. I was performing like a robot, adequately but without energy. And then, in late November, everything changed. I received an order to report to the *Luftwaffe* hospital at Clichy 'for an evaluation'.

"I presented myself at the appointed time, and a series of doctors and technicians poked and prodded me, drew blood and took X-rays for three hours. Then I was asked to wait in an examination room, and after what seemed like another hour, a brisk *Luftwaffe* physician walked in, slapped a file down on a desk, and told me that I had been declared fit once again for flight service.

"I was astonished, not knowing whether to be pleased or appalled. On the one hand, a return to flying would get me away from the miserable job I presently had, but I wasn't certain I could handle a fighter again, what with the arthritic pain in my shoulder and the weakness of my lung.

"The doctor saw the confusion on my face and told me, 'You, my fine young captain, have been recruited by General *Heldenklau*, to fly transports in the East, where I am told our forces are having some temporary difficulty.' *Heldenklau* was a joke among our troops. '*Heldenklau*' literally means 'Hero Stealer', and the phrase 'recruited by General *Heldenklau*' applied to people combed out of rear-area support jobs for active service at the Front.

"All sorts of people who thought they were safe in specialist jobs found themselves suddenly under orders for transfer. For example, *Luftwaffe* radio technicians were being assigned to panzer divisions as radio operators, and superfluous naval gunners were manning field artillery, all gathered in by the mythical *Heldenklau*.

"'You have experience with the JU 52, no?' the doctor asked. I admitted my considerable experience, and the energetic young doctor signed a few papers in my medical file, handed the file to me and told me to report to the *Luftwaffe* Personnel Division the next morning for reassignment. As I rose to leave, the young medic heartily shook my hand, congratulated me on my opportunity to assist our army in its 'noble Christian crusade against godless Bolshevism', and departed with a hearty '*Heil Hitler*', leaving me utterly dazed.

"Somehow, I got back to my hotel, and spent the evening in the café-bar, pumping anyone who had any information about why transport pilots were so urgently needed in the East, drinking more than I should have in the process, and spending quite a bit on drinks for others. Everyone I spoke to with any insight at all mentioned a temporary emergency situation at Stalingrad, a city on the Volga, deep into Russia.

"Finally, I collared one *Luftwaffe* major, who was in the Intelligence branch, and asked him directly what was going on. The major, who preferred expensive brandy, first gave the '*Deutsches Blick*' — ah, excuse me. This was what we called in those days the German Glance, to see if anyone was listening. He looked over one shoulder and then the other. Then he told me in a near-whisper, that although newsreels and newspapers had claimed for weeks that the city was on the verge of falling to our forces, or had already been taken, something had gone terribly wrong.

"Now, it seemed, the Soviets had an entire infantry army, a lot of our Rumanian and Hungarian allies, part of a panzer army — altogether something like three hundred thousand men — surrounded in the area. And he told me that Herman Goering had promised Hitler that the encircled forces could be supplied from the air, hence the urgent need for transport pilots.

"The next morning, when I reported to the Personnel Office, papers were stamped, forms were completed and orders were typed. I got a couple of painful injections and I was issued fur-lined cold-weather flying gear. On top of the pile of boots and warm clothing was a steel helmet, which seemed ominous. Then I was handed orders to report immediately to Orly airport in Paris, for priority transport to a place called Tatsinskaya.

"I asked a lieutenant working in the supply centre where Tatsinskaya was. The lieutenant, who walked with a limp and wore the Eastern Front medal ribbon, briefly glanced up from his clipboard and said, 'I'm not sure, *Herr Hauptmann*, but you can bet it's somewhere on the bad side of old Mother Russia.'"

CHAPTER 17

"What happened after that is something of a blur. The flight to Russia was over two thousand kilometers, and our plane had to stop here and there on the way. The journey also involved a lot of reunions, as I kept bumping into people I had flown with in Spain, or with whom I had trained for the Austrian airline. I also saw JU 52s from all over the *Reich* gathering on the airfields where we stopped. There were *Lufthansa* airline aircraft, military and industrial courier planes, even a few transports in North Africa paint schemes. I also saw Heinkel 111 bombers being readied for use as improvised transports, and even a few old JU 86s, which I hadn't seen since Spain. It seemed every training school had been closed down, and every pilot mobilized for this task.

"Some of these aircraft were brand new, with fancy passenger seating, which *Luftwaffe* technicians were busily ripping out. Other planes looked clapped-out, with oil leaks, banged-up sheet metal and bald tyres. The ground crews were working at top speed to replace worn parts and generally get all of these machines ready for winter transport operations, but there were so many planes that the work was backed up, so we had to lay over for a few days in Ukraine.

"While we waited, I was given a brief refresher course, along with a few other men who had not been flying for a while. It was good to fly again, and I wasn't as rusty as I thought I might be. I felt confident when we resumed our journey, particularly when the pilot asked me to fly the next leg, from Zaporozhye, Ukraine, to Tatsinskaya, Russia."

Peggy stopped the recorder and rubbed her temples. She tried to imagine what it must have been like, yanked out of Paris and plunged into active operations. While she warmed up her coffee, she looked up Zaporozhye, and then Tatsinskaya, about two hundred and sixty kilometers from Stalingrad, now called Volgograd. With the geography clear in her mind, she turned the playback on again.

"We landed in Tatsinskaya on 30 November 1942, and I was appalled by the confusion, the crowding of aircraft on the field and the dreadful lack of facilities. There were a few primitive buildings and the ground crew were at first forced to work in the open in terribly cold weather. The accommodations for pilots and ground crew were inadequate, miserable, lice-ridden hovels in the nearby village, or wood-sided structures with canvas roofs.

"People were sleeping wrapped in an overcoat, wearing a fur-lined flying helmet, gloves and two pairs of woolen stockings. I remember the first few days, but after that everything is a jumble.

"We flew every day the weather allowed, trying to supply an entire army with the hundred or so aircraft that were serviceable each day. The flying was absolutely terrifying, first because of the atrocious and rapidly-changing weather. There was damp fog, which caused planes to ice up, and blowing snow often caused white-outs.

"Snow accumulated on the runways at Pitomnik, the airfield in the centre of the Stalingrad *Kessel* — 'kettle' or 'cauldron' — that is, the surrounded area. Snow built up and drifted on the runways because the garrison at Stalingrad didn't always have enough fuel to operate their snow ploughs. Also, there were Soviet fighters and heavy anti-aircraft fire throughout the trip, but we were escorted by our own fighters and we flew different routes each trip to avoid the flak. Most of our losses were caused by weather problems, mechanical failures and pilot fatigue.

"One bright spot was the other pilot I was assigned to work with. Notice, Peggy, I don't say 'assistant', because he was more experienced than I, and we were of equal rank. Ernst Ludwig, a man in his mid-forties, had been a *Lufthansa* pilot and knew a great deal more than I about the commercial version of the JU 52. He knew, for instance, that certain models had an advanced heating system for the flight deck and a few other specifics of these aircraft. He made certain that we were assigned to one of the ex-*Lufthansa* airplanes, thus we flew in a bit more comfort than others. He and I traded off as pilot and co-pilot, and I was astounded by his handling of the aircraft.

"Ernst was an absolute master of the '*Tante JU*', or 'Auntie JU', as the soldiers called her, because she brought them good things like a dowdy, kindly visiting aunt bringing a big bag of goodies. Ernst could make the 'Auntie' dance like a teenage ballerina. Working with Ernst made each day a little easier, and I valued his knowledge, skill and pleasant personality.

"We were all determined to keep the surrounded troops supplied until they were relieved, so we used certain drugs that the authorities made liberally available to us, drugs like Pervitin, a powerful stimulant meant to keep us awake and alert. Some pilots had used it in the battle for England, but I didn't care for it. Trouble was, it caused one's heartbeat to increase, unusual sweating, and produced bad dreams that disturbed what sleep we did get. Some of the men became addicted to these drugs and a few became quite disturbed and had to be restrained. Despite all that, in the grind of flying these long missions in Russia, I used it myself sometimes.

"Between the stress of flying in terrible conditions, anxiety even when not flying, lack of proper rest, and discomfort from cold, lice and irregular meals, we were simply miserable."

Peggy could tell Max had turned off the recorder, then the tape resumed.

"It took over three hours to turn our aircraft around after landing in the *Kessel*, because our cargo had to be unloaded, which required quite a bit of time. The unloading crews were overworked and often poorly clad, so there were always delays. Then we had to load wounded and others selected to be flown out, so each flight took about six hours, one-and-a-half hours each way, and about three hours for turnaround. It was theoretically possible, then, for each aircraft to make two round trips per day, but the horrible weather, need for maintenance, and crew fatigue made that impossible most of the time. "Also, we sometimes had to make long detours to avoid flak, so some flights could take longer, maybe as long as eight hours. It soon became clear that we would not be able to adequately supply the surrounded units, but we soldiered on, hoping that ground forces under Von Manstein would somehow be able to cut a path through the surrounding forces and liberate the trapped army. Von Manstein was considered by many to be our finest commander, and everyone clung to the hope he would succeed."

"But, of course, by 19 December, that attempt had stalled. I remember the date, because I crashed the same day. We had almost reached Pitomnik, our second trip of the day, with a load of fuel, ammunition and food, when we suddenly lost power. All three engines failed, one after the other, and I had to crash-land on a flat snowy area I hoped was in German-held territory.

"I found out later, that two other aircraft had experienced the same problem, and the mechanics said it was caused by water contamination of our fuel, which froze the fuel system. They suspected deliberate damage by Russian saboteurs.

"I managed to glide the plane down and land more or less normally, but then the landing gear broke through a crust of ice into deep snow, and the aircraft abruptly tilted down, nose first, and came to a sudden breathtaking stop. Ernst was briefly knocked out, and I was nearly strangled by my parachute straps. The plane creaked, groaned and shuddered, and then became deathly quiet. Ernst moaned and stirred, hanging in his harness. Blood was dripping from his chin, which had struck the control wheel. 'Where are we?' he asked, his voice oddly distorted.

"I struggled to release my seat harness, and when I finally got the buckle to release, I fell forward onto the control panel, bruising my forehead. 'I'm not sure, Ernst. I just hope we are within German lines.'

"The aircraft had settled with its tail high in the air and its front buried in snow. I thanked God the cargo had not shifted and crushed us both against the windshield. Part of our cargo was large, heavy drums of fuel, three of which had, in fact, broken loose and slammed forward. We were saved by the fact that this ex-*Lufthansa* aircraft had a small private first-class compartment just behind the flight deck. The rolling drums had crushed those partitions and then stopped, though at least one of them was leaking.

"'We have to get out,' I said, and then I noticed white-clad figures rising from the very earth all around our airplane. I rubbed my eyes. Sheer terror gripped both of us. Was this a Pervitin-induced hallucination? Were these Russians? Rumanians? Germans? I heard

Ernst whispering the Lord's Prayer and, as the soldiers say, 'The coffee water was boiling in my guts' while these spectral figures advanced on us through a gloomy haze of ground fog. I reached for my little Walther pistol, determined to take one or two with me; after which, I thought, I might just shoot myself. Ernst read my intent, and drew his peashooter as well. My hands were shaking and my teeth chattered. Then I heard someone speaking in Bavarian-accented German, and I nearly threw up with relief.

"It turned out we had crashed in the middle of a frontline bunker complex occupied by an infantry regiment, and the approaching ghostly figures were ground troops clad in all sorts of white camouflage. Bedsheets, white curtains, even whitewashed canvas were worn over their dark uniforms.

"'Welcome to Stalingrad!' bellowed one young soldier —obviously the man in charge — while some of his men helped us out of the cockpit. Others were scurrying around under the plane, catching leaking fuel in pots, ration carriers, even steel helmets, and pouring what they gathered into fuel cans. Others crawled back into the cargo area, and one of them shouted down to the man in charge, 'It's like Aladdin's cave, *Herr Leutnant.* Everything we need and more.' He sounded grim, disappointed, as did the lieutenant, who called back, 'You know the orders, Fritzl, we are not to touch anything.' The soldier answered with a string of rich Bavarian curses.

"At this point, the infantry '*Sani*', or medic, spotted Ernst sitting down suddenly in the snow, still bleeding heavily from his chin. He went and examined Ernst briefly, then turned to me, noticed the large bruise on my forehead, and hustled us both into the unit's medical post. The medical station was in an underground bunker, just a hole in the ground with boards and canvas over the top, all covered with snow. There was a small stove, which raised the temperature a bit, but also smoked a lot. Everything in the bunker was stained with dirt and sooty smudges from the stove.

"The medic put Ernst on a makeshift cot and expertly applied a dressing to his chin, then asked me a few questions about my injury. He turned back to Ernst and told him he was sure Ernst had a dislocated jaw, and that we would both be seen by the regimental surgeon when he made his rounds later that evening.

"The medic told us to wait in the bunker, and while we waited the lieutenant we had seen earlier arrived and introduced himself. 'Ah, good evening, *Herr Hauptmann*,' he said, first saluting then shaking my hand. 'First, let me introduce myself. I am *Leutnant* Eric von Hoffmann, commanding third company, Fourth Infantry regiment, of the 29th motorized division, which, as you can see, is no longer motorized, as we have no fuel. We have many men from Bavaria, as you might have guessed from my young sergeant's language, for which I humbly apologize' — and he grinned.

"I gave my name, which raised an eyebrow, and asked why his men could not take some of the supplies, since they were the intended recipients, after all.

"'Orders, my dear Von Waldberg; orders backed by the threat of execution for anyone tampering with cargo before the Field Police gather it in for "proper distribution", which means, as far as I am concerned...' — and here he lowered his voice so the medic would not overhear him — 'to stuff the faces of those bastards at headquarters while my men go hungry. My men and I are supremely pissed off that this gift which has fallen to us from heaven itself must be left for the Chain Dogs. Left for them to pick up, even though we ourselves are as poor as church mice and haven't had a decent meal in nearly a month.'

"I asked him how the Field Police knew what was on the airplane and he told me that it was his understanding that the contents of each aircraft were transmitted by radio-teleprinter from Tatsinskaya, in case of just such an event as this. He said, 'Therefore, we are, may I say, thoroughly buggered.'

"'Maybe not,' interjected Ernst, his speech slurred by his injury. He beckoned Von Hoffmann closer to his cot, glancing at the medic, who was scribbling a report in the corner. Von Hoffmann took off his helmet and sat next to Ernst on an upturned crate.

"'Bruno,' said Von Hoffmann, 'perhaps you could check on Sergeant Brandt's cough?' The medic stood, nodded, and left the bunker.

"Ernst continued, 'There is something about this particular type of airplane that most *Luftwaffe* people don't know, let alone Field Police.' I could tell Von Hoffmann was struggling to understand Ernst, but he nodded along. 'There is a compartment at the rear of the plane which is only accessible from outside the aircraft. This compartment is meant for passenger luggage, but I noticed it was being loaded with parcels at "Tazi" before we took off.'

"I began to interrupt. But Ernst held up his hand to me and said, 'This is the second time I have seen this, Max, so I got a glance at the addresses on the packages, while I pretended to check the tail wheel. These are not army supplies, but private mail addressed to a high-ranking civilian *Reichsbahn* employee at a place called Gumrak. I also noticed that those parcels are not on our manifest.'

"I asked Ernst what he thought was going on. Why would a railroad bigwig be receiving private packages, no matter what his rank?

"Ernst believed that some civilian in the *Kessel*, with the connivance of other railroad people, was pulling a fast one. He suggested that the civilian might be selling this stuff at inflated prices, and living high on the hog, to boot.

"'And they are not on the manifest?' asked Von Hoffmann. 'No, I checked it twice,' Ernst said, slurring and holding up two fingers to make his point. 'What do you think is in those parcels?' I asked him.

"Ernst mumbled that some of the packages were grease-stained and he could smell ham, but he wasn't sure what was in all of the packages.

"Von Hoffmann jumped to his feet, slapped his thighs and clapped on his helmet. 'Well then,' he barked, 'let's by God go and find out!'"

CHAPTER 18

"Von Hoffmann hurried out of the bunker, and we could hear him calling to his men. I was getting ready to follow him when the regimental surgeon arrived and told us to sit while he examined our injuries. He looked Ernst over quickly, then told him to open his mouth wide. Ernst complied, and the doctor gripped his lower jaw with a thickly-gloved right hand, his thumb in Ernst's mouth. He put the other hand on Ernst's forehead and yanked. Ernst yelled, cursed, then felt his face and said, 'Oh, that is so much better', and his speech was nearly normal.

"'In a couple of days, the swelling will go down and you'll be good as new,' the doctor said, and turned to me. The doctor asked me if I had any problem with vision or a severe headache and whether I had bled from my ears or nose. When I said no, he held up two, three, then five fingers and asked me to count them, then shone a bright light in my eyes.

"When he finished the exam, he told me I was fine and that I should apply ice to my forehead to reduce the swelling. 'You won't have any trouble finding that around here,' the surgeon said, smiling. He told us each a few things to watch for, shook our hands, wished us luck and left the bunker.

"When we got outside again, Von Hoffmann's men had secured a rope around the tail of our airplane and, chanting in unison, levered the plane back to a near-normal position. 'It helps to have a few mountaineers around,' Von Hoffmann called cheerily, as his men carefully opened the rear compartment and hustled its precious contents underground '*im Augenblick*' — in the blink of an eye. 'Be careful, Fritzl, that stuff must be divided fairly and carefully rationed,' Hoffmann called after his NCO. '*Jawohl, Herr Leutnant,*' the man answered, with a huge grin, and he vanished into the earth.

"It was full dark now, and colder than I had ever felt in my life. The cold simply took one's breath away and even made it difficult to see, as moisture froze our eyelashes and people had to keep wiping their eyes. Removing a glove to touch metal instantly made the flesh adhere. I was told that during the first winter in Russia, soldiers had simply died after defecating outdoors from congealing of the lower bowel.

"The snow at such temperatures was like tiny slivers of ice, which were very slippery underfoot and rose in blinding clouds whenever the wind picked up.

"The regimental surgeon told me that the official ration allotment of twelve hundred calories per day was inadequate for troops working in -20°C weather, that the men were losing weight and their energy levels were low. He said the extra supplies would be a great benefit, and thanked Ernst and me for our co-operation."

Peggy shivered, paused the cassette player and helped herself to a cookie and a cup of tea. She felt guilty about her comfort, and remembered the time when she was a kid and the oil heater in their house had gone out during a bad cold snap. She, Pete and Celine had been forced to get into the bed and huddle together until the repair guy came.

That was bad enough, but she hadn't had to go out and work in the cold. Peggy shivered again and put on a sweater, though her room was a comfortable 70°F.

She switched the tape on again. Max's voice continued, "The cold and the seemingly constant grey overcast created an oppressively gloomy atmosphere, but the men seemed to be working cheerfully, sweeping away their footprints with tent canvas, joking and singing. I asked Von Hoffmann if he was afraid the Field Police would suddenly show up and create a problem. He laughed and said, 'The Field Police are like the sun. They only show up in the daytime. There are too many Russki infiltrators about and they don't like to use their headlights because of the Russian night bombers, the Night Witches. We won't see them until morning.'

"Another group of infantrymen arrived carrying long metal poles of the sort used to support camouflage nets. They were preparing to shove the tail back into the air, leaving the aircraft in its original post-crash position. 'Wait,' said Ernst. 'There is one more little secret you need to know, Von Hoffmann. Behind the pilot's seats, built into the rear bulkhead of the flight deck, is a small emergency tank holding fifty liters of fuel — this is also exclusive to the *Lufthansa* passenger model and the Field Police will not know that the fuel has been drained if your men are careful removing and replacing the covering panels.'

"'*Lieber Gott im Himmel!*' shouted Von Hoffmann, grabbing Ernst in a suffocating bear hug and kissing him so hard it made Ernst wince with pain. 'You are literally a lifesaver!' He told us there was almost no wood here for heating or cooking. They had been using oil from their vehicles' crankcases for heat, but could not cook their raw horsemeat rations with that because the oil fumes contaminated the meat and made the men sick. 'This will supply our little gasoline cookers for a month!' he said.

"Von Hoffmann shouted a few more orders to his men, and within an hour, with Ernst's instructions, the fuel had been drained into jerrycans and hidden away. The men then shoved the airplane back into its previous position, posted sentries, and settled down for the first adequate meal they had eaten in nearly a month, and Ernst and I went back to the medical bunker and lay down to wait until morning.

"An hour or so later, a strange apparition appeared in our bunker. It was a small, dirty, very thin figure, wearing an odd combination of German and Soviet uniform items. He was bearded and unkempt, but he had a twinkle in his eye and seemed quite cheerful. He was carrying two mess tins containing a thick savory-smelling soup, which seemed mostly based on ham and white beans.

"He pulled two spoons out of the top of his boot and gestured to us, saying '*ess, ess*', encouraging us to eat. Neither Ernst nor I were very hungry, especially after this little man pulled two pieces of dark bread out of the pocket of his greasy greatcoat and offered them to us as well. His nails were absolutely filthy, his hands grubby and the bread looked as if it had sprouted a fine, furry coat of mold. That took care of my appetite. That, and the thought that I was quite well-fed and Von Hoffmann's people certainly needed the food more than I.

"We declined his offerings, and the fellow shrugged and left. 'What in God's name was *that*?' asked Ernst. I explained that I thought the man was a 'HiWi', a *Hilfsfreiwilliger* — that is, a Soviet soldier, often a PoW, sometimes a deserter, who had decided to survive by helping the German army. We had such helpers around Tatsinskaya, but we pilots had little contact with them, and ours looked cleaner, at least from a distance.

"Ernst and I had a hasty snack of crackers with fatty meat paste from our emergency rations, and settled down in the smoky bunker, wearing all of our flight gear and under three blankets each.

"Surprisingly, we had the best sleep either of us had had in a long time. Maybe it was all the activity out in the cold, maybe the release of tension having survived our crash, which affected me the most, because I always get sleepy after a time of great stress. Maybe it was just the dark, quiet atmosphere in the bunker, but we both slept soundly until the little HiWi returned just after dawn, stomping down the steps, shouting a message, '*Komm, Komm, Leutnant, Leutnant, Komm!*'"

CHAPTER 19

"Moaning and complaining, we crawled stiff-muscled out of our bunker to find the chief NCO, the man the troops called *Der Spiess*, which your army would call the First Sergeant, standing over Von Hoffmann, who was lying on a stretcher, breathing but not moving. This grizzled professional soldier was wringing his hands, fighting tears, and begging Ernst and me to help.

"I was flabbergasted. These men, these First Sergeants, were the toughest men in an army of tough men. This sergeant had decorations from the First War, as well as an Iron Cross ribbon with the clasp for a second award, the Close Combat Badge and the Wound Badge in Silver, denoting two major wounds. I did something I never thought I would do to such a man — I reached out and touched his shoulder and asked what we could do.

"The sergeant recovered enough to tell us what had happened — that Von Hoffmann had been shot by a sniper while making his morning rounds. 'Damned sneaky Bolsheviks,' he muttered. 'They skulk around after dark to get in position, lay out there in the snow and cold all night, and pick off someone at first light. We killed one a week ago and it was a female. Can you believe it? They are using women as snipers! We knew they had women flyers, but snipers?'

"Then the surgeon spoke up, telling me Von Hoffmann had been shot in the right shoulder, fracturing his collarbone and causing severe bleeding. He told me that Von Hoffmann could not walk to the evacuation hospital at Pitomnik airport because that would increase the bleeding and probably kill him. He asked if we would help get him to the airport, and I asked how we would do that.

"The doctor told me that the Field Police and a work group would soon arrive to transfer our cargo, and that they could transport Von Hoffmann and the two of us to a point very close to the airport. Ernst asked why they couldn't just take us right to the airport, and the doctor replied that scarcity of fuel prevented the Field Police from driving the extra two miles to the airport, and that we would have to pull Von Hoffmann from the main road to the airport on a little *ajka*, a Russian-style sled.

"He told us the unit would send one of their HiWis to help us, and added that he didn't think it would be very difficult for two well-fed men to walk that distance. My reply was that two miles didn't seem too far to drive, even with such little fuel.

"The First Sergeant interrupted to tell me that the road to the airport was always crowded with a huge mass of vehicles, and they burned lots of fuel as they idled in long traffic jams. It was actually faster to travel the last few miles on foot.

"Also, he said, our assistance as *Luftwaffe* pilots might help to get Von Hoffmann on an airplane quickly. 'We have sent wounded to Pitomnik before, and many of them died while waiting in poorly-heated tents for a place on an airplane. I cannot bear to think of this good young officer dying that way. Please help him!'

"Well, that left us no choice, and a few hours later we left the bunker complex on the back of a Field Police truck. Two trucks had arrived after full daylight with a work crew of HiWis, who quickly unloaded our airplane under close guard to prevent pilferage.

"No questions were asked about any irregular cargo or the empty reserve fuel tank, though the crew searched the aircraft thoroughly and drained the JU's other fuel tanks into containers, which, along with all the other items, were loaded onto their trucks. Finally, we carefully lifted Von Hoffmann onto one of the vehicles.

"There had been an argument between the First Sergeant and the *Feldgendarme* NCO about this. The Field Police sergeant said his unit was not responsible for transporting wounded, and the infantry First Sergeant insisted they help Von Hoffmann. This conflict was resolved when four or five rough-looking infantry soldiers holding submachine guns joined the conversation and the field policeman backed down.

"After we got Von Hoffmann — who had been given a sedative — into the truck, we were joined by the same HiWi we had met earlier. The impish little fellow secured a small boat-shaped sled to the rear of the truck with a rope, then clambered up into the cargo bed with us, chattering away with the other HiWis, all of whom were sharing vile-smelling cigarettes, chewing sunflower seeds and spitting out the shells. Then off we went, me and Ernst cradling Von Hoffmann on his stretcher while our truck bounced along on the uneven road, and the little sled bobbing along behind us."

At that point, the tape player clicked off. The cassette had ended, and Peggy set up the player to continue Max's narrative, eager to hear more of the story. As she did that, she thought, *"This is incredible, a first-person narrative about Stalingrad? That alone would sell lots of books!"* She could hardly wait to start verifying and transcribing the material. Peggy quickly got the machine running again, and after the usual muttering, clicking, and a little static, Max's voice became clear.

"Well, Peggy, up to this point, our forced landing and the events afterwards were difficult but bearable. Von Hoffmann's injury was regrettable but, according to the doctor, survivable if he received reasonably prompt treatment. Von Hoffmann became more alert during the journey as the sedative wore off. He was cheerful and had little pain, though we had to keep reminding him to keep still and not move about.

"So, all things considered, we thought of ourselves as fortunate, and everything seemed to be going according to plan when, after about an hour, we arrived at the crossroads where the road to the airport intersected our route.

"We had noticed heavier traffic for the last mile, and our truck had been forced to slow down; but now, as we stopped at the first checkpoint before the airport road, the scene was congested and chaotic.

"I stuck my head out from under the canvas covering our truck bed and saw every sort of vehicle the *Wehrmacht* owned backed up on the roads, creating clouds of exhaust in the cold air. There were halftracks, horse-drawn sleighs pulled by skinny Russian horses, motorcycle/sidecar combinations, staff cars and trucks from every country Germany had invaded.

"Alongside the slowly-moving columns of vehicles, on both sides of the road, wound a long grey parade of ragged troops. Some were walking with stretchers on their shoulders, carrying wounded comrades; others limped slowly along using branches as canes or crutches; other groups seemed to be marching as squads, led by NCOs who cursed the slower-moving soldiers, yelling at them to get out of the way.

"Looking out into the fields alongside the road, I could see grey humped shapes, some half-covered with snow. Were these men who had collapsed? Why was nobody tending to them?

"'They are dead, in case you were wondering,' said the field policeman who lowered the truck's tailgate and helped us put Von Hoffmann into the little sled. 'Some people just can't make it, so they sit down beside the road and die.'

"'Why is nobody helping men like that?' I asked the policeman.

"'Look around, *Herr Hauptmann*. This is Stalingrad. There is very little medicine, few doctors, no food and no place to get warm. Those fellows might be better off — at least their suffering is over.'

"'My God, is it like this everywhere?' I asked him.

"'You'll soon find out, sir,' the man answered, as he slammed the tailgate and moved off, yelling, 'OK, OK, I'm moving, damn you!' at the drivers behind us who were honking their horns at our truck.

"The four of us — me, Ernst, Von Hoffmann in his sled and our HiWi — paused there for a moment as the truck pulled away, marvelling at the incredible traffic jam and slow-moving columns of troops.

"I gave Von Hoffmann half of a pain-killer pill the doctor had given me from his dwindling supply, and Ernst covered him with his greatcoat and put his fur *Luftwaffe* cap on the young lieutenant's head. Ernst still had his fur-lined flying helmet and leather flight jacket for protection from the cold.

"Our HiWi began to point to the road behind us, holding out his arms like wings and making airplane sounds. He grabbed the rope tied to the sled and walked away, pulling Von Hoffmann, while Ernst and I followed along, gazing at the chaos, shaking our heads.

"The next two hours was a journey into hell. As we stood in line for the checkpoint, we saw the police stopping soldiers, even officers, at the intersection and turning them back, becoming aggressive if the men resisted.

"At one point, a field policeman drew his sidearm, driving an officer away who was arguing and trying to show him some documents. When it was our turn, a policeman carefully examined our papers, initialed Von Hoffmann's wound tag, then waved us on.

"We joined a seemingly endless line of soldiers and trudged along the two miles to the airport. It took us over two hours because of the slow-moving masses in front of us. Along the way we saw trucks broken down in ditches alongside the road. A soldier told us that if a truck broke down or ran out of fuel, it was simply pushed off the road by a tank kept available for that purpose.

"One of those trucks was an ambulance, and Ernst went to look through the rear window. He came back, crossing himself, and told me there were six dead men inside. Ernst and I discussed what we were seeing as we shuffled along. We could not understand how our disciplined, experienced and well-trained General Staff could have gotten us into such an unholy mess.

"Suddenly, Von Hoffmann spoke up. We hadn't noticed that he had become alert and was listening to us. He told us that many warnings had been ignored, that at least some of the Soviet build-up had been spotted before the army got surrounded. He also told us that there had been repeated warnings about the weakness of the Hungarian and Rumanian troops guarding the army's extended flanks.

"'So what happened? Why did no one pay attention?' I asked Von Hoffmann.

"'*Gröfaz* is responsible for all of this. We might have moved German units to the flanks, but *Gröfaz* wanted to conquer the city bearing Stalin's name and said no troops could be spared from the assault. We might have been able to break out in November, but *Gröfaz* said no, he would not leave the Volga; so here we are, sitting ever so deep in shit!'

"'Who is *Gröfaz*?' Ernst and I asked in unison.

"'You don't know about *Gröfaz*? It stands for *Grosste Feldherr aller Zeiten*, the greatest military leader of all time! I'll bet you can guess now.' Of course we now realized he meant Hitler. Such talk could get people killed, I told him.

"'Look around you, Waldberg — what could be worse than this disaster?' Von Hoffmann had become agitated, and began gesturing with his injured arm, which made him wince. I gave him the other half of the pain pill, and after a while he relaxed and became still, so we plodded slowly on.

CHAPTER 20

"I asked Ernst if he thought Von Hoffmann was right, and he answered that between *Gröfaz* and *der dicke Hermann*, or Fat Hermann Goering, somebody had definitely put his foot into it, and it was our job now to get out, to survive; and by the way he told me, make sure he, gesturing to Von Hoffmann, survives as well.

"By now we were trading off helping our HiWi pull Von Hoffmann along. On one of my stints, the little man pointed to himself. *'Georgi,'* he said, *'Georgi Ukrainia, Stalina kaput.'* I laughed and said 'Max' and he nodded. *'Georgi HiWi, Georgi gut HiWi'* — and here he did his airplane imitation again — *'Georgi gut HiWi Deutschland?'*

"I glanced at Ernst, who shrugged, then, despite myself, I answered, *'Da, gut HiWi Georgi Deutschland.'* The little man suddenly stopped and knelt on the frozen road in front of me. He bent over until his forehead touched the snow, lifted my right foot, placed my boot on his head and chanted, *'Hetman, hetman, gut HiWi Georgi Deutschland, spasiba, spasiba hetman.'* Then he stood and we began pulling again, while I tried to figure out what *'hetman'* meant and how on earth I was going to keep such a silly promise.

"'So, *hetman*, how are you going to pull that off?' asked Ernst, who had been watching Georgi's performance. I answered that I wasn't sure, and asked him what '*hetman*' meant.

"'Oh, my friend, you have been dubbed a chief or boss by our small friend, and he has promised you lifelong service and loyalty. I have seen this before, early on, during our invasion of Ukraine. Local people would approach our troops and do what Georgi did. They were delighted to see us, because they thought we were liberators, freeing them from Stalin. Women would bring pitchers of water and offerings of bread and salt, welcoming our soldiers. Then, when we didn't break up the Soviet-style collective farms, started shooting people for minor infractions or for no reason at all, and herding people off for forced labor, that goodwill disappeared.'

"I just nodded, and on we went, Ernst and Georgi pulling Von Hoffmann for a while. I began to notice that my right foot was becoming numb. I thought maybe my boot was too tight, so I sat down on the fender of an abandoned truck and started to tug at my boot, meaning to remove it and rearrange my socks, or do whatever else it took to loosen it a bit.

"'Jesus, sir, don't do that!' a passing NCO called out. 'If you take that boot off, your foot will swell up and you'll never get it back on, and you'll lose your foot for sure!' He was leading a small group of men, and he didn't stop, just kept on walking.

"His greatcoat was open and I noticed he wore the infantry assault badge and other decorations indicating he was an old campaigner — what we called an '*Alte Hase*' or old bunny, someone who had been around a bit. I decided to follow his advice and called after him, 'What should I do? I can hardly feel my foot.'

"'Just keep on walking, sir. You can deal with the problem whenever you get where you are going,' the man barked over his shoulder as he marched on.

"So, on I went, hurrying a bit to catch up with the others, then falling in behind. I worried about my foot. It felt like I was walking with a block of wood on the end of my leg, but even that concern faded away as we approached the airport.

"A huge mob had gathered around the checkpoints at the gate, and heavily-armed field police were roughly shoving people into orderly lines. There were more scenes of conflict, people shouting at the police, police ordering men to turn back. There were loud arguments, and in one case, a physical struggle as a man tried to shoulder past a policeman. The fellow was subdued and led away, sobbing.

"Then a policeman spotted our little group and directed us to a checkpoint manned by *Luftwaffe* officers as well as field police. We were questioned by a major with aviator badges, who examined our papers carefully. That is, he examined my papers, and Ernst's, then listened closely to the story of our crash and subsequent journey.

"The major stepped away to a table where an NCO looked up something in a large stack of papers, and nodded when the sergeant pointed to one of the documents. He returned to where we waited and quickly checked Von Hoffmann's wound tag, then stamped our documents and waved us through. Nobody at the checkpoint paid the slightest attention to Georgi. It was as if he was invisible.

"'Go to that big blue tent and drop off your wounded man, then go out to the flight line and you will be directed to an airplane,' the major said, pointing to a cluster of tents in the distance. He told us that pilots and flight personnel had priority. He turned to the next person in line as we walked away.

"I glanced at Ernst. He nodded and we quickly moved off until we got close to the tents, then turned towards an area where we could see aircraft being loaded. Von Hoffmann yelped as the sled bounced on the rough ground, and Ernst cautioned him to stay still. He told Von Hoffmann that when we got close to the planes, he would have to stand up and walk between us until we got on to an aircraft. He also told him not to talk to anyone — we planned to say he had a head injury and was temporarily dazed.

"As we got close to a group of JU 52s, Ernst and I helped Von Hoffmann to his feet. Ernst pointed to one of the planes, which by now I had learned to recognize as an ex-*Lufthansa* machine.

Von Hoffmann leaned on me as Ernst took off with our HiWi into the fog and snow, and when Ernst came back, we joined a line of men waiting to board that aircraft. Once again, we were noticed by a field policeman, and waved to the front of the line. As we passed the waiting troops, some of them cursed us, saying things like, 'If you damned flyboys would do a better job, we'd have enough to eat' and other insults. Von Hoffmann started to reply, but Ernst shushed him and we hustled him forward, trying not to jostle his injured arm.

"We came to the cargo door, and one of the pilots helped us aboard. I recognized the man from Tatsinskaya. 'My God, Von Waldberg, Ernst Ludwig, we thought you both were dead! Glad to see you' — and he hugged us both, pounding us on the back. He turned to Von Hoffmann and asked us who he was. Ernst told him in a low voice. The man nodded and directed us to a place at the rear of the cargo hold, where we could sit on the floor with our backs against the bulkhead. 'Best I can do, I'm afraid,' the pilot said. 'This plane will be totally filled up in a few minutes, so make yourselves as small as possible and try to keep warm. I'll see you at "Tazi" and help you out.'

"With that, he returned to directing the men loading the aircraft, and, true to his word, within minutes every spare centimeter seemed to be occupied. Ernst and I squeezed close together, Von Hoffmann tightly in between us, which kept him warm and immobilized his injured arm.

"Stretcher cases were loaded in after us, the wounded men groaning as they were moved around.

"When the entire floor space was filled, other wounded men who could walk and sit up were directed to makeshift seats along the sides. Last, a few unwounded men were allowed to enter the cargo hold and curl up wherever they could find space.

"There was room next to us for one unwounded man, who stepped carefully across the stretchers and joined us against the back bulkhead. He introduced himself, and said he was a radiotelephone specialist being flown out because of his training. He said the other unwounded men on the plane were either technical experts or couriers, and after a few minutes he fell fast asleep.

"I looked around and wondered whether we could get off the ground with such a load. I had never seen a JU packed so tightly. Our planes had not been so heavily loaded on our earlier flights, but now there seemed to be greater urgency to fly out wounded men and specialists.

"Later, I learned that Von Manstein had conceded the failure of his breakthrough attempt the day before. The commanders were trying to evacuate as many men as they could, aware that there would now be no other way out.

"Finally, just before the door was closed, there was a commotion. A portly man wearing a dark blue uniform with rows of unfamiliar decorations was trying to board the aircraft, and arguing fiercely with the pilot. 'I am required in Berlin for urgent consultation with *Reichsminister* Speer. Get out of my way.' An officer near the door called out to a nearby field policeman, who tapped the man on the shoulder and told him to present his papers. 'I've lost my papers in an air raid, but I am ordered to Berlin, to make an important report,' the man bellowed.

"The field policeman asked the man who he was, and said he did not recognize his uniform. 'I am the Chief Railroad Police Inspector for this region. My *Reichsbahn* rank is equivalent to an army colonel. You can check with my headquarters at Gumrak. I have been ordered to report in Berlin at once. Now leave me alone!'

"At the mention of Gumrak, Ernst prodded me in the ribs and whispered in my ear, 'Gumrak was where those mysterious packages were addressed, remember?' I nodded, and Ernst hid a smile. 'This might be the railroad bigshot who was smuggling food.'

"The man kept arguing, but the field policeman had heard enough. He ordered the man to walk away from the airplane, dropping his hand to his sidearm. The railroad man stepped back, but kept shouting, 'Give me your name, Sergeant. I'm going to report you to the Führer!'

'OK,' the policeman said, 'and you can tell him my promotion is overdue as well! Now come along and we'll sort this out.'

"I asked Ernst quietly what he had done with Georgi, and he answered that he had managed to stuff him, undetected, into our rear luggage compartment, and hoped that he would survive the trip in the small unheated cargo space. I shivered, hoping so as well.

"Then the door was closed, the engines revved up and we began to move, while I prayed that this seriously overloaded airplane would get off the ground.

"Peggy, I had been flying for a long time, but I never had a flight as scary as that one. The plane barely made it aloft, and I thought we were going to go off the end of the runway, but we finally got airborne. Then, as the aircraft ascended, Ernst got a severe headache and nosebleed; and finally, after three miserable bumpy hours, we landed at Tatsinskaya in the middle of a blizzard. The co-pilot came back to help us off the airplane.

"We needed that help, because our legs had gone numb, but we limped off and helped Von Hoffmann to a waiting ambulance. When we dropped him off, I told the medic about my foot, and Ernst mentioned his problems with bleeding, so the medic gestured for both of us to get into the vehicle. Ernst asked the medic to wait just a moment, and walked stiffly off behind the tail of our aircraft, through a mist of ice crystals.

"The medic assumed, I think, that Ernst needed to relieve himself, and turned to other patients. Just to make sure he was distracted, I asked him a couple of questions. Ernst quickly came back, jerking his thumb quickly over his shoulder when nobody was looking.

"I glanced back and saw a small, dark figure staggering through clouds of blowing snow towards a long line of Russian civilians shoveling one of the runways. I patted Ernst on the back as we clambered up into the waiting ambulance and said softly, 'Georgi gut

HiWi no Deutschland,' and he, whispering, replied, 'Da, *hetman*, but Georgi gut HiWi no Stalingrad either'; then he bowed to me and we both chuckled as our vehicle pulled away towards the aid station.

"As it turned out, both of us had serious injuries. My right foot was severely frostbitten, and two of my toes were in danger of gangrene. The doctors said that was at least in part due to my ankle injury as a teenager. They felt that the circulation in my foot had been slightly compromised after that injury, but that it had only become an issue during exposure to extreme cold and a long walk on frozen ground.

"Ernst's facial injury had resulted in damage to his sinuses, and he was deemed unfit for further flying. Both of us were put on a hospital train and began a long trip back to Germany, for treatment and reassignment.

"Though we were kept relatively comfortable on the train, the trip was a nightmare. All of the troops on the train except those severely wounded had to carry weapons because of a constant threat from partisans along the route. Soviet bombing or sabotage had damaged some rail lines and facilities, rail equipment was poorly maintained so the train ride was very rough, and the wounded men cried out when the train swayed and lurched.

"The wonderful girls, the *Krankenschwestern*, or nurses, were short of help and medicine. Ernst and I helped where we could, but I was in severe pain from my foot, which was swollen and ached terribly after it was warmed up.

173

"The trip seemed to take forever. Both Ernst and I began to be quite depressed. We wondered how we could supply our troops with so few airplanes and the railroads in such poor condition.

"Then, early in the morning on Christmas Eve, four whole days after we left Tatsinskaya, our train finally reached Warsaw. There, a young *Luftwaffe* signals officer who had been injured in a road accident boarded the train and was assigned to our compartment.

"After introductions, he asked where we were coming from and he told us that, while he was waiting for transport at *Luftwaffe* headquarters, he had heard that the 'Tazi' airfield had been overrun by an armored Soviet raiding party. Many flight personnel had been killed, he said, and over seventy aircraft were destroyed. So, in one blow we had lost ten percent of the total transport capacity of the *Luftwaffe* in the East. At that moment, both Ernst and I knew that the men in the Stalingrad pocket were doomed, and our sadness became almost unbearable.

"Despite our grief, we joined in the weak cheer that went up from everyone when we finally crossed the German border; but soon, whatever joy people had felt began to dissipate. Looking out of the windows, we saw damaged buildings and bomb craters. People were picking through rubble, looking cold and hungry.

"Finally, as we approached the suburbs of Berlin, orderlies came through the cars, asking everyone to pull their window shades closed. When asked why, they responded that it was an air raid blackout precaution.

'Blackout?' the signals man sitting with us asked. 'How can this be a blackout precaution when it's not dark yet?' 'Regulations then, sir; just do it, please,' the orderly answered.

"Ernst tapped the young officer on his knee before he could protest further. 'It's not about the blackout, lad. They don't want people to look in. They don't want people to see how many of us there are or how miserable we look. It's all about morale, my boy, all about morale.'"

CHAPTER 21

"Our train arrived at the Berlin *Hauptbahnhof* well after dark. We had twice been forced to sit waiting on sidings as priority trains roared past, loaded with troops and equipment to reinforce the desperate situation in the East.

"We, the walking (or, in my case, hobbling-with-crutches) wounded were directed by harried railroad and medical personnel to various waiting transports. I was sent to a bus destined for one hospital, Ernst to an idling truck headed for a different destination. We embraced and shook hands outside the station, wished each other luck, promised to keep in touch if we could, and went our separate ways.

"I was hospitalized for ten long days, while the quacks tried to save at least part of my foot. I quickly became aware of the contrast between my earlier hospital experiences in France and this one. The hospital near Paris had been comfortable, even luxurious; the staff, both French and German, courteous and kind.

"This time, my 'hospital' was a drafty old warehouse building, hastily converted to handle an overflow of injured from the Russian Front. The nurses and orderlies were overwhelmed, the doctors brusque, efficient and not given to prolonged explanations. The place was noisy, dirty and smelled bad because of the nature of our injuries. It was jammed with men suffering various forms of weather-related extremity injuries, such as frostbite, chilblains, trench foot or, as in my case, gangrene.

"Two of my toes had turned black, and had no feeling. The rest of my foot remained red, swollen and blistered, and I developed a fever. My treatment consisted of applications of various salves and periodically soaking my foot in a basin with a peroxide solution, none of which accomplished a damned thing.

"I lay on my cot each night, my foot throbbing, often unable to sleep because of pain or men crying out, snoring, or muttering in their sleep. I thought back over all of the things I had seen over the past few years. I thought about Spain, Poland, France — all victories, but all complicated by dark events. Then England, definitely a defeat, and blunders by our command to boot. I thought about what my grandmother had said, and what young Alfons and a weeping Rion had told me of atrocities.

"I thought about Rachel, being hunted like an animal God knew where by people like me. I prayed she was safe and at least had enough to eat and a place to stay warm. What would happen to her if she was caught?

"Then I thought about Stalingrad, what I had seen there and the terrible mistakes that had been made. I thought about my comrades at Tatsinskaya crushed by

Red Army tanks, our precious planes burning on the runways.

"I thought about all of the losses, all the lies, all that senseless terror and murder — for what? My hope for victory, even survival, was gone. Optimism, enthusiasm and faith in German power had died the death of a thousand cuts. How could I have been such a fool?

"Every morning I woke, if I had slept at all, to another day of pain and misery. Amputation was the only cure for many of the injuries these soldiers had suffered, so amputations occurred every day. I thought about a book I had read about the American Civil War, how amputated limbs had piled up outside the surgeons' tents; and now here we were, about eighty years later, still sawing off arms, legs, fingers and toes wholesale. I imagined a growing pile of them somewhere in the basement.

"Therefore, I was not terribly surprised when one morning a surgeon, gloved and gowned, showed up at my bedside, accompanied by a burly orderly with a surgical tray. In less than twenty minutes, with the orderly holding my leg down, he had lopped off my blackened toes, the big one and the one next to it, with a tool that looked like shears for cutting up poultry. He sutured up the stumps, applied an antiseptic, slapped on a fresh dressing and was gone.

"After the swelling went down, I had very little pain, and I was actually happy about the amputation. For one thing, the procedure got rid of my fever, and the swelling and redness in my foot began to go away.

"I also assumed that the loss of my toes, added to my earlier injuries, would get me discharged. I felt that getting out of the war at the cost of only a couple of toes was an enormous bargain, given the price thousands of others were paying.

"However, as you know, Peggy, that was not to be. To my utter astonishment, I was ordered to report for re-assignment only four days after leaving the hospital, while I was still recuperating in an officers' hostel. I arrived at the Berlin replacement office, still using crutches, which I didn't really need, though I did have a pronounced limp.

"I wore my oldest uniform, and tried to look as ill as I could. A *Luftwaffe* colonel, an older man with World War I decorations, reviewed my service record with me, and asked if everything there was correct and in order.

"I agreed with the history, but emphasized my injuries. After all, I had suffered a concussion after my crash in the Channel, a second head injury in Russia, four broken ribs with a collapsed lung which had reoccurred in Paris, and now a frozen foot and subsequent loss of my toes. I had headaches, I told him, and walked only with pain and a bad limp. That, of course, was a fib, Peggy. My limp was more an issue of balance than pain, and I soon developed a nearly normal gait, as you have seen.

"I did not feel ready for re-assignment, I said, and wondered what sort of job the *Luftwaffe* could find for a man in my condition.

"Certainly, I told him, I'm in no shape to be flying transports any more, because I knew I wouldn't be able to handle the pressure involved in kicking rudder pedals and stamping on brakes required by the JU 52.

Fighters, I said, are absolutely out of the question because of my lung injury.

"The doctors had told me that because of the frostbite, my right foot would forever be unusually sensitive to cold, which I was already experiencing in the damp Berlin winter of 1943. I practically pleaded with him not to put me at a desk somewhere. I had done that, I said, and simply couldn't stand it again, at which point I sort of ran out of things to say.

"The colonel glared at me over his spectacles, his face flushing. Did I not wish any longer to serve the *Führer* and Fatherland? he asked. While thousands were sacrificing themselves for the Thousand Year *Reich* — what did I wish to do: scurry back to my alpine cave somewhere in Austria and hide while the Red Tide rolled over Germany?

"He roared and fumed, his wattles shaking, pounding on the desk. 'You aristocrats are all the same,' he bellowed, 'out for all you can get, then bolting the minute things get tough. I saw your kind in the Great War. I ought to have you court-martialed for defeatism!'

"Oh, God, I thought, another Nazi fanatic. Why do I keep running into these guys? First the doctor in Paris, and now this World War I relic sits behind his iron-plated desk, and bullies people who have seen what is

180

really going on. I simply shut up and waited for him to conclude his monologue and give me the bad news.

"He ran on for another minute or so, so loud one of the clerks stuck his head in the door and asked if all was well. Eventually, he ran out of steam, cleared his throat, and levelled his forefinger at me while he read me my new orders. It turned out I was ordered to report within thirty days to a *Luftwaffe* base at Mont-de-Marsan, France, where I was to learn to fly another type of airplane, the huge JU 290.

"I had seen one or two 290s during my career, and I knew they had hydraulic-assisted controls, which meant I wouldn't be slamming my foot against rudder and brake pedals, but I still had severe doubts about my ability to fly this gigantic aircraft.

"I knew they flew at high altitude, scouting for Allied convoys, according to popular magazines. I also knew that an aircraft at high altitude was cold as hell, and what would I do about that?

"I left the office deeply depressed, sick to death of the war, the *Luftwaffe*, and yes, even sick of flying for the first time in my life. I was also wondering if I could make it home and then to southern France in thirty days. *'Or maybe that blowhard colonel was right,'* I thought. *'Maybe there was an alpine cave I could hide in until all of this madness was over.'*"

CHAPTER 22

The tape snapped off, startling Peggy, who had become immersed in the story. She found the next tape, and noticed that Max had written a date on the cassette a full week after the previous one.

Before playing the next segment of Max's narrative, she heard the sound of the postman's truck and decided to fetch the mail. She noticed fresh snow on trees and the outside staircase, *again*. The air was very cold, with heavy clouds promising yet more snow.

She began to sweep off the stairs, but then saw the postman getting out of his truck and went down to meet him. He had a special delivery package addressed to her, which she signed for and hurried back upstairs to open.

Peggy had forgotten about the uniform cap Ed Williams let her borrow after she interviewed him. Now, here it was, neatly packed with tissue and a typewritten letter from Mr George Atkins, an expert in WWII-era militaria, based in Michigan. She had discovered Atkins' appraisal service in a military collectors' magazine, and sent him the cap shortly after she got it from Ed Williams. She was hoping to have it authenticated and had also asked Atkins if he would try to decipher the writing on the sweatband.

Mr Atkins' detailed letter included photos of a label and factory marks she had not noticed when she first looked at the cap. Atkins had even analyzed a sample of the thread used to sew the item together, and noted the number of stitches per centimeter, which, he said, was consistent with German commercial sewing machines of the period.

He concluded that the cap was genuine, that it was of early-war manufacture, and that the insignia on it indicated it had belonged to an officer of the *Luftwaffe* signals branch. Other photos of the cap were included, along with illustrations from reference materials confirming Atkins' findings.

As to the writing on the sweatband, Atkins reported that he had examined the inked letters under bright light with strong magnification. He was able to make out only the first four letters, NOTK, which seemed to be followed by one or perhaps two more letters.

He also stated that he was convinced the cap had been immersed in seawater at some point, since crystals trapped in the fabric proved to be sea salt. The letter concluded with an offer to purchase the cap, and a hefty bill for services rendered.

Peggy's hands shook as she finished the letter. *'This is it,'* she thought, *'this is proof!'* All she needed to do was show the cap to Max, who might be able to identify the owner, and then get an affidavit from Ed Williams. But how could she get to Max's cabin? It had been snowing on and off for days, and even the asphalt roads were tricky. Her little car would never make it up the unplowed trail to Max's.

Of course, she could ask Grocery Bob for a ride in his four-wheel-drive truck the next time he delivered supplies. In the meantime, before the next grocery delivery, she was going to follow up on her Freedom of Information Act request to see the 1944 FBI file, and also go through the next tape Max had made.

So, after she drove to Rockland and placed the cap and Atkins' material in her safety deposit box, she visited the Grocery King and was disappointed to learn that Bob was not going to see Max for "a couple of weeks", according to Bob's father. Bob was in Portland, at the VA, his father said, getting some therapy, so he couldn't go sooner.

Between ringing up customers' groceries, the man told Peggy that Max maintained good reserves every winter for situations like this, when the weather was bad. After Peggy assured him, she was Max's friend, he promised to call Peggy before Bob made the next trip.

"There's a lot of things Bob can't do since he came back," his father said, turning quickly away, "but he sure as hell can handle that truck — I can't think of five men hereabouts who could do that so well."

Peggy thanked the man, did a few more errands in Rockland, then drove carefully back to Owl's Head and loaded Max's next tape. She felt a distinct letdown, since the day had started on such a high note.

Max's voice came up on the recorder, and Peggy immediately noticed that his voice was weaker than usual, and that he was coughing and clearing his throat a lot. She forced herself to concentrate on what he was saying.

"Peggy, my voice may be difficult to understand, and I might have to turn the machine off now and then. I've caught a cold, and it might be hard to talk for long stretches. Anyway, the day after my meeting with the angry colonel, a courier arrived at my hostel with the formal copy of my orders, travel vouchers and ration cards for the trip. It was intended for me to travel by train through Germany and across France, but I knew a bit about wartime rail travel by then, so the next day I went out to Tempelhof airport, hoping to hitch a flight to Austria.

"If I could get a flight to Vienna, then I could make it home for a week or so before going on to southern France. If I got stranded along the way and was late reporting to my new assignment, what were they going to do? Send me to the Eastern Front? I eventually did manage to wangle a flight out of Berlin to Vienna, then hitched a ride on an army cargo truck to Kufstein.

"Things had changed in my sleepy little town. The local inn where I had met Goering was under heavy SS guard, the stores had very little on display, and the fuel station was closed and shuttered.

"I asked what the SS were doing at the *Gasthof*, and the driver said it was very hush-hush, then gave the German glance, one shoulder, then the other, and told me the rumour was, that high-ranking, French prisoners — hostages, really — were being held there.

"'No gas for civilians any more,' the truck driver also told me, noticing my interest in the vacant gas station. 'Everybody has gone back to horses or they are using contraptions that burn wood or coal to run the vehicles.'

"I remember thinking again of what my grandmother had told me back in '41 — *'Two-front war, downfall of Germany'* — and I shuddered as we pulled up in front of *Schloss* Kesselstein, my boyhood home." Max started clearing his throat again, and the recorder clicked, indicating another pause.

Peggy was worried, and wondered what was going on with Max. She became even more determined to go see him as soon as possible.

Meanwhile, she continued to listen and take notes as Max resumed his narrative.

"My time at home did not go as well as I had hoped. My grandmother was anxious and overworked. She was extremely busy looking after her flock of people in hiding, a group that now numbered twenty, including six children. She was, of course, glad to see me, but appeared almost as happy to learn that I had been issued an extra ration book along with my travel orders. She told me that feeding so many people had become very difficult due to restrictive rationing and chronic shortages of things like meat, eggs, milk and fats, like butter or lard.

"'Please go greet your mother,' she said, 'but then come back and I'll have someone take you to the market. Buy all you can, Max, we are much in need.'

"I asked her why she was unable to work with local farmers 'under the table', as she had been doing on my last visit. I thought she was going to bite someone, so fierce was her response.

"'The damned bureaucrats are everywhere these days, Max,' she growled, blue eyes flashing. 'They are counting every pig, sheep and ox. Even horses have been subject to a census, those that haven't been requisitioned by the military. They have tightened everything up, and my contacts tell me they are stripping the countryside to support the big cities. That's where the regime thinks political unrest might start if shortages get too bad.'

"I clearly remember the gist of what my grandmother said next—

"'The people around here are afraid, especially since SS showed up in the village. If it were not for the youngsters in our *schutzenverein* group, we would be in real trouble for food. They bring us rabbits and other game they catch which, used creatively, help us a great deal. Even the damned Nazis cannot count every hare, pheasant, squirrel and fish in the Austrian Alps, thank God. Now go see your mother.'

"My mother was also very busy. She had been contracted by the Ministry of War in Berlin, which everyone called the *Bendlerstrasse* because of the street where it was located. Mother worked as an interpreter, spending long hours on the telephone, or working with documents that were delivered and picked up by motorcycle couriers.

"She told me that her classification as an essential war worker got her extra rations which, along with the money she earned, was a help in managing the needs of their clandestine dependents. She told me that in addition to the SS I had seen, there was a battalion of regular army troops in the area, which also made people nervous.

"I told her I was heading into town as my grandmother asked, and wondered if there was anything I could bring her. She answered no, but asked me to mail a letter for her at the post office, and told me that even though I had proper coupons, some of the items I wanted might not be available.

"Then she said, 'Oh, Max, just one thing, if you could get some cigarettes or even a little tobacco, I would appreciate it. With all of this stress, I'm afraid I have taken up smoking. It helps me relax.'"

The machine clicked and clicked again, and it must have been off a while, because Max's voice was stronger, but his speech was a little slurred when he came back on. *Schnapps*? Peggy wondered.

"Well, hmm, what next? Oh, *ja*, Peggy, I changed into my old civilian clothes and got a ride to town in grandmother's old buggy, pulled by a skinny black horse driven by the family's estate manager, a man I liked and trusted, named Willi Goetz. Goetz told me that he would meet me at the local *Bierstube* in an hour and dropped me off in the village square.

"I made the rounds, haggling with merchants, and used up all of my coupons except for the tobacco ration.

It seemed there was none to be had, so I was disappointed as I entered the *Stube*. Goetz was not there yet, but I was twenty minutes early, so I ordered a brandy at the bar. The barman said there was no brandy, no schnapps, only rum, which I disliked, so I ordered a beer. The beer was truly vile, weak and watery, so I shoved it aside and decided to simply sit and wait for Goetz.

"'They've rationed or confiscated most of the barley, so the beer is awful, isn't it, Master Waldberg?' said a voice from behind me.

"I looked around to a table near the back wall and almost immediately recognized one of my schoolmates, a fellow named Tomas Klaibisch, from a winegrowing family in our neighborhood. He looked older than he should, I thought, then I noticed an empty left sleeve pinned to his shirtfront. He rose and came to sit next to me, and we shook hands, greeting each other warmly, hugging in the Austrian fashion.

"Klaibisch motioned to the barman and said he thought I would like some of the house special. The barman hesitated, but Klaibisch told him that I was an old friend and a good man, and not to worry. The man nodded and reached under the bar, producing an unlabeled bottle containing an oily clear liquid. He poured two glasses, one for each of us, and pushed them across the bar. Klaibisch raised his glass in a toast and said, '*Prost und prost ex!*', which was local slang for 'drink it all at once'.

"I did, with some misgivings, and found that after the first incredibly acrid bite, the stuff was not bad at all, almost like a second-class peppermint schnapps. I said as much to Klaibisch, who told me it was made locally. In fact, *very* locally.

"It was distilled, he said, from potato peelings, and flavored with local mint. It was carefully aged, he said. When I asked how long it was aged, Klaibisch said that he walked up from the basement with each batch *very* slowly, and we both laughed.

"Tomas got me another, with ice this time, and motioned me to his table. At that point, Goetz, the estate manager, walked in and announced he was ready to take me back. Klaibisch told him that he and I needed to talk, and that he would get me home, if that was all right with me. I noticed that Tomas winked at Goetz. So I knew our meeting was not accidental, but what the hell, I thought.

"I said indeed it was OK, and gave Goetz the things I had gotten from the market. 'Damn! No tobacco today?' Goetz asked.

"'None,' I answered, and he left, cursing under his breath.

"Well, Tomas and I had a long, rather boozy lunch. We switched from his moonshine schnapps to an inferior white wine and he told me his story, involving service as an infantry officer, first in France, then North Africa, and I told him mine. He spoke of the setbacks in Africa and I told him what I knew of Stalingrad.

"Finally, just before we left, Klaibisch went to the bar and came back with four packets of army cigarettes. He gave them to me, refused payment, and drove me home one-handed, in an old Opel, holding the steering wheel with one knee when he needed to shift gears. I was too tipsy to be frightened then, but it scares me now to think about it, driving like that on those snowy mountain roads.

"When we stopped at the gate of the *schloss*, Tomas leaned over to me and spoke very softly and carefully into my ear, holding my lapel tightly. 'Max, remember this while you are away. We will look after your mother and grandmother, and we will protect those people they are hiding. We will help take care of them until the right time comes, and we will then make sure that Austria is once again run by *Austrians*, not a bunch of political thugs sucking up to the damned Germans. Will you remember that, Max?'

"Well, Peggy, all I could think of was what Rion had said in Paris, about 'his friends' taking care of things. There was an American baseball player from the 1950s who supposedly said, 'It's déjà vu all over again', and that is how it seemed. So I asked Tomas, as I had asked Rion, 'Who is "we"?'

"Again, exactly as Rion had told me in Paris, Tomas answered that it was best I did not know.

"The next morning, I found Goetz in one of the barns, and handed him one of the packets of cigarettes Tomas had given me. The man almost cried, he was so grateful. Then I asked him how Tomas managed to be

191

so generous — how it was he had access to such things as unrationed tobacco.

"Again, the German Glance, then he told me that my old school friend Tomas Klaibisch was an unofficial local boss, perhaps best described as an unelected mayor. Goetz sat down on an overturned bucket, lit a cigarette, inhaled deeply, sighed, then offered me a puff — which I declined — and continued his story.

"According to Goetz, Tomas' business had started with the manufacture and distribution of his popular bootleg schnapps, which began soon after his discharge in early 1942. That soon led to his purchase of the *Bierstube*. After that, Goetz told me, Tomas had become involved in a number of enterprises. 'If you want to buy almost anything without paperwork, under the counter, untaxed and unregulated, Tomas is your man,' he said.

"He also told me Tomas was thought to be involved in other, more dangerous activities, which 'it was best not to know too much about' — yes, that line again. Goetz stood then, carefully snuffed out the half-smoked cigarette between spit-moistened fingers and tucked the remaining butt into his hatband. Then he left, giving me a handshake, another expression of gratitude, and a wink.

"I stayed at home for another two weeks or so, trying to be of use, but it soon became clear that I was more of a hindrance than a help. The estate staff, people in hiding, mother and grandmother had developed an efficient supply system of sorts, in co-operation with local farmers and merchants, a system in which I had no role.

"I noticed wagons coming and going, people slipping in and out after dark, and once, late at night, I thought I saw Tomas' Opel near Goetz's cottage. Finally, my mother and grandmother made it clear that the *Schloss* was no place for an active-duty officer.

"Danger to me aside, should their operation be discovered, my grandmother told me my presence frightened some of the local folk. I told her I understood, and that it was time for me to get going anyway, that I would see them again as soon as I could. I wished them both luck and said I would pray for their safety. I put my uniform back on and left the morning of 28 January 1943 for Munich airport, hoping to catch a ride back to Berlin, then on to southern France.

"The trip to Mont de Marsan was terrible. The weather that harsh winter of 1942-43 was simply awful. There were constant delays due to bad weather, lack of aircraft and shortages of parts, pilots and fuel. Trains were unreliable because of Allied bombing and other problems.

"I ended up stranded in Berlin on the morning of 3 February 1943, the very day the announcement came out that the German 6th Army at Stalingrad had surrendered. An absolute orgy of National Socialist mourning followed!

"Each hour, dark Wagnerian music blared out of loudspeakers on every street corner, followed by mournful male choral singing, mostly the old quasi-hymn '*Ich hatt' einen Kameraden*', a traditional dirge mourning the loss of friends in battle. Public ceremonies were held, torch-lit marches arranged, symbolic coffins buried, wreaths placed, and there was constant processing by torchlight.

"The nation was swamped in a tidal wave of mawkish choreographed official mourning, all in the service of whipping up hatred and anger against the 'Mongolian hordes' — the barbarians who had so unfairly slaughtered our fine young crusaders at Stalingrad.

"The message was that the Bolsheviks had triumphed not through superior tactics or military skill, but instead just overwhelming our brave boys with massive waves of brutish peasants — at least that was the Nazi Party line. Those of us who had been there and thought about it, knew better.

"I called everyone that I thought could help, because I simply had to get out of there, and after twenty or more difficult and poorly-transmitted conversations, plus a hefty bribe, I eventually managed to secure a ride on a mail plane. I finally arrived, after God knows how many stops, at Mont de Marsan France on 9 February 1943, a day late according to my orders."

At this point it was Peggy who turned off the recorder. She had noticed that Max's voice was speeding up, his pacing faster. She sensed he was pushing himself, as if there was some deadline she didn't know about. She sat, drank tea, and thought about that, then decided to continue the tape and pay closer attention to Max's tempo and tone.

"My assignment was to a unit called *Fernaufklärungsgruppe* 5 — yes, Peggy, that is one of those lovely compound German words. It means 'long-range reconnaissance group'. The group's mission was flying out over the Atlantic to locate Allied convoys bound for England or Russia, and report their location to naval headquarters, which would send submarines or other aircraft to attack them.

"When I reported to the officer in charge, he was not disturbed by my one-day tardiness. 'You are most welcome, Von Waldberg, and I understand the difficulties of travel in the *Reich*. We are having similar difficulties here, now that certain criminal elements have become more active.' I asked him what was happening and he told me that the Vichy government had announced plans to draft young people and force them to work in German factories. This had driven thousands of them into the arms of what he called bandit groups hiding in the mountains thereabout.

"Those groups had become more active, he told me. They were blowing up trains, stealing supplies and generally raising hell in the countryside. They were also killing individual German soldiers whenever they could get away with it, so he advised me to see the unit armorer to have my sidearm checked, then report to my new commander, one Major Krause.

"Krause, he said, was training pilots for the Junkers JU 290, a large four-engine ultra-long-range aircraft which was to replace the older Folke-Wulf 200 'Condor' for maritime reconnaissance. He was also, it turned out, a man I would come to despise."

CHAPTER 23

"I started on the famous Condor, flying as co-pilot at first, then taking over as pilot. The Condor was a wonderful airplane, easy to fly and agile for an aircraft of that size. Earlier in the war the Condor had been tasked with finding convoys, reporting their location, and then attacking individual ships with bombs and rockets, or strafing them with their guns.

"But as Allied anti-aircraft measures and radar improved, the Condor proved vulnerable, and it also could not fly far enough to patrol all desired areas. They were gradually being replaced by the JU 290, an airplane with a longer range. So, after becoming accustomed to the Condor, I was transitioned to the monster 290 and worked up on that airplane.

"The 290 was not meant to attack shipping, but to operate at high altitude beyond the range of anti-aircraft weapons and locate shipping visually or with radar.

"I don't have time to go into a great deal of detail, Peggy, about my training. I'll just say that I adapted fairly quickly to four-engine aircraft, which mostly required attention to synchronization of the engines, and the constant monitoring of lots of gauges. By June of 1943, I was assigned to a crew, regularly doing reconnaissance flights.

"We either flew the Condor or one of the two JU 290s that had arrived by then. As I said, our mission was searching the Atlantic for Allied convoys en route to England or Iceland, because Iceland was a staging point for ships bound for Russia. When we located a convoy, we radioed messages to navy headquarters, so submarines could be sent to attack those ships.

"The main problem I encountered was mind-numbing boredom. Flying nearly over thousand miles, even at two hundred and twenty miles per hour, takes more than nine hours. We flew out into the Atlantic, then we flew circular search patterns, one overlapping another, sometimes for sixteen hours. So, we flew for long, tiring periods, sometimes as high as two miles above a monotonous blue-grey ocean in a frigid, droning airplane.

"We seldom even saw the convoys we located, which were detected by our radar operator at a range of about sixty-two miles. Though other aircraft were attacked by Allied fighter aircraft, and some planes were lost, we saw nothing like that the whole time I was there.

"I was even more bored by the fact that I was required to fly as co-pilot, which meant simply sitting there most of the time, uncomfortable in my parachute, monitoring gauges and supervising the transfer of fuel from one tank to another. We had two pilots, a flight engineer, radioman, radar operator and three or four gunners, for a total crew of eight or nine.

"The other crew all had something to do, even if it was chatting with one another. Of course, the pilot, the aforementioned Major Krause, was flying the aircraft, leaving me with little to do but try to stay awake.

"Even if it had been permitted to doze, Krause would have prevented that. Krause made every flight miserable.

"Krause had started needling me when I first reported to him, complaining about my being a day late, claiming he would have me charged with overstaying my leave. I calmly pointed out that the officer commanding the unit had noted my tardiness and dismissed it. Then he started in on his constant theme: my decorations, noble birth, prior experience and his lack of all three.

"'It's not all about medals and ribbons here,' he continued, noting my Iron Cross and other decorations. 'It's about steadiness and dedication, not glory.' He continued to explain that my title would not help me here, implying that recognition of my wounds and other awards were due only to my connection with the '*vons*' he seemed to resent so much. I noticed immediately that he seemed quite young to have the rank he held, and that his tunic was all but bare of any decorations. He caught my glance.

"'Oh, yes,' he said, rising from his desk, 'I haven't had the honor of serving in the glamorous fighter arm, but we'll soon teach you here what true service is all about — steadiness, dedication and unshakeable faith in victory. That's what is needed to win this war, despite what snobbish aristocrats and those running the army think. We'll soon teach you, my dear *Von* Waldberg, what *real* service is!'

"Peggy, my first impulse was to throw myself on this pompous young ass (he could not have been more than twenty-five years old) and strangle him. He was a slight man, even smaller than I am, and I could have easily overcome him. But then I thought of my mother, my grandmother, and my need to survive this war, which I was pretty sure was already lost, my need to save my family, and find Rachel, if possible, so I let his insults pass.

"I did tell him, though, that fighter service was not my only contribution to the *Reich*'s victory, that I had flown in Russia in support of Stalingrad, and been wounded in the process. I advised him to read my service record before we spoke again, saluted, turned on my heel, and left.

"That night in the mess, I was approached by another pilot, who introduced himself and asked if I was among the men to be trained on the 290. When I answered that I was, he sat down and we talked for a while, about his experiences and mine, which were similar in that we had both flown the JU 52, though he had served in Africa, battling heat instead of cold.

"After a while, he told me a bit about Krause. 'Watch that one,' he said. 'Krause is the nephew of *Generaloberst* Hans Jeschonnek, Goering's Chief of General Staff. He was rapidly promoted doing a desk job in Berlin, then posted here about a year ago. He wanted wartime flying experience for his résumé, so Uncle Hans sent him here, where he could technically see combat but remain reasonably safe.' Apparently, Krause had also made himself unpopular in the mess with loudly stated political opinions.

"Krause was universally disliked by crewmen as well. He was notorious for roaming around the base, yelling at enlisted men for having their hands in their pockets, failing to salute properly or other minor infractions. The man wished me luck working with Krause, bought me a drink, and left.

"Krause proved to be a competent instructor and pilot, though he flew without any finesse and sometimes had trouble with rough landings. Krause seemed unable to properly gauge distance to the runway on landing, and never seemed to realize he was still six meters off the ground, high in the cockpit, when the wheels touched the runway.

"This resulted in some hard landings, but not so hard as to be dangerous, though the enlisted crew joked about it until I gave them a stern talking-to. Krause may have been a pompous loudmouth, but he was still an officer and chief pilot, though he did not seem to enjoy flying.

"What he *did* enjoy was trying to goad me into some outburst that he could use to get rid of me, by charging me with insubordination. Every slight mistake during training resulted in sarcastic criticism: 'One would think a pilot of your vast experience would know better than that' or 'Surely, *Von* Waldberg [he always emphasized the *Von*], a man of your sophistication should be aware...' He nagged me about always wearing my parachute, claiming that it 'demonstrated a lack of confidence in his flying skill', and once reported this objection to the commanding officer.

"The CO talked with me about my reason for the 'chute, and silenced Krause on that topic, whereupon Krause started complaining about my receiving 'special treatment', referring to an electrically heated boot I had been issued for my cold-sensitive right foot.

"That matter was promptly swatted down by our flight surgeon, who told Krause that the boot was an 'accommodation for an honorable wound' and was none of his business. Krause sulked for days, but soon perked up and developed a new means of trying to annoy me.

"On our long flights, he would lecture endlessly on the glories of National Socialism, the wisdom of the *Führer* and how the 'titled dunderheads' of the General Staff were letting him down — that all of those military aristocrats should be shot for incompetence and replaced by younger men infused with 'National Socialist Ardor', who would then win the war; presumably men just like Krause himself.

"I simply declined to play along and tried to shield myself by constantly wearing radio headphones 'in case there was an important message', when, in fact, I had tuned my radio to a music station in Sweden one of the gunners told me about.

"This went on for nearly two months until suddenly, around mid-August of 1943, Krause was transferred. He simply disappeared — there one day and gone the next. I was astonished and delighted. I was immediately appointed chief pilot of our aircraft and acquired a perfectly pleasant younger man, a graduate of the Condor, as co-pilot.

"It turned out Krause's distinguished uncle, *Generaloberst* Hans Jeschonnek, had shot himself at his headquarters after he blundered by ordering Berlin's anti-aircraft batteries to fire on a group of German night-fighter aircraft gathering over the capital. Since Krause no longer had a powerful patron, our CO simply pushed him out, getting him sent to an obscure office job somewhere in Occupied Denmark.

"After that, Peggy, my life was boring, but not entirely unpleasant. By October, we had taken delivery of all our JU 290s, and I was flying them exclusively. I flew missions routinely, fighting the monotony by letting my co-pilot take over from time to time and walking about the aircraft, talking to crew members, learning a little about our radar equipment and trying to see to it that everyone was awake.

"I played chess with our radio operator, announcing moves over the intercom while we each kept our own board, drank endless cups of bad coffee, and listened to music when I could. Flying over the North Atlantic in winter was difficult, but we were often flying above the weather, so most of the danger was during take-off and landing, and I had learned a few tricks for slick runways in Russia.

"By spring of 1944, our unit began to experience a very sharp and violent increase in local resistance activity. The *resistants* had been emboldened by our defeat at Stalingrad, reinforced by our clumsy attempts to force young people to labor in Germany, and were heartened by the imminent possibility of Allied landings somewhere on the European mainland, probably in France.

"A huge increase in radio traffic between England and France was detected by our signals staff beginning in March of '44, and it became very dangerous to travel from place to place in France without an armed escort. Many of us, previously housed in requisitioned villas in the town, moved into less comfortable quarters on the base itself.

"Then, one night in April, a group of French insurgents penetrated the base, not five hundred meters from our ready room, and set fire to a hangar containing two aircraft.

"Thankfully, one of our drivers was a slightly disabled ex-infantry sergeant from the Eastern Front, and he quickly threw together a defence group of drivers, cooks and mechanics who drove the intruders off. Two bodies were found in the morning, one of them a mature man, the other a young French woman, a teenager. Her body was surrounded by spent cartridges and she was lying on a British Sten gun with three empty magazines beside her.

"She appeared to have died covering the retreat of the others. I still get a lump in my throat when I think about it, how frightened she must have been, and how brave.

"In July of 1944, because of the Allied landings in Normandy in June and the imminent threat of another landing in the south of France, our *Gruppe* was sent back to Germany, but I got orders instead to report to a *Luftwaffe* base at Bergen, Norway, for a 'special assignment'. *'Ach, Gott, what now?'* I thought, as I packed my bags."

CHAPTER 24

"On the flight to Bergen, I reviewed my situation. I was thirty-three years old, trapped by events I could not control. That lack of control was the most galling thing of all. I was a pilot, and pilots ought to be in charge; yet here I was at the mercy of an evil regime which was certain to lead us all to destruction, and there was nothing I could do about it.

"I considered trying to defect to neutral Sweden once I got to Norway, but then what would happen to my family? If I did manage to survive in that way, how could I ever face myself again? How could I ever go back to Austria if it was known I had deserted?

"I looked around the plane, a beat-up 'Old Auntie' JU 52, and studied the faces of the other men aboard. Most were *Luftwaffe* ground crew or administrators, their faces uniformly grim. Even the younger ones, some in their late teens, looked worn out.

"I wondered what I looked like, but I was sure I looked older than my age. What would happen to us when we lost this war? Surely the Allies, especially the Soviets, would extract a fearful retribution for what we had done in the name of the Third Reich.

"I tried to sleep as our plane droned on, but my feeling of helplessness and a sense of impending doom were overwhelming, and I was fatigued and irritable by the time we landed at Bergen late on the night of 15 July 1944.

"Then things got very strange indeed. When we landed, one other officer and I were told to remain aboard while the other passengers departed. Then a ground crewman came aboard and the aircraft taxied a few hundred yards further down the runway, to a small bus waiting beside the tarmac.

"The crewman directed us to board the bus and asked us not to speak to each other. He drove for a few minutes until we stopped at a guard post, where heavily armed Field Police accompanied by snarling dogs carefully checked our orders and our identification.

"I noticed the area we were entering was surrounded by a stout fence topped by bright lights and barbed wire. *'What on earth am I getting into?'* I wondered.

"We reboarded the bus and were driven a mile or so to another formidable checkpoint, this one equipped with guard towers, searchlights and machine guns. Finally, we arrived at a large well-appointed villa, probably someone's country estate, where we were checked in by a young Field Police officer and each assigned a room.

"We were directed to please settle in, get some rest and be prepared to report to a briefing at eight a.m. The officer gave us each a box lunch, asked us to stay in our quarters until morning, and once again we were requested not to speak with one another. I was worn out, so I gobbled down the food and a bottle of beer that came with it, and fell into a deep sleep.

"The next morning, I was awakened, given breakfast, then, with eight other officers, escorted by armed police to a large hall with rows of folding chairs. At one end of the space was an easel holding a map board covered with green cloth and a lectern on a raised dais. Another group of officers entered by a different door, also escorted by Field Police, and we all took seats facing the dais.

"By studying the colors of shoulder board and cap trim around the room, I could determine that some of the men were aviators, some flight engineers, a few navigators, but one group had insignia I was not familiar with. I nudged the fellow next to me, a pilot officer, and pointed to the unfamiliar color. '*Luftwaffe* meteorological personnel,' he whispered.

"At that moment, a door at the rear opened and we were called to attention as two *Luftwaffe* officers — a general and a colonel — one grey-clad officer bearing an SS rank insignia, and a captain of Field Police entered the room and took positions on the raised platform. As best I can remember, Peggy, this is what the general said,

"'Please be seated, gentlemen. I am *General der Flieger* Radtke.' He indicated the other officers and gave their names, but omitted the Field Police officer, who sat down next to the easel and handed the general a wooden pointer. 'I am here today to describe to you a mission for which you will be asked to volunteer. This undertaking, if successful, could change the course of the war, and upon its completion every man who participates will immediately be awarded the Knight's Cross of the Iron Cross by the *Führer* himself, and advanced two grades from his present rank, regardless of seniority.'

"The men in the audience shifted in their seats, murmuring to one another. 'This must *really* be dangerous!' the pilot next to me said softly. I nodded. *'God help us, another hare-brained war-winning scheme,'* I thought.

"Ever since the war began to go badly for Germany, everyone had been talking about '*Wunderwaffen*', miracle weapons that would win the war for us, weapons the all-knowing *Führer* was 'holding in reserve until just the right moment', they said.

"My thinking was that if the Allied landings in Normandy had not been 'just the right moment', I couldn't imagine what would be, but I kept that to myself. There had been false alarms — the V-1 flying bombs had been touted as 'war-winning weapons', and they hadn't made much difference. Airplanes with jet engines were supposed to deter the raids pounding our cities, but they made hardly a dent in the bomber streams.

"The general went on, 'We have been thinking for years about how to strike at the Americans in their homeland. The *Führer* believes, that if the Americans begin to suffer the sorts of terror bombing we are undergoing, they will soon drop out of the war or propose favorable peace terms.

"'In fact, after much careful study, *Doktor* Goebbels' propaganda ministry feels that even the *threat* of bombing will cause such fear and panic among the American population that they will rise up, overthrow the tyranny of Roosevelt and his clique of Jewish bankers and demand peace! Americans are too soft for total war, and that is what we are about to bring them!' At this point, the general nodded to the Field Policeman, who pulled the cloth away from the map board.

"There was a collective gasp. The large map showed the path of a proposed flight from Bergen, past Iceland, across the Atlantic and over Canada, to a point in the American Midwest marked with a large 'X'. The flight path then continued to a point off the US coast, quite close to the state of Maine, where it abruptly ended, oddly enough, in the ocean.

"I sat there dumbfounded, Peggy. As far as I knew, we didn't have an airplane that could make that round trip, and even if we could get an aircraft that far and back, how many bombs could it carry? And why bomb the American Midwest? Why not bomb New York or Washington?

"The ending of the flight path in the ocean off the American coast suggested a seaplane, but even our biggest Blohm and Voss aircraft couldn't make that flight without refueling somewhere.

"I was doubtful but curious as the general continued, 'That "X", gentlemen, is the site of the gigantic Willow Run plant near Detroit, in the American state of Michigan. That plant manufactures thousands of B24 bombers and other important war machines using American mass production techniques. Knocking out that plant will slow down American production for years! Just as important, since that plant is located deep in the American heartland, destroying it will show the Americans that *nowhere* in their country is safe from our vengeance.'

"He went on, Peggy, getting louder, 'This mission will force America to protect *all* of her cities from air attack, diverting thousands of guns to anti-aircraft batteries, and sending as many as a million troops to man these defenses — guns and men that might otherwise be destroying our own cities. Many aircraft will have to be withdrawn from Europe to guard American skies, instead of escorting the terror bombers which are killing women and children.'

"His voice rose again here, till he was shouting, 'Blackouts will have to be re-imposed, costing many man hours and causing much inefficiency, and our success will embolden the already large peace movement in the USA to demand a just negotiated peace' — he began pounding on the lectern — 'The American people will soon think twice about what it means to be involved in total war with the Greater German *Reich. Sieg Heil, Heil Hitler*!'

"At this point, the two other officers stood, began to applaud loudly and bellow '*Heils*'; so, of course, the assembled officers had to stand and join the barking chorus. I noticed the Field Police captain taking careful note of everyone's reaction, so I faked a coughing fit, hiding my face in my handkerchief while I tried to figure out how to get out of this latest fiasco." Max started coughing again, and Peggy could hear him moving around, glass clinking, and muttering for a minute or two. Then the tape ran out.

Peggy quickly inserted the next tape Max had sent. She was frantic to hear the rest of the story, and felt this tape and the one remaining would not be enough to get her to the end. Her hands trembled as she started the playback. *"Damn!"* thought Peggy. *"Now I really have to get up there — the suspense is killing me."*

The tape clicked on, there was more coughing and moving about, until Max's voice came on, starting unintelligibly at what seemed some distance from the microphone; then he seemed to move closer and said, his voice faint, "I am sorry, Peggy, I was sort of talking to myself and taking some medicine, but now I have figured out where I left off, so let's go on." Max cleared his throat and continued.

"When things quietened down and everyone was back in their seats, the officer in grey took the podium. As he stood, I could see the 'SD' patch on his sleeve, and his rank badges indicated an equivalent rank to *Wehrmacht* colonel, as best I could tell. I never got a full understanding of the SS rank system. The SD stood for

Sicherheitsdienst, or security service, and men like this were much feared in Hitler's *Reich*.

"Falling foul of the SD could land a person in the clutches of the Gestapo, a short way of saying *Geheim Staatspolizei*, the secret national police, who answered only to Himmler. I sensed a chill in the room.

"The SD colonel was exactly as one might imagine. He was tall, cold-eyed, and spoke with a guttural north German accent. He began like this, as I remember, 'Gentlemen, you should be proud that you have been selected to choose to participate in this momentous task. Let me point out a few details of the security arrangements we will ask you to adhere to. However, whether a man volunteers or not, he is to remain in this ultra-secure location until the mission is completed.

"'A preliminary briefing will be given this morning, and small-group sessions to study the mission will begin immediately after the major presentation. In addition, all mail and other communications with the outside world are strongly forbidden; you are requested to please place your *Soldbucher*' — that is, Peggy, our service ID booklets, our only valid identification — 'in the basket at the front of the room. Finally, violation of any of these regulations is punishable, by order of the *Führer*, with the death penalty, to be administered immediately, without trial, in this place. Are there any questions?' There was some murmuring, but no questions.

"The SD man sat down and the *Luftwaffe* colonel, at a nod from the general, rose to speak. He wore the

Waffenfarbe, or specialty color, of the *Luftwaffe* technical branch, men who were mostly based at Rechlin, a town in Germany where most of our aircraft research was done. The colonel nodded to the Field Police captain, who removed the previous map board and placed a different chart on the easel. This graphic gave a number of figures and what looked like a schedule.

"The man began, 'The plant at Willow Run is over four thousand kilometers from Bergen, by the route that has been selected.' Again, murmuring in the room. The man acknowledged that and continued, 'Yes, I know what you are thinking. We do not have an aircraft that can make a round trip of over eight thousand kilometers, so this flight will be a one-way trip.

"'What is expected is that certain specially-designed aircraft, which we will show you later, will leave Bergen at about eleven p.m., fly past Iceland at high altitude before dawn and then across the Atlantic, entering Canadian airspace around Battle Bay, Labrador. The aircraft will then cross a huge waterlogged, virtually uninhabited area of Canada, and arrive over Detroit/Willow Run just before dusk the next day.'

"He then said, 'There will be two flights. The first will confirm the route and navigation, photograph the target area, then fly out towards the ocean, arriving near a place called Owl's Head in the American state of Maine at around eleven p.m. their time. The area is sparsely populated, and there is a prominent landmark there. We have calculated moonrise, moonset, full moon, and so forth, and will schedule the flight to arrive off Maine with no less than three-quarter moon and clear skies.'

"The unease in the room increased, men raising their hands and nudging one another, some actually uttering nervous laughter.

"The colonel continued, 'I know, I know, but hear me out. The first plane will rendezvous with a submarine off Owl's Head, drop the exposed film canisters and other information with parachutes, then perform a water landing near the sub, transfer the crew to the U-boat, and be on the way back home. The second flight will follow the same route and schedule, but this plane will carry ordnance, which it will drop over the target, then depart the same way as the first.'

"The audience began to shout questions, but the speaker held up his hands, saying, 'No questions just yet, please. You will now be assigned to small groups and given a written outline of this critical mission. Each group will consist of a hypothetical crew, that is, a pilot, co-pilot, flight engineer, navigator and radio/radar operator. In your groups you will prepare written questions or comments for discussion after lunch. That way we can eliminate duplicate questions, and our staff will have time to prepare adequate responses.'

"The Field Police captain came to the podium and began reading off the names of officers for each group. As groups were assigned, each was directed to a numbered table in the adjacent dining area. Groups contained two pilots, a navigator, and a flight engineer, as the briefing officer had noted. In addition, a *Luftwaffe* signals officer was assigned to every table. Then orderlies came round, passing out numbered folders, which each officer had to sign for, giving the technical data and other details of the flight.

"I mostly listened as my group discussed the mission. One man, an engineer, seemed particularly sceptical. He asked about the practicality of a water landing, saying, 'Why not just bellyland in a field some place, hop out and ask which PoW camp we'd be going to?' 'How much damage can the bomb load of this airplane cause anyway?' 'If the *Amis* — that is, Americans — can build thousands of bombers, they ought to be able to fill in a few bomb craters, no?' Heads nodded in agreement and a few snickers broke out.

"Other officers questioned different aspects of the mission, and I volunteered to write down our list of questions. After an hour or so of discussion and a light lunch, we reconvened in the original meeting area while the officers at the podium went through our questions, eliminating duplicates. Then the colonel from the *Luftwaffe* technical branch rose and began his answers.

"On the issue of the water landing, the man said that it was important that the Americans believe our aircraft completed a round trip, so they continue to fear further attacks. Photographs will be published after the second mission to support that claim. Only by deliberately sinking the plane in deep water could that deception be maintained. Also, the Americans will be frantic for information after the attack, therefore any prisoners would probably be tortured until they cracked.

"He continued by describing the ordnance that would be deployed over Willow Run as 'a weapon that would create utter chaos and render the area uninhabitable for years'. There was muttering in the room, comments about poison gas or germs, both of which were forbidden by the Geneva Convention. 'Please, gentlemen, come to order. This new weapon is not mentioned in the Geneva Convention, you have my assurance on that.'

"Other technical questions and discussions followed, but I was already certain I was not going to volunteer for this mission. I was convinced that the war was already lost, and all I wanted to do was get back to Austria alive, and stay in the mountains until the end of my life.

"I was also pretty sure that if we had something so fearsome, the Allies had such things, too, and that if we used ours, they would use theirs. I wanted no part of it and said so later that day when I was asked to make a decision — though I didn't say I thought the war was lost. Saying that could get a person shot. Then I was asked to turn in my briefing book, with the requisite signatures, and directed to return to my quarters for further assignment.

"I thought that was the end of it, Peggy, though I knew I would have to stay in the compound until the mission was complete; but I wasn't idle during the next couple of weeks. I was kept busy double-checking flight plans, fuel consumption charts, moon phases, tide tables and weather reports, working with other officers who had also decided to sit this one out. I learned to my amazement that one of our submarines had placed an automatic weather station in the Canadian Arctic, which allowed us good predictions of weather off the coast of Maine.

"I was also shown the aircraft, two six-engine monsters put together mostly from components of JU 290s. The planes were classified as JU 390s, but everyone who worked on the project referred to them as *Amerika* Bombers. They had folding cargo ramps at the rear like the 290, and technicians were testing loading techniques on one plane for a very bulky square container, a big box so heavy it required a tracked vehicle to push it into place inside the aircraft.

"One technician said to another that the damned thing seemed as heavy as lead, to which the second man replied, 'It *is* lead, *Dummkopf,* so the radiation won't get out!' *'Radiation?'* I thought, happier than ever not to have signed up for this mission.

"Then, in late July, as I was checking fuel consumption charts for the twentieth time, I was told that I had a visitor and was asked to report to my quarters.

"I opened the door to my room to find an old friend sitting at my desk. He was a man I met at *Gymnasium…* er, high school you call it, and he was in almost all of my classes. His name was Georg Heinemann, and we were close in school. Heinemann was interested in technical things like I was, and after graduation he went on to university to study engineering, then he served in some capacity in a scientific branch of the government. He had been to our home many times. We had hunted, fished and flown paper gliders together.

"He was, what we called in German, a *Duzfreund*, a person with whom you were so familiar that he could address you with the familiar *Du* rather than the more formal *Sie*. He had spent a lot of time with my family, and I always thought he had something of a crush on my mother. He was one of the most affable and charming people I have ever met.

"I was glad to see him, but quite surprised by the black uniform he was wearing, bearing the SS rank equivalent to, I thought, major. We greeted one another, and he caught my reaction to his uniform. 'Don't be upset, Max, I'm not an SS thug. The uniform and rank are pretty much honorary, granted by *Reichsfüher* Himmler to those performing special tasks. The uniform and my SS pass get me through gates when needed, that is all.'

"Then he caught me up on the news from Kufstein, where he had just spent a short leave. He was, as always, suave and amusing, and he even had some news from other school chums, so I was enjoying our conversation immensely.

"I told him most of my story while we had a pleasant lunch, then he asked me if I had heard the latest sensational news. I told him that we were pretty much insulated from the world here, that this place was a cross between a barracks and a monastery.

"He cleared his throat, gave the German Glance and told me that a group of officers had attempted to assassinate Hitler at his headquarters in East Prussia. I was astounded and feigned outrage when he told me the plotters had planted a bomb in Hitler's conference room, then attempted a coup in Berlin to take over the government.

"The plot was thwarted only when it became apparent that Hitler had survived the blast, and some of the conspirators were shot that very night, among them the young *Graf* von Stauffenberg.

"Then he leaned closer to me and put his hand on my knee. He said that this was the reason he had obtained passes to see me here. 'You see, Von Waldberg, many of the would-be assassins were of the Prussian nobility, and now those around Hitler and Himmler are searching high and low for anyone they think might have been involved' — his voice broke and he wiped his eyes — 'and, my dear friend, I am afraid the SD has come to suspect your mother. Many of these aristocratic plotters were associated with military headquarters at the *Bendlerstrasse* and... and they attempted to communicate with foreign governments to arrange a ceasefire after the *Führer* was dead.'

"Heinemann lowered his voice. 'The Gestapo have suspicions that your mother was involved in the translation of documents, and they are holding her and your grandmother under house arrest at *Schloss*

Kesselstein.' I was utterly dumbfounded. The room seemed to spin, and the death's head on Heinemann's uniform cap suddenly seemed larger and more ominous.

"Heinemann continued, 'I can see you are upset, Max, and so am I. We all know your mother would never be involved in such a plot, but the bullyboys of the SD and Gestapo suspect anyone of noble birth, especially someone who worked for the *Bendlerstrasse* — but I may have a solution. I understand you are involved in a top secret undertaking that might change the course of the war. If that is true, I am sure I can convince the thugs to back off, lest they compromise your mission. What do you think?' he asked, as he sat back in his chair.

"I recovered my composure enough to explain that I had declined to participate in the actual mission, but that I was doing important work to support the flight. Heinemann's face went white. He trembled slightly and looked as if he was going to burst into tears. His voice broke again as he said, 'Oh, my friend, please say it is not so. I've come all this way to see you so I can return to Berlin and assure the authorities that your service to the *Reich* is invaluable at this time, and I'm afraid, if I tell them you've decided not to fly... well, it would not sit well with them, and I'm afraid there might be negative consequences for your family. Is there any way you could change your status and perhaps participate?'

"My stomach felt like a lump of cold iron had settled in it. Peggy, I was trapped."

CHAPTER 25

Peggy turned off the tape and headed down the chilly outside stairway to help her mama in the bakery for a few hours, as she did each morning she wasn't working at the newspaper. Peggy loved the sharp contrast between the intensely cold outside air and the steamy cinnamon-laced fragrance of the bakery, and using the outside stairway let her check the curbside mailbox.

She considered Max's dilemma while she worked. She wasn't sure whether Heinemann had been genuinely concerned with protecting Max's family, or whether he was a shill to coerce Max into flying this perilous mission.

Peggy thought about a phrase she had heard attributed to a famous Hollywood actor: "It's all about sincerity. Once you can fake that, you've got it made." Heinemann had certainly seemed sincere in Max's recounting of the episode, but Peggy's years of big city news reporting had left her a bit cynical, doubtful of everyone's motives.

On the other hand, why would there be a need to bully Max? Surely plenty of fliers had volunteered, so why bother to threaten an ageing pilot with physical limitations to make him participate? It didn't make sense, she thought, and decided to call Grocery Bob's father again to try to arrange a ride to Max's place. She really needed to talk to Max, and find out what he was thinking during this encounter. She also sensed a climax approaching and wanted to be sure she was with Max again before that happened.

When the week's orders were all prepared and stacked, she ran back upstairs, cleaned up, and called the Grocery King. She was told, to her delight, that Bob would be back from the VA hospital the next week, and that a large order was being prepared for delivery to Max's cabin the following Saturday. Peggy decided to finish the last two tapes, then get her notes in order and gather everything she needed for a visit, including the all-important uniform cap.

"First things first," she thought, and switched the recorder playback on. Max's voice came on at once. "So, the very next morning after Heinemann's visit and a long session of *schnapps* and contemplation in the mess, I marched into the commandant's office and announced my willingness to participate in the mission, which was now referred to by all of us as the flight of the America Bomber.

"The commandant rose from his desk, clapped me on the shoulder, wrung my hand and all but hugged me. 'I am delighted, Von Waldberg. We have had some trouble staffing the first flight, and I am short an engineer and, until now, a co-pilot.' I asked why there were not enough volunteers, especially for the reconnaissance flight, given the powerful incentives that were being offered. 'Well, there have been difficulties,' the colonel answered. 'Some of the men are eager but unqualified, not having enough experience or skill. Others are qualified, but they are all signing up for the second flight.

"'Perhaps they consider the actual delivery of ordnance more important than scouting and photography, though having those photos is nearly as important as the bombing itself. Others are just not volunteering at all, as you know.' I asked why the photographs were so important. He asked me to sit, and offered me a drink, which I gratefully accepted despite the early hour as I had a bit of a *schnapps* headache.

"The colonel sat down behind his desk and began, 'The planners in Berlin are quite realistic, giving this mission a seventy/thirty chance of succeeding; that is at least for the first flight, a seventy percent chance of success. If the first flight is completed and the film gets back to Germany, we will have obtained some leverage with the Americans, whether or not the second plane ever takes off. You see, Von Waldberg, if for any reason the second aircraft cannot make the trip, the pictures will be published in German newspapers, those of our allies and neutral countries, proving that America is vulnerable to attack.

"'A crew will be photographed in front of the JU 390 before and "after" the flight, demonstrating that we have ultra-long-distance capabilities and prompting all of those responses *Reichsminister* Goebbels is hoping for, which are the reassignment of weapons, personnel and aircraft to the American mainland rather than

Europe, and perhaps panic and a demand for peace among the US population.' He lit a cigarette and asked what had changed my mind.

"I immediately understood why so many men had volunteered for the second flight, but I kept that thought to myself as I answered that the plan seemed feasible, and that my previous reluctance to volunteer had been overcome as I studied the mission during my research for its support. I asked the colonel when I could begin training and who the primary pilot would be.

"The colonel told me that the primary pilot had not been officially selected, as there were two candidates, both equally qualified. Both pilots had been asked to serve as co-pilot for the second flight if not selected for the first, and both had agreed.

"Training and testing were proceeding for those men. As soon as the decision was made and the crew completed, training would begin in earnest for the reconnaissance flight. The colonel stood and thanked me for my change of heart. Shaking my hand again, he was escorting me to the door when he asked if I had any more questions.

"I told him I was curious about the reference to 'radiation' related to the big box being loaded aboard one of the airplanes. The colonel froze, closed the office door, abruptly indicated I should be seated, and sat down next to me. 'Where did you hear that, Von Waldberg?' he asked me, his face grim. I told him what had happened and he questioned me closely regarding the time, date and other details.

"Then he told me in clipped, authoritative tones that I was not to mention this to anyone, nor was I to ask about the subject ever again. 'This topic is *strengst verboten* [strongly forbidden] and *Hauptgeheim* [top secret],' he said. When I agreed to his instructions, he warmed up again and took me to the door, saying that I would be contacted as soon as arrangements were complete. As I left, I heard him yelling to his adjutant to contact the project security officer at once.

"I went back to my quarters, musing about this meeting. I was certain that many of the men who had volunteered for the second flight did so because they thought the flight would never happen. I think they had calculated the first flight would be detected or fail for technical reasons and that they would then have credit for having volunteered without having to make the flight. Also, I was more curious than ever about the reference to radiation, and determined to find out what that was all about, secret or not.

"A week later, despite snooping and eavesdropping as much as I could manage without being obvious, I was still in the dark about the mysterious reference to radiation. But I was assigned to a crew and we met and discussed each person's role in the flight while we awaited the arrival of the primary pilot, who we were told was training elsewhere.

"We were introduced to a mock-up of the aircraft and rehearsed our separate tasks under the direction of a stand-in pilot, a man whose combat injuries had made it impossible for him to fly at high altitude. This went on for two weeks, day and night, with physical testing in between mock flights. Then we were told the chief pilot had arrived, and the five of us were directed to report to a meeting room at once.

"We assembled as instructed, speculating about who the pilot might be and why he had not been training with us. The commanding officer arrived and we stood to attention. A pilot officer dressed in a flight suit and leather helmet walked behind the colonel as he approached the podium and I caught a glimpse of his face — *"God help me!"* I thought, as I recognized him. It was that bastard Krause, the pompous ass promoted to major only due to family connections, who had made my life miserable at Mont de Marsan.

"The look he gave me as he pulled off his helmet and faced us from the podium was one of pure venomous glee. I wanted to throw up, but instantly hid my discomfort behind an icy grin. I was not going to give the little shi... er, the little stinker the satisfaction of seeing me flinch. He seemed disappointed as he began his talk.

"Krause's little speech was his usual combination of bombast, belittling others, boasting, lying and spouting the party line. I looked around and saw eye-rolling from the flight engineer and the *Luftwaffe* signal branch photographer. The other crew members, the radio/radar operator and the navigator, both of whom were young guys in their late twenties, maintained neutral expressions — probably, I thought, due to all their years of attending Nazi Party functions.

"Krause finished his introduction or pep talk and the colonel brought him around to meet each of us. When he came to me, he gave me that look again and said he was glad to see me. I asked if he had enjoyed Denmark. At that point our young navigator interrupted, nudged Krause and, giving him a wink, asked if the girls in Denmark were all as beautiful as he had heard.

"Krause frowned at him, stiffened, and gave the youngster a short, curt lecture about the importance of duty, saying he had had no time for such frivolous things during his important assignment in Denmark, having spent every hour paying attention to duty, not chasing skirts, and he advised the navigator to do likewise. This time, as soon as Krause turned his back, the eye-rolling was unanimous, except for the colonel, who turned away shaking his head.

"Well, it all went downhill from there, at least in terms of Krause's relationship with the crew. He was sarcastic, caustic, quick to find fault and generally even more obnoxious than he had been in France.

"He got into disputes with our flight engineer routinely, and tried to have him transferred. The rumor was that the CO had chewed Krause out, and for a few days Krause was subdued, but then he started picking on the communications man, who simply ignored him, a technique I had adopted myself and recommended to him.

"Krause, it turned out, had been training at the *Luftwaffe* research center at Rechlin, where another JU 390 was based, and he flew the thing well enough, except for his usual bumpy landings. With an aircraft even taller than the 290, he had even more trouble than before figuring out where the wheels were in relation to the runway.

"Eventually, we arranged for the flight engineer to stick his head out of the aft access door and call off the altitude until, finally, Krause got the hang of it. Krause had never been deft as a pilot, and we assumed he was made chief pilot because of his rank, which was higher than any of ours. One had to admit, though, that Krause had a great deal of experience with large aircraft, and that was probably a factor as well.

"Our flight engineer, a very experienced and decorated combat aviator, started needling Krause in subtle ways, praising Krause for his cleverness in flying so long in wartime without any wounds or other injuries. He also speculated about how dangerous Krause's duty in Denmark must have been, what with all the bombing and so forth.

"When Krause responded hotly that there had been very little bombing in Denmark, the engineer responded mildly that he humbly apologized for his mistake. Krause then realized he was being mocked, flushed bright red and stormed off.

"After the next training flight, Krause publicly dressed the engineer down for his impertinence and then inadvertently let slip the information I had been seeking. 'You think I was sitting on my arse in Denmark, do you? Let me tell you, the work I did there helped us to develop the war-winning weapon we will soon deploy over Detroit. Do you know who the primary atomic scientist in the world is, my smart-mouthed little engineer?

"'Of course you don't! Well, his name is Niels Bohr, and he founded the Bohr Institute in Copenhagen and was trying to work with our own great physicist Professor Heisenberg to develop an atom bomb. My job was to shuttle important personnel and materials for this vital project, and unfortunately it was so secret that no awards were granted for such service…' He trailed off at this point, aware he had said too much.

"The engineer then asked quietly if there was indeed such a bomb ready for delivery by the second flight. Krause evaded the question, saying Bohr had sneaked off to Sweden and that he had been told by one of the physicists that Heisenberg remained uncertain about the basic principle of such a weapon. Krause then added, almost to himself, that the physicist had smiled and winked when he said that, though Krause didn't know why.

"Then Krause collected himself and returned to his diatribe. 'Mark my words,' he shouted, red in the face and waving his fist in the air, 'the bomb we will drop will be just as effective as an atom bomb, and the radiation from it will render the entire area unusable for the rest of the war.' Then he stopped abruptly and threatened to report all of us if we said anything about any of this, so we each went about our business.

"I knew then and there I was incapable of helping poison thousands, maybe tens of thousands of innocent civilians, and a plan began to form in my mind. The plan matured slowly as we began to wrestle with the logistics of the flight, and by the time we were ready for take-off, it was very clear, what I had to do. I bided my time and waited.

"To save fuel, it had been decided to lighten the aircraft as much as possible, so any extra equipment, including defensive armament, ammunition, unnecessary partitions — even the little stove and other equipment from our tiny galley — were removed. Extra fuel tanks were attached under the wings, which could be jettisoned as they ran dry, another innovation for this flight.

"In addition, to save fuel we were to use rocket-assisted take-off, which we were able to practice only twice due to the scarcity of appropriate rockets. I must say, Peggy, that was what you Americans would call a 'hoot'. The kick of those rockets pushed us back in our seats, and we left the runway as if catapulted into the sky. I hadn't had that much fun flying since my glider days as a kid. The other crew also enjoyed it, except for Krause, who got a little pale each time.

"These measures, the experts said, increased our range by about two thousand kilometers, raising it from six thousand kilometers to about eight thousand, enough to make the one-way trip with a bit of safety margin, but not much.

"Finally, after over a month of constant training, the crew was working together in a very efficient manner, and even Krause had settled down to a demeanor which, if not pleasant, was tolerable. Each task of the flight had been analyzed and the crew assigned to complete every one of them, or so we thought.

"When we were issued electrically-heated flight suits, sidearms and flight schedules with charts and tables listing every task and the projected time for each, we were certain our take-off was imminent. We also received a final security briefing from the SD colonel, who ended his talk by handing us each a cyanide vial in a little brass container which looked like a pistol cartridge. We were given to understand that if capture was imminent, we were to kill ourselves rather than reveal the nature of our mission under torture. I dismissed that suggestion, but tucked the thing into my flight suit.

"After a pause for weather prediction and a final recalculation of every variable we the crew and the experts could imagine, we lifted off — no, blasted off — with a roar and a bellow, fire flame and smoke, well before dawn on a clear starry night in late September of 1944. The flight engineer, a captain named Nordland, had somehow patched a recording onto the intercom system, an old marching song called in English, 'We're Marching Against England' — but every time the song mentioned 'England', Nordland bellowed 'America'.

"Rising so fast with the rocket-assist boosting the airplane and hearing that old song, even I, as war-weary as I was, began to feel some enthusiasm. Then I remembered my plan, and that feeling went away."

CHAPTER 26

"We gained our six thousand-feet cruising altitude quickly, and then, after an hour, began to climb much higher to pass Iceland at our maximum altitude of nineteen thousand feet, more than two hundred miles offshore of Iceland's coast. Rekyjavik, a major assembly point for Arctic convoys, was bristling with anti-aircraft and protective air patrols, but we were flying so high and fast, perhaps we simply sneaked by.

"Also, we quite often overflew Iceland for reconnaissance, so maybe they thought we were that sort of mission, and let us go in order to capture and decode our radio transmissions. For whatever reason, we flew on unmolested and, after an hour or so, returned to cruising at six thousand feet. I noticed during our passage near Iceland that Krause became increasingly edgy, causing an odd incident.

"Because of the intense cold at high altitude, part of our aircraft had been insulated. Some grey powdery material had been sprayed on the inside of the cargo area, then covered with brown sticky paper which sealed it and held the stuff in place. Someone had miscalculated, though, and as we ascended past about twelve thousand feet, the insulating material expanded so much that some of it burst through the paper coating with a sharp popping sound, and soon grey dust was floating around inside the airplane.

"Krause decided we were under attack, and began to shout orders to gunners we didn't have while he jerked the plane about in what he probably thought were appropriate evasive maneuvers. I tried to calm him down, but he ordered me to the rear of the plane to determine where the enemy was. I then realized that Krause had never heard the sound of bullets hitting an aircraft and couldn't tell the difference between those mild popping sounds and actual impact explosions. He also probably thought the dust was smoke.

"I left my seat and found the other crew members hanging on for dear life. The engineer showed me what had happened, grinning like a monkey. I went back and told Krause what was going on. He told me to take over and went to the rear of the pilots' compartment to use the urinal. When he returned, he had settled down, but I thought I smelled alcohol on his breath.

"He was steady for the rest of the long overwater flight, merely muttering to himself between required communications about fuel, wind speed and other details. But then, as we began to climb again, approaching the coast of Canada, he tensed up once more. I could feel his hands shaking on the control yoke as we both pulled back to gain altitude, and I told him all was well, that the area around Battle Bay, Labrador, was almost entirely deserted, and it was unlikely we would be detected.

"Krause told me sharply to pipe down and mind my own business, and we both went on oxygen again, inhibiting further conversation. We got past Battle Bay and returned to six thousand feet shortly thereafter, then switched on the autopilot to save our energy for the evolutions scheduled later.

"I went aft as scheduled to get us each a sandwich, and when I came back there was that alcohol smell again, and Krause seemed to be dozing in his seat. I put the sandwich on the console next to him and decided to let well enough alone. I popped a Pervitin pill to stay awake and watched as wretched, monotonous, potholed country rolled by below us, while Krause snored softly beside me.

"Finally, after what seemed an eternity of fighting to stay awake, another Pervitin and three cups of coffee now gone stale and cold in my Thermos, we approached Detroit just as dusk began to fall. We had seen a few lights here and there during our passage of Canadian muskeg country, but here was Detroit, brightly lit, as if there was not a war going on. We could see roads clogged with cars, headlights blazing, and smoke belching from foundries, factories and railroad locomotives. I jogged the controls and Krause snapped awake.

"He sat up, noticed the bright lights below and muttered, 'Detroit, *ja*?' Then he immediately took over without any explanation or apology for his long siesta, or even a hint of gratitude, ordering me to go aft and help the photographer set up for our airdrop, as outlined in our protocol. My heart started to beat faster, as I began the first step to carry out my own plan.

"I found the photographer crouched over the transparent dome in the plane's belly, snapping away with a selection of cameras. They ranged from an enormous black movie camera to a small hand-held Leica with a 75mm lens. As he worked, he unloaded each movie film cassette, still photo plate, or small 35mm roll and handed them to me.

"As we had practised so often, I placed the large movie cassettes in bulky round cans, and placed the smaller rolls in film canisters, like the ones sold today, but made of metal rather than plastic. What the photographer didn't notice was that I had pocketed five canisters of the 35mm film and replaced them with similar canisters I had carried in my flight suit's extra pockets.

"After the prescribed two passes over the Willow Run area, the photographer and I lugged the film containers to a spot near the aft cargo door, and placed them in a large waterproof flotation bag secured to a small parachute, which in turn was attached to a static line which would automatically open the 'chute once the package was kicked out of the door. Then I returned to the cockpit to begin the next phase of my plan.

"As I took my seat, I carefully tried to judge Krause's attitude. As usual, he seemed sullen and withdrawn, so I tried to break the ice by pointing out the incredible carpet of bright lights passing below. 'They'll be shut off soon enough,' he snapped. 'Our weapon will shut all of this down and give us time to develop our other wonder weapons — you just wait and see.' I responded that therefore it was crucial that we get back to Germany to help plan the second flight. He snarled, '*Und, Herr Hauptmann?*'

"I then asked him the key question, my last chance to satisfy my conscience, to do the right thing instead of what I wanted to do — I asked him, in view of his somewhat awkward experience with landings, whether he would allow me to perform the water landing.

"Krause exploded, becoming so agitated he yanked back on the control yoke and the big aircraft bounced as he shouted, 'Yes, that's just what you would like, isn't it, you titled piece of shit? You'd love to steal my thunder, my last chance to distinguish myself in this war. Oh, yes, of course the brilliant, handsome, well-born Baron von Waldberg performed the tricky landing, while the poor *Lumpenproletariat*, working-class little Krause was kicking shit out of the door...'

"I interrupted, reminding him that everyone who returned would receive the Knight's Cross, no matter what they did on the mission, but he would have none of it. 'Yes, yes,' he bellowed, so loud the flight engineer asked if everything was all right. 'Get back to your post!' Krause yelled, then continued to excoriate me — 'The newspapers will get the facts, you would be the hero, and I would be the second-rate crewman. Not a chance, you snobbish bastard; you do your job and I'll do mine.' And then he subsided to his customary muttering, working himself up for another outburst.

"At that point, the navigator came up on the intercom with the co-ordinates for our course to Maine, and Krause and I had to start taking notes. I sat back and started to input compass settings into our navigation/fuel consumption calculator. I had done everything I could. The die was cast."

Peggy turned off the playback, noting that the tape was almost finished. She eyed the final cassette Max had sent her on Grocery Bob's last trip. She studied the label and saw that Max had recorded this tape a full week after the one she had just finished. She looked at her watch. It was three p.m. *"Should I listen to this last recording now?"* Peggy wondered. Celine would have some things ready for delivery, but not until a bit later, so why not? She went downstairs, chatted a bit with Celine, got a nice hot *croissant* and coffee, then settled next to the tape machine with her notepad, loaded the cassette, and switched the playback on.

"The flight to Maine was uneventful, though Krause became jittery once more when we spotted another aircraft below us. The navigator identified the plane as an American commercial airliner, and it soon disappeared." Max's voice was weak, and Peggy had to turn up the volume to understand what he was saying.

"As we approached the coast, lights on the ground became increasingly rare. Soon, we were flying above a nearly totally darkened landscape, though a brilliant three-quarter moon gave some illumination. I began to prepare for my pre-landing — actually pre-ditching — tasks as outlined in our protocol. I placed our flight logs, schedule books and a couple of small calculating devices into a satchel and left the cockpit.

"The navigator was busy making a position check using a fix on a star, and the flight engineer was transferring fuel into various tanks around the plane to correct our balance for the water landing. The radio/radar man was also occupied, so it fell to me to assist the photographer with the photo airdrop and destruction of sensitive material.

"The radio/radar operator was crouched over his receiver, searching for a homing beacon from the submarine, when I tapped him on the shoulder. He passed me his code machine, code book and radio log, which I placed in a special lead-weighted disposal bag, along with the material from the cockpit. I dragged the bag aft and gathered up all of the flight engineer's notes and calculation sheets, a few of which were destined to be dropped to the waiting submarine along with the film, the rest to be consigned to the deep in the weighted bag. I filched a couple of the calculation sheets and a chart and zipped them into my flight suit. *'So far, so good,'* I thought.

"I added a few maps and charts from the navigator's table and laboriously slid the heavy bag along the deck to the aft cargo door, where the photographer was waiting. We separated out the materials to be added to the film packet and those to be jettisoned. My heart was beating so fast and hard, I thought the photographer would hear it.

"We pulled open the cargo door and gasped in the frigid slipstream. All was ready. Once we were over the sea and well away from shore, the photographer and I would throw out the weighted bag; then, on the signal from the radio operator that the submarine was in contact, we would kick the flotation device with the exposed film and other material out the door, whence it would descend to the sea by parachute, to be recovered by the sub's boat crew. Those items would be used for planning the next flight, the flight that was to drop the bomb. At least, that was the plan. *'Not if I can help it,'* I thought.

"The photographer nudged me and pointed towards the ground. 'Look, the lighthouse!' he shouted over the roaring draft from the open door. I asked loudly where the lighthouse was, moving closer to the opening. He pointed again and I stuck my head out into the chilly slipstream and spotted the whitewashed lighthouse in the moonlight, on a height at the edge of the sea a couple of miles ahead of our aircraft.

"The cold wind felt good on my sweaty brow, damp from exertion, excitement and the side effects of the stimulant Pervitin. I turned back to the photographer, nodded vigorously, then faked a stumble and tumbled out of the door backwards with what I hoped was a convincing shriek, free-falling through the cold night as the giant aircraft passed above me.

"After the plane had passed, I pulled the ripcord and my faithful ever-present parachute deployed perfectly, though it gave me quite a jolt as it snapped open, and I lost my special insulated right boot. Thankfully, I still had my ordinary shoe on that foot. I felt elated, free for the first time in years, delighted that my plan had worked perfectly so far and exhilarated by the bird-like feeling of floating towards the earth on a gorgeous crisp moonlit night.

"I looked down and saw what I had hoped to see, a small group of buildings a few miles inland and dense dark forest below me. I had read a bit about parachuting, but most of the material was from military manuals and had to do with dropping troops in open country, not parachuting into a coniferous forest. Parachuting into giant pine trees proved to be a very bad idea indeed.

"People have told me since then that as one approaches the earth in a parachute, everything seems to speed up, and I found that to be true. Rather than floating, I seemed suddenly to be hurtling towards the ground at a terrifying rate, and my eyes got very round as I picked up the details of claw-like evergreens that I was going to impact at considerable speed. Then, with a tearing crash, breaking branches and the taste and odor of pine needles slapping me in the face, I hit a tree hard, swung in towards the trunk, and was knocked unconscious when my head hit a thick scaly branch."

Peggy heard Celine calling her from downstairs, and realized it was time to make deliveries. She reluctantly turned off the playback, got dressed and went about her tasks, all the while thinking about what she had heard.

CHAPTER 27

Editing note: The following information was discovered by means independent of Ms Pederson's interviews with the aviator Max von Waldberg. An associate of Ms Pederson tracked down *Leutnant zur See* Wilhelm Göttgens' obscure self-published postwar memoir in a German library, realized it held information relevant to Von Waldberg's story, and had it translated to English. This excerpt, which has been lightly rewritten for better reading (Göttgen's style is very stilted and pedantic) and for clarity, will be inserted at this point in the final text in the interest of continuity. For reasons unknown, Göttgens, now deceased, wrote in the third person.

Leutnant zur See Wilhelm Göttgens watched with intense admiration as the great aircraft came across the bow of the submarine a few hundred feet off the surface of the water. The aluminium skin of the aircraft was painted dark green and black, like shadows in the light of a bright three-quarter moon. The big machine's landing lights were making bright patterns on the dark water.

The submarine had received the plane's radio burst and answered it, and then they had heard her coming, a low droning, and had seen her light signal and flare. The sub's crew had answered as they were instructed, with a shielded light and their own quick star shell, and had positioned the boat properly. Göttgens ordered recovery crews on deck, manned the bridge machine guns and deck gun and alerted sick bay to expect to receive casualties. In all respects, the U-1230 was entirely prepared to recover the aircraft's crew.

First, they had picked up the package that the plane had dropped on its first pass, the boat crew homing in on the 'chute and magnesium flare bobbing on the waves. They quickly snared the container and returned to the ship. Göttgens turned to his Captain and said, "They seem to know what they are doing," as the plane circled back, apparently preparing to ditch about a hundred and fifty meters from the sub, into the light wind, on a course parallel to that of their vessel. The plane flared out, lifted, came about, and the engines cut out as it drifted towards the sea.

"Boat crew off," he ordered, after the captain nodded, and a new crew of five bounded to the rubber boat, the first crew having been worn out by rowing to pick up the earlier packet in the cold sea. All of this was part of the plan that they had all rehearsed so often in the Gulf of Danzig. They had spent a week lying on the bottom, breathing the fuggy air of an immobile submarine, surfacing only at night to recharge batteries, "*Schnorkelling*" a couple of times per written orders of the *Oberkommando der Marine*, naval HQ, maintaining radio silence the whole time, and blackout discipline to boot.

Göttgens was proud of the crew, mostly youngsters, and his crew chiefs, survivors of a campaign with enormous casualties. They had managed this claustrophobic ordeal very well, and he had been sure to see that they got out on deck during their long voyage to the American coast, in places where they could not be detected by aircraft or surface ships. A few bottles of schnapps he had managed to wangle out of a tight-fisted quartermaster had helped to raise morale a bit on the long trip, and he and the captain had seen to it that meals were properly prepared.

The men were happy, even though they weren't sinking ships. They had been sworn to secrecy and knew that their mission was something important, so they griped only minimally and did their jobs well.

Once the submarine had gained the eastern coast of America, they had had to settle into the incredibly dull routine of waiting, sitting on the bottom of the Gulf of Maine after having identified the prominent Owl's Head lighthouse tower through the periscope. By this stage of the war, it was near-suicide for a U-boat to surface anywhere near the American coast in daylight, as there were constant surface and aerial patrols by the US Navy and Coast Guard. Over two hundred and forty U-boats had been lost already in 1944, and the captain was taking no chances with his big new submarine.

They lay on the bottom all day thereafter, for four full days, surfacing only at night to ventilate the ship and recharge their batteries, ignoring fat merchant ships, the sort of targets that win aggressive sailors Iron Crosses, and waiting for something, Göttgens knew not entirely what, to happen.

He was happy to be on deck now, breathing fresh night air in the conning tower, next to his Captain — a man he admired greatly, hoping that this recovery might help bring an end to such surreptitious missions and that they could soon go back to what he felt was the real business of U-boats: sinking enemy ships. Göttgens held his breath as the great bird slowly settled to the sea, tail down, reaching, reaching, then touching the waves, at first about two hundred meters from the sub.

It looked picture-perfect, tail down, nose up, skipping, once, twice. Göttgens even saw the lights in the cockpit as the beautiful craft drew abreast, and he thought he saw the shadow of a pilot, but then there was a hard bounce and then another, the black sea creaming white around the dragging tail of the aircraft, and then the entire tail section, the whole rear quarter of the aircraft, flipped upward with a screech of tearing metal they could hear on the sub over two hundred meters away, and the great aircraft slewed away from the submarine. Then the tail section dropped, dragging into the sea like a giant scoop, still attached to the plane, acting like a sea anchor.

The plane stopped abruptly, a charging dog at the end of its chain. The front of the plane slammed into the sea, briefly going under, then bobbing sluggishly back up, but very low in the water. Then the aircraft rolled toward its side, and after a stunningly short time, disappeared beneath the waves, the creamy wake from her landing seeming to swallow her up.

Göttgens sucked in a deep breath, stunned, as he heard his Captain exclaim, "God in heaven! Order the boat crew back. We'll check for survivors after the sea settles." And so they did, both the crew boat and the sub itself trolling through an expanding petroleum slick for two hours, calling out softly, picking up an item here and there, a floating life vest, a seat cushion, a few gas cans, some other odds and ends; but no people, no bodies.

"They were probably all belted in," the captain mused. "Never had a chance, poor bastards. We'll stay on station till just before dawn, just in case someone got out, *Herr Leutnant*, then we'll submerge and proceed with our voyage. May God have mercy on their souls."

They patrolled mournfully, calling out now and then for a couple of hours; then, as the sky began to lighten, they dived and set course for their next destination.

"At least we recovered whatever it was they dropped," Göttgens said to the captain as they set off.

"*Ja*," the captain replied. "I just hope it was worth it."

Göttgen's memoir continues, describing other wartime activities and his postwar career in the

German merchant navy. None of that information is relevant to Von Waldberg's story, so it is not included here.

CHAPTER 28

When Peggy had finished her deliveries, she raced up the snowy outside steps rather than going through the bakery. She knew Celine would want her to stop and have something to eat, but she was dying to get back to Max's story. While making her rounds, she reminded herself to tell Max about this — that she had left him hanging in a tree. Smiling at that, she switched on the playback and adjusted the volume.

"Around dawn, I became aware of an intense itching sensation on my face, and woke to discover a mass of flies crawling on me, probably attracted to the blood that was all over my helmet and the side of my head. I reached up to assess my injury and at first thought I had fractured my skull, as my fingers contacted a spongy mass covered with clotted blood.

"I thought I was a goner for sure, that my brain was exposed and I'd never survive such an injury. Probing a bit further, I realized I was feeling the blood-soaked woolly lining of my leather flight helmet, which was torn open by impact with the tree. My scalp was lacerated, but my skull seemed intact. I mentally thanked the maker of that helmet, and added a short prayer of gratitude to St Joseph of Cupertino, the saint who was said to levitate and thus became the patron saint of pilots. I also wished I could levitate myself out of that tree.

"It took nearly an hour to get down to the ground. I had to saw through my parachute harness with a rather dull survival knife until I was hanging by a single thick leather strap, then carefully ease myself out of the tangled parachute cords and plant my weight on the bough below me. Our parachutes had a quick-release device, but if I had used that, I would have fallen out of that very tall tree. With my feet firmly on a stout branch, I cut the last strap and finally had a chance to look around.

"Peggy, I was stunned. In Germany and Austria, the forests are carefully managed, almost like parks. The underbrush is cut back, except where needed for animals to shelter, and diseased or fallen trees are quickly removed. Well-kept trails are maintained, many with signs directing hikers to various scenic places, villages or *Gasthofs*. The *Forstmeisters*, wardens, and their dogs patrol regularly and nothing happens in the woods that they do not know about.

"This forest was an incredible jumble of huge pines, tangled underbrush and decaying fallen trees everywhere. There were huge black boulders, many the size of small houses, scattered around, some covered with scaly moss so they blended in with the trees. Even from my perch about a hundred feet up, I could not see a single trail or road. There were no buildings in sight, nor could I hear any sound of engines or other human activity. My spirits fell as I laboriously lowered myself from limb to limb and finally reached the ground.

"I sat on a fallen log under the tree, nearly worn out. The Pervitin had worn off, my head ached terribly and the wound in my scalp was bleeding again. Also, I was covered with sticky pine sap and the damned flies were buzzing around my head, irritating me no end. Then I started thinking about what sort of dangerous animals might be living in this uncontrolled wilderness.

"Except for some parts of Eastern Europe, bears and wolves had been eliminated, but here? I was thinking that lots of wild animals were about, and here I was bleeding all over the place. I quickly bandaged my head, leaving the helmet in place. I pulled out my puny sidearm and crawled under a huge tangle of brush and fallen limbs, trying to decide what to do next. Soon, I was sound asleep.

"When I woke, it was bright daylight, the sun directly overhead. I buried the paperwork and all but one of the film canisters I had taken from the photographer under the tree I fell into, since it was marked by my parachute and therefore could be located. I kept one roll of film with me.

"I felt much better and decided to walk in the direction of the buildings I had seen earlier. I pulled out my compass and set out along the course we had been following just before I 'accidentally' fell from the plane.

"I walked for six days, slept in thickets or under rocks. On the second day it started to rain, and rained steadily all that day and night as the temperature fell. I ate meat paste and crackers until those ran out on the third day, and I drank water from creeks or low spots.

"I was a wreck. My flight suit was tattered and ripped from thorny branches and a bad fall I took when I tripped over a wet rock and tumbled into a stony ravine. That fall also broke my compass, but that no longer mattered. The large rocks all around me probably contained iron or some other magnetic metal, so the compass needle had been swinging about wildly. I suspected I had been walking in circles, and knew I was hopelessly lost.

"I was ravenous, dazed from hunger and blood loss. I was wet to the skin, chilled through and through and shivering uncontrollably. My head still hurt, and worst of all, my right foot had gone numb again, and was now painful with every step. On top of everything else, the cursed flies kept following me, nipping at me all the time, and gigantic mosquitoes were thick and bloodthirsty, adding to my misery.

"Utterly exhausted, cold, starving and at the end of my tether, I sat on a rock and wept from frustration, angry at myself. How could I have been such a fool? What sort of idiot jumps into an uncharted wilderness with four cans of food, a few crackers and an injured foot? Why hadn't I been more careful in rationing my food?

"How had it come to this? I was trying to do the right thing as I saw it. I had decided I could not serve the Nazi regime any longer, and simply couldn't deal with helping them drop some long-lasting poison on thousands of innocent civilians. I was certain that I was going to die alone in these dark woods, and my bones would be scattered by animals. Nobody would ever know what became of me; I would have failed to complete my mission and those thousands would die.

"I looked at my pistol. I had taken to carrying it in my hand, hoping to spot a rabbit or squirrel for a meal, and also because I had heard noises in the brush that suggested a large animal might be following me.

"I contemplated shooting myself, but the pistol, the small-caliber Walther PPK, seemed risky. The last thing I wanted was to be seriously injured but still alive when the scavengers showed up. There had been debates among my colleagues in Russia about whether it was better to put the pistol in one's mouth or at one's temple, and grisly tales about people who had survived such attempts, paralyzed or blinded and maimed.

"Then I remembered the cyanide capsule the SS man had given me before the flight, and placed my pistol on the rock next to me, patted around all the pockets of my flight suit and finally found the tiny bullet-like container. I unscrewed the threaded lid with trembling fingers and spilled the glass ampoule into my hand, and sat there for a while, thinking about everything I had been through, about Rachel, my mother and grandmother, tears streaming down my cheeks.

"I thought about trying to write a letter, since I did have a notebook and pencil, but my hands were shaking and my whole body was trembling. It was damp and looked like more rain coming, so a note or letter would have soon dissolved anyway.

"I thought about Spain, France, Poland, flying over England, Russia — all the things we had done in the name of the *Führer*, and felt my life had been wasted in the service of an evil regime, just because I wanted to fly.

"I didn't think God would condemn me for killing myself under these circumstances, but I said a prayer anyway and prepared to put the ampoule in my mouth.

"Just then, I heard the sound of an engine, which sounded like a truck laboring uphill not far away. I put the ampoule back in its container, put it in one of the pockets of my flight suit, stuffed my pistol back in its holster, and took off as fast as I could hobble in the direction of that wonderful sound, thanking Joseph, the levitating saint, as I went.

"The engine noise stopped, and my heart sank, but then I realized I was very close to the vehicle I had heard, because I could actually smell exhaust fumes, so I continued in the direction I thought the sound had come from. After a few minutes, I heard a man shouting just ahead of me, then terrible snarling and growling drowned out the shouting. Mustering enough energy to cover the last hundred yards fairly quickly, I broke out of the underbrush onto a crude trail, just two ruts in the mud.

"A small, sturdy-looking green vehicle was sitting on the trail, and I noticed a white pine tree image painted on the front of it. It appeared to be transport for an

American *Forstmeister*, and I was delighted to have found someone in authority to surrender to. I limped past the little truck and, looking to my right, discovered the source of all that shouting and roaring.

"In a clearing next to the trail, a man in a green uniform was on the ground and a gigantic bear had him by the leg, flinging his body back and forth while the man shouted and punched at the animal with no effect. I was thunderstruck for a moment, as the sight was utterly surreal, something out of a Teutonic horror story; but I had enough presence of mind to pull out my Walther and fire a shot at the snarling monster. The bear swatted at the bullet wound as one would swat at a fly, and turned to me, the man's leg still firmly in its mouth.

"I turned to try to flee, but looked back when I heard the man yelling even louder than before and saw that the bear had torn the poor fellow's leg off, and was shaking it as a dog shakes a dying rabbit. Horrified, near-paralyzed with fear, I emptied the entire magazine of my pistol into the bear, and it promptly turned and rushed me, dropping the man's leg as it charged, bellowing in rage and pain.

"The Walther's bullets seemed to have had little effect, other than to irritate the monster, and the next thing I knew the damned thing had knocked me to the ground and was crouched over me. Its foul smell was overwhelming, and saliva was flying everywhere as it shook its enormous head, pawing at what were probably bullet wounds from my sidearm. I prepared to die a painful death, pounding the animal with my empty pistol.

"Then there was a thunderclap, or so it seemed, then another, a smell of gunpowder, and the reeking beast collapsed on top of me, gave two giant, shuddering, gasps, defecated with a hideous blast of flatulence, then became perfectly still.

"I lay there, unable to move the carcass that was pinning me down, barely able to breathe because of the weight on my chest. The animal's blood, saliva and excrement were everywhere. Something shifted the dead bear's massive forearm, letting in a few glorious breaths of fresh air.

"A man's face appeared, peering at me trapped under the huge furry mound. Then he said something like, 'Hey der. You just hang on der a minute, fella, and I'll get you outta der, but I gotta go get da yeep to pull dat der bear off ya, OK?' I nodded weakly, and lay there wondering what on earth a 'yeep' was.

"Of course I know now that was Pete's way of saying 'Jeep' when he was worked up, but it seemed odd at the time. You see, I had never seen what you folks call a Jeep, because I never had contact with American soldiers."

Peggy heard laughter in Max's voice on the tape, and she had to laugh as well. *"How just like Pete,"* she thought, then realized that Pete's accent wasn't an act, like some people thought, but that his accent got thicker when he was *scared*. That explained a lot, and made her admire Pete even more.

"Well, I heard the engine start up, lots of cursing, banging and pounding, and some business with chains, and finally the weight of that damned stinking dead bear was pulled away and I was able to crawl out from underneath, blinking in the daylight. 'So where the hell did you come from, anyways?' the warden, who I now know was Pete, asked. He was leaning on the vehicle, holding a large rifle, and I realized that it must have been he who shot the bear. *'Mein Gott, how had he survived having his leg torn off?'*

"I told him part of my story, that I had very important information and would only talk to the FBI. Then I handed Pete my pistol, a totally symbolic gesture, since it had no bullets.

"Pete pounded me on the shoulder, so hard it made me wince. He also told me what a doofus — his term — I was to try to kill a full-grown bear like that with such a popgun, but that I had saved his life and he was grateful. Grinning, he accepted my surrender.

"I asked him what had happened, and desperately, if he had anything to eat. Pete told me to go and open a compartment at the back of the 'yeep' and I would find some sandwiches, a soda and a bottle of schnapps.

"Pete said he was a little worn out, and needed to sit for a while and work on the straps for his leg. He said he could get around a little, but his prosthetic leg wasn't working right, as he hopped off towards a big tree, using his rifle as a crutch.

"I limped away thinking, *'Ach, artificial leg, that explains it!'* I got the food and drink, and Pete and I sat with our backs to the tree, with Pete's big rifle between us. Then I ate one of the most delicious meals I have ever had in my life, especially the bread, which smelled heavenly, while Pete told me his story.

"Pete told me he had been tracking a deserter from the Naval Air Station at Owl's Head, an American Indian from a reservation in the American southwest. He said the Navy had told him that the man had been caught doing something bad where he lived, and the judge told him he could either enlist or go to jail, so the guy joined the Navy and then deserted after being assigned to the Owl's Head Naval Air Station.

"Pete said he had been seeing signs for a couple of days, a campfire site here, a footprint there, but on the day we met, he had noticed buzzards circling, followed them, and come upon the carcass of a young cow moose that had been killed by a bear. Next to that dead moose lay the partially eaten corpse of a man dressed in Navy dungarees and a torn P-coat. 'I figured the guy thought he had stumbled on a free meal, and the bear got him,' Pete said, between bites of his sandwich.

"'But then I made a dumbass rookie mistake. I put down my rifle and bent over to roll the Navy guy's body over and get his dog tags. When I straightened up, I heard a noise and turned around to see a young bear cub at the edge of the clearing. Well, shit, fella, my hair stood up fer sure and I knew I was in for it then, 'cause when you see a cub like that near a kill, ya gotta know momma bear ain't far away. She grabbed me before I could turn around to get my rifle, knocked me down and was about ta do me in when you showed up with that crappy little gun and saved my bacon!'

"'You are entirely welcome,' I said, eyeing his sandwich.

"Pete went on after we both had a healthy swig of surprisingly good American schnapps, 'Lucky for me, mamma got hold a' me by my wooden leg, and when she went after you, I crawled over to my rifle and shot her.' Then Pete told me about his artificial limb, and gave me the uneaten half of his sandwich, which I wolfed down in seconds, wishing he had more.

"We sat for a few more minutes, then Pete said we had to get out of there because there was what he called a 'big blow' coming. Pete said we could leave the Navy guy there for a while, that he would call the Navy base when he got back to the house. He'd give them the co-ordinates and they would come and get him. I was relieved, because I knew I hadn't enough strength left to help load a corpse into the vehicle.

"We studied the set-up of the little truck and worked out a way to drive it with two good legs between us. Pete's prosthetic was poorly attached because the straps were torn, and he had large bruises on his hips and stump. My right foot by now was almost useless, with very little feeling. It ended up that I worked the clutch and brake with my left foot, and Pete steered, operated the throttle with his right foot and shifted the gears. Then, with a whole lot of stopping, starting, gear-grinding and creative tri-lingual swearing, mostly from Pete, we got the Jeep to Pete and Celine's cabin."

CHAPTER 29

"We must have been quite a sight when we pulled up at Pete's. A petite, pretty woman, who I now know was Celine, came out at the sound of the engine, and seeing us, looked like she was going to faint. She said what sounded like a short prayer in French and rushed over to hug Pete, but he told her to wait, saying, 'Honey, we both got covered with bear poop and blood; we're gonna hafta clean up before we come in. Please bring out a coupla blankets. We'll go in the shed and then be right there. Oh, and bring me my old crutch, please.' The woman reluctantly went inside, then came back with the things Pete asked for.

"Pete and I limped into Pete's little tool shed, stripped, leaving our torn, smelly and stained clothing in a heap on the floor. We draped the blankets over us and, supporting one another, made our way to the cabin.

"When we got there, the fragrance was magnificent, overwhelming. The woman, who I now know was your mama, was baking cinnamon rolls of some sort, and seeing the look on my face, she gestured for me to sit at the table and she put three of those incredible rolls in front of me, with a steaming mug of coffee laced with cream and schnapps.

"She gave the same to Pete, who was on the phone with the Navy. After that, I'm afraid, I fell sound asleep in my chair, my face in the empty plate, according to Pete.

"At some point I was vaguely aware, half-awake, of being sponge-bathed by Celine and helped into clean pyjamas, then onto a lovely soft cot. I remember marvelling at how strong she was for her tiny frame, and how Pete's snoring seemed to shake the whole cabin.

"I slept for a whole day and night, waking briefly in the morning to eat some more of Celine's wonderful baked goods, before going back to sleep for another half day. When I finally became fully awake, Pete told me he had called the sheriff, and the sheriff had called the FBI, after making sure I wasn't going to escape from Pete's custody.

"Pete told me he said, 'Escape? The poor fella just walked around in the woods for six days without no food, then got beat up by a big old bear, and he's got something wrong with one of his feet. He ain't goin' nowhere.' There was a huge storm outside, Pete told me, what he called a 'Nor'easter' with some early snow, and nobody would be able to get to Owl's Head from Boston for at least another day, maybe longer. 'Just take it easy, come and sit with us, and tell us your story.' I stayed with them for two more days, and we talked a lot, and by the time Kelly, the FBI man from Boston, arrived, we had become good friends.

"When the FBI agent, Kelly, showed up with a sheriff's deputy, I was dressed in my flight suit, though it was stained and ripped. I had cleaned it as best I could after I stopped Celine from burning it along with some of Pete's smelly clothing. I told her that I had to be in uniform when I surrendered, lest I be considered a spy.

"Kelly looked me up and down, and asked if that was the only thing I had to wear. Pete intervened at this point and said as long as Kelly understood that I had surrendered in uniform, he would give me a clean coverall. Pete also gave me an old knapsack which held my personal items, my damaged flight suit and the film roll I had taken from the aircraft. With that, we were off on the train to Boston, and eventually an FBI safe house.

"The trip was very difficult for Kelly, who was extremely grumpy the whole time, probably because there was no alcohol available on the train, after he had emptied the flask he had with him. The trip was unpleasant for me as well, because my foot began to ache terribly and my whole body seemed to be one gigantic bruise.

"The storm had caused a lot of flooding, and tracks were washed out in some places and under water in others. Our train seemed to have low priority, as we often sat on sidings while trains loaded with trucks or troops passed by. When we finally got to Boston late in the afternoon after two days cooped up on a slow-moving train, Kelly brusquely turned me over to two other agents and promptly disappeared.

"The new agents, who looked much more alert and professional than Kelly, brought me to an old brownstone mansion converted to apartments. There, I was processed, searched, fingerprinted and assigned quarters. I had a luxurious shower and was examined by a medic, who re-bandaged my injuries, applied a soothing salve to my aching foot, cleaned and dressed my head injury and gave me an injection of some sort, saying it would prevent infection in my wounds.

"Then I was given a change of clothing, a sort of pajama-outfit with medical symbols on it, and escorted to a brief interview with a very young American junior officer who spoke excellent, if American-accented, German.

"I told him I had parachuted from a German airplane over Maine, and asked him to immediately recover and assess the film from my knapsack, stressing that the information on it was critically important, and that there was little time to prevent what could be an enormous calamity. 'Come now, *Herr Hauptmann*, a German airplane over the state of Maine? Tell me another. I think you are a spy brought here by a submarine. I believe you were sent here to obtain information but got caught, or you came here to tell us some fairy tale to mislead us.' I reminded him quite tersely, in English, that I had turned myself in, was in uniform upon my surrender, and thus entitled to the protections of the Geneva Convention.

"Very tired, injured and in pain, I emphasized I wouldn't say more until the photographs had been examined. After a little more bluster, and warnings that spies like me could be shot, the youngster reluctantly ordered a guard to take me to my room, where I slept like a dead man until the next morning.

"The next day I was awakened early, given coffee, a boiled egg and toast, then escorted once again to the interview room. It was a very different setting this time. The young officer was there, crowded into a corner on a folding chair, but the room was dominated by three important-looking men of my age or older. The first, who seemed to be the oldest, was dressed in civilian clothes, a very well-tailored and expensive suit. Two other men, both in uniform, were at the table. One had eagles on his collar, the other silver oak leaves.

"The man in the suit began, asking me where I obtained the pictures on the film roll turned over the day before. I explained a bit and his eyebrows rose. Continuing that I had hidden other material after I landed, I told them I was prepared to co-operate fully providing they would consider a few requests which I believed they could grant.

"The officer wearing eagles broke in here, asking just who the hell I thought I was, making demands when I was no more than another damned arrogant Nazi prisoner who ought to be happy to be safe and sound. At that point the man in civvies intervened and the other fellow muttered, 'Sorry, Bill... I mean general', which got him a very sharp look.

"'See here,' the general, if that's what he was, continued, 'we are pleased you have brought us this information, but we are under no obligation to you.' I told him I quite agreed and was perfectly content to be sent to the nearest PoW camp and let them figure out how to prevent a catastrophe involving one of their major manufacturing centers and its civilian population.

"Eagle man broke in again, smacking the table and abruptly pointing out that there were 'many ways of obtaining information from stubborn people', at which point the man in the suit asked him to go and try to find a map of Maine. The eagle man, who I now know was an *Oberst*, or colonel, pointed to the young junior officer, saying he could fetch the map, but the older fellow gave him that look again, and the colonel left the room.

"Thereafter, our conversation became much more productive. I was asked to outline what I wished them to do. I told the men I had two major concerns. I wanted them to promise me that they would check on the security and well-being of *Fraulein* Rachel Liebeskind, believed to be in or around Paris, and gave them the name of Inspector of Gendarmes Jean Rion, who ought to be in contact with her if she was still alive.

"I told them next I was very worried about my mother and grandmother, and explained the circumstances of their detention, giving them the name of Tomas Klaibisch, a person of influence in that area of Austria. I wanted to be assured that steps would be taken to protect my family from the SS. I also asked if I was in any danger from other prisoners, since I knew they would guess I was sharing information with our captors.

"Then I asked if something could be done to safeguard my family's property and try to guarantee the safety of the people that had been sheltering there. The colonel returned with an encyclopedia containing a map of Maine, and I was asked to explain my activities after I jumped from the aircraft.

"After about an hour of answering those questions the best I could without revealing too much, the general seemed to be satisfied with that part of my story, though the colonel continued to glare at me with unconcealed hostility.

"The officer with the silver oak leaves cleared his throat and the general said, 'Go ahead, John.' The man then informed me that all of the men in our facility were specialists of one kind or another, all had been offered an opportunity to co-operate, and that all of them were providing important information to the Allies, so I was in no danger from them.

"The meeting ended with the general telling me that they would discuss my requests with the appropriate agencies and convene again when they had something to tell me. I answered that until then I was unable to give them any further information, which earned me a derisive snort from the red-faced colonel, and a curt nod from the general in civilian clothes.

"An armed soldier was waiting outside the door to take me back to my quarters, and as we climbed the stairs, I heard a loud voice from the room we had just left. I could not make out the words, but guessed all was not going well for the surly colonel. A muffled snicker from my guard confirmed that impression."

CHAPTER 30

"For the next eight days, I was kept away from other prisoners, seeing only the guards who walked me to meals taken alone in a small pantry. I caught glimpses of other prisoners, all wearing floppy green fatigue uniforms, but was not allowed to speak with any of them.

"Bored to distraction, I begged one of the guards, who seemed sympathetic, to get me something to read. The man came back after a while with a stack of American magazines, called *Life*, *Time* and *Saturday Evening Post*. I thanked him profusely and spent the rest of my solitary confinement reading and re-reading every word of those publications.

"I was amazed at the news from an American perspective, and at first quite sceptical, but the articles seemed refreshingly free from the sort of clumsy propaganda occurring in such things at home. I was also struck by the optimism expressed in these magazines, and while I did not understand some of the American idioms, or completely trust what I was reading, I got the impression that life here was nothing like the misery we were told prevailed in America.

"Advertising showed goods for sale that were unheard of in heavily-rationed wartime Europe. Recipes and illustrations of meals implied a bounty beyond my imagining.

"Pictures of smiling American children made me ill when I contemplated what would happen to so many of them if a fiendish radiation weapon was employed, so I prayed the authorities were following-up as promised.

"In the afternoon of the eighth day, I was given a clean set of khakis and, to my surprise, taken outside to a waiting sedan. This carried me and two guards to a large office building in downtown Boston, where I was taken to a conference room, much bigger than the one I had visited previously.

"Some of the people I had seen before were there, seated behind a large table. The powerful older man I had met earlier was there, this time in a uniform bearing two silver stars. The young officer was there, off to the side with a notepad, and the man with the oak leaves, who I knew by now was a lieutenant colonel, was also present. In addition, there was a naval officer, a man in civilian clothes and an officer in an Air Corps uniform.

"Behind those seven people were three other men in civilian clothing, sitting against the rear wall. The belligerent colonel, I noted with relief, was not in the room.

"I see the tape is running out, and I'm a bit tired, so I will summarize. The lieutenant colonel told me that Rachel was safe in Paris, but ill with amoebic dysentery from contaminated water. She had been living rough in the mountains until Paris fell, then was brought to the city and put in a hospital, where she remained. He told me they would provide me with information as her treatment continued.

"I was then addressed by the man in civilian clothes, who spoke with an upper-class British accent. He told me that his organisation was quite impressed with Tomas Klaibisch's operation, which was far better organized than similar resistance groups they had worked with in France.

"Tomas's group had discovered by chance that the Gestapo was going to arrest my mother and grandmother and had hustled all the people in hiding out to various locations in the countryside in the nick of time.

"He went on to tell me that mother and grandmother were secure. They had first been confined at *Schloss* Kesselstein, then transferred to another local castle, a place called *Schloss* Itter, where they were being held, probably as bargaining chips, along with a group of high-ranking French detainees. Contact had also been established with other elements of the Austrian resistance, who would assist the Allies in looking after our property and protecting those who had been sheltered there.

"Finally, the naval officer informed me that two dead German airmen had been found washed up from the sea near Owl's Head lighthouse and asked me to look at pictures that had been taken at the scene. I looked, and the room seemed to shrink. I instantly recognized the two bodies as those of the photographer

and the radar operator. I felt as if I was going to faint—
"

Max began to cough, or maybe he was becoming emotional. His voice failed, and the tape was turned off.

"Damnit!" thought Peggy, noting the tape was almost finished. *"Two days until Grocery Bob comes, and then I'll be able to talk to Max. I can hardly wait."*

Somehow, Peggy got through the next couple of days, distracted at work and spending all her time at home, sorting through the material she had accumulated to prepare a list of questions for Max. She went through the list over and over, and checked the uniform cap and its accompanying letter half a dozen times.

Finally, on a bright chilly Saturday morning, with the neighborhood shining under a blanket of freshly-fallen snow, she heard the rumble of a powerful engine and a loud horn. Looking out of the window, she saw Bob's big red truck idling in front of the building.

Peggy quickly gathered her files, scooped up the box with the uniform cap and letter, and put five fresh cassettes in her jacket pocket. She hurried out the door to the outside stairway, waving at Bob so he knew she was coming, and started quickly down the snowy steps. After only a few seconds she slipped, missed the handrail, and tumbled all the way down the stairs. Putting her right hand out to break her fall, she heard a distinct pop, and felt terrific pain in her wrist and shoulder.

Despite the pain, she let out a foolish laugh, feeling silly and embarrassed, and tried to stand. That was when she noticed that her right wrist was severely deformed, curved where it shouldn't be curved, and that her shoulder wasn't working. She sat there at the bottom of the steps, her files scattered about, staring at the strange shape of her lower arm.

Suddenly, Bob was next to her, holding a small olive-drab pack with a caduceus stenciled on it. He opened the pack, pulled out a large triangular bandage and deftly fashioned a sling, into which he placed her arm. She looked at him, a little dubious, and Bob, his speech very difficult to understand, placed his hand on his chest and said, 'Muh, muh, muh, medic', and then something about dogs, collies, which she couldn't figure out, but she decided to trust Bob and relaxed as he secured the sling with a swathe around her torso, then said, 'I guh, guh, get muh, mama, y-y-you st, st, stay', and he ran to the front of the building to alert Celine.

Like many brain-injured people, Bob had difficulty modulating his voice, spoke with a stammer and tended to speak in over-loud bursts, so he had difficulty communicating with Celine, and finally simply took her by the elbow, saying, 'K-k-kom, k-kom', and led her to Peggy, now weeping at the bottom of the icy stairway.

Between the two of them, Bob and Celine got Peggy to the truck and Bob drove them both to the emergency department in Rockland. Then Bob explained with great difficulty that he was leaving to go to Max's place, because more snow was coming. He didn't want to get stuck, and Max was probably in need of supplies.

When the doctor examined Peggy's arm, he asked who had immobilized it. She told him, and the doctor said, 'Well, he did a hell of a good job. Tell him that for me.' Then he said, she had dislocated her shoulder, told her she had sustained what was medically labelled a 'Colles' fracture of the wrist and that she wouldn't be able to use her right arm for a month or more.

After three long hours, during which her shoulder was painfully relocated and her broken wrist repositioned, then encased in plaster, Peggy and Celine returned to the bakery in a taxi, to find Bob's big truck parked in front of the building, with Bob sitting on the running board, his face in his hands, blubbering like a baby. Bob was a large, burly, bearded man, and it was disconcerting to see him in such a state. Peggy touched him on the shoulder and asked him what was wrong.

"Muh, muh, Max is duh, duh, dead," he howled, and for the second time that day Peggy found herself suddenly sitting down in the snow.

CHAPTER 31

The next five hours were confusing. Peggy was absolutely stunned, surprised at the depth of her feelings for a man she had known only a short time. She responded numbly, phoning the sheriff's office after an inconsolable Bob finally made it clear that he had to get home, had to see his doctor, had to lie down. He then drove off, still crying.

The sheriff sent a man with a snowmobile, as did the forest service — machines that could make it through the snow to Max's cabin. One of them was towing a toboggan.

A couple of hours after getting directions from Peggy, the men were back and asked Peggy to look at a body they had discovered in the remote cabin near Birch Point. One of the men pulled back a blanket from the dead man's face and asked Peggy to identify him.

The deputy told the women that it was clear Max had died before Bob arrived, so any suggestion of a crime was almost certainly eliminated.

Peggy staggered a bit, astonished by Max's appearance. He had lost so much weight since she had last seen him — his face was emaciated, his cheeks sunken. Max's lips were grey-blue, and his closed eyes were hollow. She was momentarily unable to respond, so Celine stepped up and told the officer that the dead man was Max Wald, that he was a distant relative of her late husband Pete.

Celine said he had gone through bad things in Norway during the war, and chose to live alone in the woods after he came to the US.

The forest service man said he remembered Pete telling him about Max when he, the warden, was a trainee, and the sheriff's deputy wrote that down.

Peggy, recovering from her shock, started to interrupt, but Celine's expression made her pause. The warden, an old friend, gave Celine a hug, shook Peggy's hand and told them the cabin had been secured, and that after the medical examiner established cause of death, Celine would be free to deal with the place as she saw fit, as she was the owner of record.

After the men left, Peggy stumbled upstairs and went to bed, irritated by unaccustomed clumsiness due to the weight of plaster on her injured arm. She was also groggy from the pain medication she had been given and fell into a deep sleep.

Peggy stayed in bed for two days, getting up only for the bathroom and to eat a bite or two from what Celine brought her.

She was deeply depressed. She was in pain and medication made her even more fatigued. On top of that, she could not type with the awkward cast, and she couldn't afford a typist, so work on Max's story completely stopped. Peggy had made a huge investment of time, effort and emotion in compiling the work, and she was afraid she would never be able to complete it without Max.

She missed Max terribly, not just because of the impact his death had on her work, but because she had become very fond of him.

She couldn't drive her manual-transmission vehicle either, so she felt isolated and hopeless. She had no way to get to Max's place even after the sheriff gave permission, because Bob had needed to go back to the VA for treatment for an acute relapse of his PTSD, according to his father.

"Max was Bob's friend," the man said when Peggy called him. "Max really *listened* to Bob, and understood what he had been through. Max's death is a great blow to Bob, and I know he'll recover, he always has, but it's going to take a while."

A letter from the Medical Examiner, addressed to Celine, asked for instructions about "the disposition of the deceased". Celine explained to Peggy that Max had told her he wished to be cremated, and she called the coroner with those instructions.

The Medical Examiner's letter ruled out any sort of foul play, but stated that shards of glass were found in Max's mouth, suggesting poisoning, probably with something like cyanide. No note had been found, but given the circumstances, the Medical Examiner ruled the death a suicide.

The report also said Max had been terminally ill at the time of his death, with a lung disease probably related to asbestos exposure. Peggy felt she should have questioned Max more closely about his chronic cough; she felt guilty for not being more perceptive.

Driven into a deeper depression by the autopsy's findings, Peggy neglected her appearance, her hair uncombed, not bathing, not even brushing her teeth.

Peggy knew that she had an ethical obligation to tell her employer the truth about Max. She was a journalist, and bound by a commitment to the Rockland paper. Her editor had hired her when she really needed a job, and had been kind to her since. She knew what she had to do, but the prospect made her heartsick.

She was sure that when the story broke, it would be picked up by news services all over the country, maybe all over the world, and perhaps destroy her chances for a successful book whenever she did recover.

That thought put her back in bed for another day, but the next afternoon she gathered herself together enough to call the newspaper and speak to the editor, who promptly put a stenographer on the phone in a three-way call. Over the next hour, Peggy told her story, outlining the information she had to document her findings. She also told the editor she was working on a book about Max, then broke down in tears after hanging up the phone. More depressed than ever, Peggy went back to bed.

When she crawled out from under the covers again, she found two newspapers Celine had left on her bedside table. The first, her own *Courier-Gazette*, ran the story about Max with a banner headline above the fold: **"Recluse who lived in Maine woods since 1945**

was escaped German PoW." The story continued, giving details Peggy had provided and some stock photos of German aircraft. Peggy noted with perverse satisfaction that the editor had given her a byline.

The second paper, published in Boston, was much more sensational, the headline reading: **"Nazi Pilot Hid in Maine Woods for Nearly Forty Years — Austrian Aristocrat Aviator Escaped US Custody, Told FBI About Secret Mission!"**; followed by a near-total reprint of the *Courier-Gazette* piece. An interview with the Agent-in-Charge of the Boston FBI office appeared next.

The agent was quoted as saying that FBI records indicated that the person in question had been turned over to the PoW facility at Fort Devens after VE Day and from there he was presumed to have been returned to Germany.

He said the FBI was investigating what role, if any, the agency played in Max's case, and that further details would be released as available.

Peggy went back to bed. She knew public consciousness was fleeting and feared the story would seem stale by the time she managed to finish it, if she could finish it at all.

Finally, after five days of almost uninterrupted withdrawal, Peggy woke to the sound of a truck engine, and then Celine banging about the room, raising the shades and throwing open Peggy's bedroom windows to the chilly air.

"Get up, get up, *allez, vite, vite!*" Celine cried, shaking her. "You have a visitor; someone is here to see you!"

Peggy roused herself enough to look out of the window and saw a rental pick-up in front of the building, a new-looking snowmobile in the truck bed. Next to the truck stood a figure she immediately recognized. It was Ian — Ian MacDonald, her ex-boyfriend, a man she hadn't set eyes on for over three years, since he had walked out after yet another bitter argument about her preoccupation, which he called an obsession, with the French resistance book.

Almost without thought, Peggy blurted out, "Where in the hell, did *he* come from? Why is he here?"

"I called him," Celine answered. "Someone had to do something, *ma petit chou*; you are going downhill, falling apart. Ian said he does not have a job now, and that he was happy to help. The phone, it is ringing all day with reporters and two who said they were agents. What kind of agent do you need? I had to take the phone off its hook, and my customers, they cannot call me. You need a helper, *non*?"

"N-o-o-o!" Peggy cried. She was furious with Celine for interfering. She struggled with a flood of emotion, and remembered a German word she had learned from Max — *Wirbelwind*, meaning whirlwind, but somehow stronger. That's how she felt, caught up in a *Wirbelwind* of conflicting emotions.

She was angry that Ian had left, that he hadn't been more supportive of her work. Simultaneously, she

278

realized how lonely she had become. Peggy was confused, hurt and frightened, unsure what to do next. She also knew that Celine was right. She had to pull herself together and complete Max's story before its novelty faded. Also, she was curious. Why didn't Ian have a job? Last she had heard, Ian was a well-established investigative reporter working for a major Boston daily. He had even been nominated for a Pulitzer — why wouldn't he have a job?

As she wrestled with all of these feelings, and grief at the loss of Max, she felt all of her counter-arguments collapse, even with her anxiety about having to interact with Ian again, and decided to go along with Celine. With that decision, she felt a great weight lifted from her, and felt that she wasn't quite so alone. Somebody might be willing to help. There was a way forward, she felt, and her mood began to brighten. Then she became conscious of her appearance. *"My God,"* she thought, *"I'm a mess!"*

"Tell him, to go away! I can't let him see me like this," she cried to Celine, looking down at her food-stained nightgown and noting her untended hair, bad breath and the sleep-lines on her face. She stuck her nose into the front of her nightgown and recoiled — she absolutely reeked after nearly a week without a bath.

"I'll tell him to come back in an hour," Celine answered. "Then I'll come up and help you put yourself together."

"Tell him to come back in *two* hours," Peggy begged. "I need a shower, I need to wash my hair!"

CHAPTER 32

At the beginning, the reunion between Peggy and Ian was tense and awkward. They sat in Peggy's tiny sitting room, sipping lukewarm coffee. Both were nervous, unsure of what to say. They exchanged pleasantries between long, uncomfortable pauses, until finally Peggy's strong independent streak asserted itself, and she couldn't wait any longer.

"Why are you here, anyway?" she asked abruptly. "I don't need to be rescued, if that's why you came. I'll be fine once I get this damned cast off. You must have better things to do, what with your Pulitzer nomination and all. I appreciate your effort and it was kind of you to come, but I should be OK in about a month because that's when this thing will finally come off." Peggy stopped talking, a bit surprised at herself for this outburst, but realising how much anxiety she had been dealing with.

Ian suddenly looked very sad. "It's not what you think," he said. "Writing a series exposing abuses in the Catholic Church got me a nomination for a Pulitzer, but it didn't make me any friends in Boston. The backlash against my paper was very powerful. About ten percent of our readers cancelled their subscriptions, and the series was cancelled before it was finished. My editor got canned and I was transferred to the features desk, writing puff pieces and articles about neighborhood festivals. After a month I couldn't take it any more, and I quit."

"Surely you could get another job."

"Not a good job, and don't call me Shirley," Ian said, smiling, dredging up one of their shared jokes from the old movie *Airplane!* Peggy could not help but smile as well. "I really don't want to leave the area," said Ian, "but I can't find anything like my old job, and everything else is s-o-o *boring*! I was happy when Celine called. She said you are working on a great story and that you might need some help. I've got some money saved up and if you could find something for me to do, it'd give me an excuse to hide out for a while until I figure out what we, uh, I mean I, am going to do."

Peggy hesitated, so Ian went on. "Peggy, it's not about work. I am not the same as the man who left you. I understand now what it's like to be totally immersed in a project and then be terribly disappointed. I have come to realize what is important, and believe me, it's not my job. Let's just say I've missed you, missed you a lot, more than I can say." Now it was Ian's turn to hesitate. "So, Peggy, what do you think?"

"Whoa, cowboy!" Peggy responded, blushing despite herself. "This is moving a little too fast for me. Give me some time. Let's figure out what you might want to do, and go on from there, OK?"

"Do you have anything in mind?"

"Well, I have a thought. I would like you to take the transcript of Max's recordings and my typed notes and read them. I have them in chronological order. Then you and I can sit down and decide how to proceed. Would that work for you?"

"Sounds like a good approach. I can probably read a lot tonight. I'm staying at a motel in Rockland, and there aren't many temptations in the raucous Rockland night life. Anything else?"

"Yes, I have a question. Why do you have a snowmobile in your truck? Have you become a nature lover?" Peggy knew Ian was an entirely urban sort of person who didn't care for the outdoors.

Now it was Ian's turn to blush. "Well, Celine said you needed a snowmobile to get to Max's cabin, and I thought it would help. I spent a whole four hours learning to use it, and it's actually fun!"

"You went out and bought a snowmobile just to help me?"

"No, I went out and *rented* a snowmobile, if that's what it's called, just to help you."

Peggy laughed and said, "Well, then, if the weather is OK, we'll go to Max's tomorrow, if that's all right with you."

"OK, boss."

Together they gathered up Peggy's files and Ian prepared to leave.

Just before Ian went out the door, Peggy called to him and he paused, turning towards her.

"I'm glad you came," she said.

CHAPTER 33

Early the next morning, Peggy contacted Ed Williams, the crusty lobsterman who had told her about finding the bodies on the beach. She reached him by telephone after a couple of tries, told him she was unable to drive and asked if he would be willing to stop by the bakery. She said she wanted to discuss an affidavit verifying how and when he had come into possession of the *Luftwaffe* cap.

Ed agreed to stop by, but only after eleven a.m., because he had an appointment at the vet for one of his dogs at nine-thirty. Peggy thanked him profusely, then called Ian at his motel and asked him to come over at noon, rather than nine. Ian gratefully agreed, telling her he was tired. He said he had been up late reading her material and could use some extra sleep.

Peggy was in the bakery working on Celine's accounts when Ed's battered pick-up pulled up in front. When Ed got out, Peggy noticed he was all spruced up. His hair was carefully combed, he was freshly shaven, and he was wearing a starched white shirt with a nice-looking jacket.

"*Bonjour, Celine,*" Williams said as he entered.

"*Ah, bonjour Etienne, comment ca va,*" Celine answered, wiping her flour-dusted hands on her apron.

283

She bustled about, getting Williams' coffee and a fresh-baked croissant while they chatted in the local *patois*.

After half an hour, Peggy was able to pry Williams loose and lead him upstairs to sit with her while she explained why she needed him to sign a statement about the circumstances of finding the bodies. She explained what she knew of Max's story, telling him the cap constituted solid proof of what had happened.

"I knew they was aviators," Williams answered, "and I saw what was in the paper, and I'm glad you didn't use my name. If I sign this paper, can you still be sure my name won't be published?"

"The purpose of the document is to convince a publisher that the story is true, not for release to newspapers. If the newspapers ask after the book is published, if it ever is, I can still say that the information is on background. By the way, the man who evaluated the cap's authenticity made a sizeable offer for it. You might want to sell it. I'll make you a copy of his letter and give it to you when I bring it back."

Peggy told him the amount of the offer. Williams whistled. "Wow," he said. "I'll have to think about that."

After a bit more conversation, Williams signed Peggy's document and went back down to have another croissant and talk to Celine some more, and Peggy got ready for a trip to Max's cabin.

On her way out to wait for Ian, she spoke briefly to Celine, who was humming around the bakery. "Etienne?" Peggy asked. "I thought his name was Ed."

"Ah, *oui*," Celine answered, "Ed's father, he was *Anglais*, his mama, she was French. She named him Etienne, but his papa, he called him Ed, and when he went into the navy, he just started using that name, because it was easier than spelling 'Etienne' all the time, and he just kept using Ed when he came back."

"I didn't know you knew him well," said Peggy.

"Oh, my, we were good friends. Me, Pete, Etienne and his wife Bessie were very close after the war. Bessie, she was in school with me. Etienne, he got very sad when Bessie died and he became, how do you call it, a loner?"

"Well, that's too bad, he must be lonely."

"*Oui*, he is lonely; but tonight, Etienne and I, we go to the bingo at St Joan's." With that, Celine hurried off to check one of the ovens, humming again, while Peggy stood dumbfounded at the front door.

When Ian arrived Peggy was outside, wearing ski pants, boots and a sweater. Her hair was tied up with a bright ribbon, and she had a hooded parka over her arm.

"Wow, you look like Miss Norway," said Ian, stepping down from the truck. "Very cute and woodsy, if I dare say so."

He was dressed in olive-drab fatigues, heavy boots and an army-style fur cap, so Peggy countered, "You look like an arctic GI Joe, military *and* woodsy," and they both laughed. Peggy got into the truck and they drove quickly over snowy roads to the point where Max's rugged trail intersected the hard-surfaced road.

Ian pulled off the road at a flat spot, parked the truck and lowered the tailgate.

He rolled the snowmobile down a ramp from the truck bed, fiddled with it for a bit, then got it started, and they were off in a cloud of ice crystals and light-blue exhaust.

The woods were beautiful under a glistening blanket of snow. Peggy felt exhilarated, almost joyful at experiencing the outdoors after being cooped up in her depression, being whisked through the magnificent Maine woods. *"Fresh air and sunshine are great mood elevators,"* she thought.

Various critters, startled by the sudden arrival of the noisy machine, rushed across the poorly-defined path. They saw a fox and a coyote, and once Ian, the city boy, had to pause in awe as a doe squared off in the middle of the trail while her two fawns leapt gracefully across behind her. "Tough little lady," Ian whispered to Peggy when the deer were gone.

Ian was handling the snowmobile very well, but the ride was still bumpy, so Peggy had to put her arms around Ian to keep from falling off. This was a bit difficult with the cast on her arm, so she had to hold him tight. As she snuggled up to Ian, his scent washed over her, a smell compounded of after-shave, shampoo, nice-smelling soap and his own particular male aura. That, and the hard, flat tummy under his jacket brought back lots of memories, and she had to shake her head to clear it in order to focus on reviewing her to-do list once they got to the cabin.

After another fifteen minutes, they pulled up in front of Max's small home. Peggy unlocked the front door and they went inside. The interior was dark and very cold, the outside shutters were closed and the furnace was not operating.

Peggy flicked a switch, and to her surprise an overhead light came on. "Well, that's a relief," she said.

Ian busied himself with the propane heater in the living room, trying to get it going, and Peggy went to the bedroom, a space she had never seen. The bedroom had no overhead light, just a small lamp on a table, which Peggy turned on. The room was small, dominated by a king-sized bed, the floor covered with an enormous ferocious-looking bearskin rug. In the corner was a small potbellied stove, with a neatly-stacked pile of firewood, kindling and newspaper next to it. Peggy got busy making a fire in the stove, smiling as she heard Ian grumbling and banging about with the gas furnace.

Peggy was shivering, her teeth chattering. She spotted a thick quilt draped over a chair and pulled a pillow from the bed. Peggy thought about getting under the covers, but was put off by the idea that Max might have died there, so she lay down on the rug close to the woodstove and pulled the quilt over herself, intending to remain there only until the cabin warmed up.

Peggy was shaking and could see her breath. As the fire in the stove began to build, she buried her cold fingers in the thick fur near the bear's taxidermized head. To her surprise, two of her fingers went through the rug and touched the chilly wood floor. She looked

287

closely and realized her fingers had passed through two small holes in the fur.

Just as she understood what that probably meant, Ian entered the bedroom, wiping his hands, and announced that the furnace was working, and that the place would be warmed up in a few minutes.

"Ian," Peggy asked abruptly, "did you read the part of the story about Pete, Max and the bear?"

"I sure did. One of the best parts, I thought. Why do you ask?"

Peggy reached under the edge of the rug, stuck her fingers through the holes and wiggled them so Ian could see.

Ian was puzzled, then his eyes got very large. "I'm guessing that's not from moths, right? Is that...?"

"It's *the* bear! Those have to be bullet holes from Max's pistol! Oh my God, how just like Pete. He must have recovered the bear, had it preserved, and given it to Max as a trophy."

Ian was laughing, but Peggy could see he was trembling from the cold. "You might want to get under this quilt, just until the room warms up. The fur is soft and cosy."

"Oh, thanks," said Ian, and he started to lie down next to Peggy. She went to throw part of the quilt over him just as he sat up a bit to turn over, and her cast accidentally conked him hard on the forehead.

Ian dropped back to the rug without a sound, his eyes closed. "Oh, Ian, are you all right?" Peggy cried. She leaned close to see if he was breathing, perhaps bleeding. Ian moaned, feigning unconsciousness, but she could see his eyelids fluttering, then he was laughing. "You devil!" she shrieked. "I thought I had really injured you!" She punched him lightly in the chest.

"I'm OK, but you pack a mean wallop with that cast." He noticed she had not moved away, that her face was still just above his, her breathing a bit faster than normal, her minty breath brushing his cheek. "But, it did hurt a little. Maybe you could... kiss it and make it better?"

When Peggy still didn't move away, he put his hand on the back of her neck and gently pulled her to him until their lips met. Both of them were trembling now, maybe not entirely from the cold, and they kissed for a long time.

Within half an hour, they were both warm, quite warm, in fact, which was remarkable given that by then neither one of them was wearing even a stitch of clothing and the heavy quilt had been thrown aside.

CHAPTER 34

Afterwards, they slept a bit, and when they woke, the cabin was warmer. Peggy stoked the little woodstove and Ian went outside to open one of the shutters on the kitchen window to let in some light. That took a while because the men who had come to remove Max's body had nailed all of them shut, a standard precaution against intrusion by bears. When he returned to the warm cabin, stamping his feet and brushing snow from his boots, Peggy was sitting in Max's tiny kitchen, sorting through a stack of audio tapes.

She had made coffee, so Ian poured himself a cup and sat across from her, his knees touching hers. "What's up?" Ian asked.

"I found one tape near the recorder I gave Max, and there is another one in the machine that looks complete. There are eight tapes, but there are dates written on only those two. I tried to play the one in the recorder, but its batteries are dead. We'll have to take them all back and run through them at my place."

"Well, we had better get going. I'm not confident enough to operate the snowmobile in the dark. It's getting late and it also looks like it might snow, so we need to get on the way."

Peggy glanced out the window. "Gosh," she said, "I guess time got away from me. I didn't realize we were, well, asleep for so long."

Ian smiled warmly and touched Peggy's hand. "Best sleep I've had in three years."

Peggy leaned across the table and kissed him lightly. "Let me grab the tapes and some papers I found in the closet, and we'll get going. Could we come back tomorrow and look around more carefully?"

"Sure," Ian said.

Ian went out, secured the kitchen window and fired up the snowmobile. Soon they were on the trail, and arrived back at the bakery just before full darkness. Ed Williams' pick-up was parked in front of the building and Peggy remembered that Ed and Celine were 'going to the bingo' that evening. Peggy and Ian met Ed and Celine on their way out. "Isn't it early for bingo?" she asked Celine.

"Ah, *oui*," Celine responded. "We are going first for supper. I'll be back about eleven; see you then." Ed shook hands with Ian, and Celine kissed Peggy and Ian on the cheek as she and Ed left. Peggy noticed Celine was wearing perfume, something she almost never did.

Peggy asked Ian to come in, made them both substantial sandwiches with fresh-baked bread, and they settled in Peggy's sitting room. Peggy provided Ian with a review of where the last tape she played had ended.

"Max has just been told about his mother and grandmother, brought up to date about Rachel, and, finally, shown a photo of two of his aircrew washed up on the beach. Remember?" Ian nodded, so she loaded the first of the new tapes into the tape machine and started the playback. The label showed that the tape was made almost immediately after the last one Peggy had heard.

Max's voice on the playback was almost a whisper, and Peggy turned up the volume.

"I think that was one of the worst shocks I had during the war, seeing the bodies of those two young men. I hesitated briefly, and the general suggested a break, but I wanted to get the meeting over with so I could get back to my room and deal with my sorrow privately.

"I asked if we could continue. I confirmed the two bodies were members of our crew and gave the naval officer their names. The naval officer turned and nodded to one of the men in civilian clothes against the back wall, who was taking notes. I later learned he was an FBI agent who had been doubtful about my information until I gave those names.

"The general asked if I was satisfied with the arrangements that had been made for Rachel, my mother and grandmother, and the family estate. I answered that I was, but asked for updates when available. I wondered aloud about the fate of the people who had been sheltered there, and one of the men assured me that local anti-Nazi groups were looking out for them.

"So, we got down to business. I had written down the compass heading the plane was following just before

I 'fell', and told the group what I had seen during my descent. I mentioned that the photographer had pointed out the Owl's Head lighthouse just before I left the aircraft.

"I told them that the tree where I landed and buried the remaining films, logs and charts could probably be spotted from the air if there was not too much snow in the area, because my parachute was snagged near the top of that tall evergreen. By this stage of the war, our aviator parachutes were light yellow in color due to a preservative applied to the cloth, so the 'chute should stand out. The naval officer immediately left the room at a nod from the general, presumably to get a search started.

"Maps were brought in, and the Air Corps officer, who turned out to be a navigator, went over the entire flight from beginning to end, asking very intelligent and probing questions regarding timing, headings, altitude and so forth. Then he left the room after assuring the general that he would have a comprehensive report on his desk the next day.

"Then it was the turn of the two civilians, who asked me lots of questions about the device that was to be dropped. I couldn't help them much except tell them about the big lead box I had seen and what the technicians had said. I also said it was considered a very high-level secret and repeated what Krause had told us about the device laying waste to the Willow Run area for a long time.

"By this time, I was getting very tired and hungry, and apparently so were the others, because the general adjourned the meeting, telling everyone they would be notified for another meeting in a week or so. I was escorted back to the safe house for lunch, then to my quarters, where I flopped on the bed, overcome with sadness and guilt.

"I felt the death of those men was my fault, that I should have done something to prevent Krause from performing the landing. I felt as low as I ever have; at least that is what I thought.

"A few days later, in mid-October 1944, my grief and guilt got much, much worse.

"It started routinely enough. All of us PoWs were assembled in a large hallway, with a movie screen at the front. We had seen this set-up before because our captors occasionally showed us newsreels documenting Allied successes and, of course, German defeats. These newsreels were always followed by 'indoctrination' films meant to convince us that Nazism was an evil doctrine and that democracy was a much superior form of government.

"Well, Peggy, I didn't need any convincing about Nazism and had already concluded that the war was lost, but I enjoyed these interludes as a relief from the constant boredom of captivity.

"Also, it was an opportunity to mingle with the other prisoners, which I was finally permitted to do since the last meeting with the general. I enjoyed the little tasks I was given about the place as well — simple cleaning, helping with meals, and so forth.

"So, while some of the officers groused about being forced to watch 'propaganda' and muttered about everything being faked, I was prepared to enjoy the next hour or so. An American officer entered the room, and we were called to attention, which was unusual. While we were still standing, the officer read us a prepared statement in excellent academic German which informed us that no one was to leave the room during the presentation of the film.

"He told us the film had been obtained by journalists accompanying the Red Army in the area of Lublin, Poland, in July of that year. Nobody was allowed to speak during the film or disrupt the showing in any way. Any outbursts would be handled by Military Police, he said, indicating five burly, white-helmeted, armed men at the back of the room. We were told to sit, the lights were turned off, and the film began.

"The forty-minute movie was in scratchy black and white and the camera jumped about. It was narrated in Polish-accented German with English subtitles. The images on the screen were horrendous, showing skeletal scarecrows barely recognisable as human beings, piles of unburied bodies, shots of cremation furnaces four in a row.

"The narrator said that this was a camp constructed for the imprisonment and murder first of Red Army PoWs, then Polish Jews and others the Nazis deemed 'undesirable'. The voice went on to say the place was called Madjdanek.

"According to the film, an estimated seventy-eight thousand people had perished there, from starvation, overwork, or, to my utter astonishment, being deliberately, systematically, on an industrial scale, killed in gas chambers disguised as showers. The film showed guards of the camp, some of whom were women, wearing SS uniforms.

"I had heard, from my grandmother, from Rion the Paris gendarme and even young Alfons Dietrich, my co-pilot from the Spanish war, that Jews were being arrested, and that social activists, Communists and other dissenters or 'undesirables', gypsies and Christian fundamentalists were being rounded up and detained, even that some had been shot. But I had learned nothing like this, nothing like the assembly-line slaughter of thousands of people. I knew nothing of the disposal of thousands of bodies in crematoria to disguise the Nazis' crimes.

"Many men tried to look away, or stare at the floor, but one of the MPs, a middle-aged sergeant, would shout, "Look at the screen, damn you. Look at what you Nazi bastards have done!" and prod the offender. A young MP grew ill and had to be assisted out the door. A few Germans were sniffling and wiping their eyes, others looked pale and grim.

"At one point a German officer, an SS man, leapt to his feet, shouting, 'All of this is false; this is entirely Soviet propaganda — do not believe a word of it. Heil

Hitler!' He was quickly subdued by the MPs and taken out of the room. Later, through the grapevine, we learned he had been transferred to what the Americans called a 'diehard Nazi' camp in Arizona.

"Other officers rejected what we had been shown, claiming it was simply meant to attack our morale. Some men, though, became quiet and thoughtful after seeing the film.

"As for me, Peggy, I was appalled. I felt doubly guilty. On top of my overwhelming guilt and sorrow for the death of my crewmen and my anxiety about my family and Rachel, there was this incredible burden of responsibility for the slaughter of helpless people.

"I had served a regime that murdered innocent people, even women and children, and burned their bodies to cover up the crime. How could I go on? What would the victors do to Germany when the war was over?

"Basically, Peggy, I collapsed. I only wanted to sleep. I was unwilling to get up, perform any of my small duties, or even eat. Finally, the commandant of our detention centre showed up, yelled at me for a while and finally asked what he could do to help me.

"I need to see a priest, a Roman Catholic priest," I answered.

"The commandant said something like, 'Von Waldberg, you are entitled to access to clergy by our regulations and the Geneva Convention. I will arrange for a priest to counsel you, but it may take a while to find the appropriate person. I would like you to return to your household routine with my assurance that I will find the person you need' — or words to that effect.

"I asked why I couldn't just visit the local Boston priest who celebrated Mass for us on Sundays. I knew other men had seen him for confession. The commandant explained that because of the sensitive information I possessed, any priest who I confided in needed to have a special security clearance, and to be briefed on my situation. That would take some time, he said.

"I realized he was correct and agreed to his proposal, hoping he could find the right man soon. I also found that returning to routine household tasks lulled my anxiety, keeping my mind occupied and leaving less time to brood and worry.

"Eight days after my conversation with the commandant, the general convened another meeting and I was again given a clean khaki uniform and transported to the large meeting room. The cast of characters seemed the same as before, except for the two men who had asked me about the device meant to be dropped over Detroit. They were not present, and as far as I could tell had not been replaced.

"The general began the meeting by informing me that my parachute had been spotted and a team from the nearby naval air station had recovered the material I buried. The young lieutenant placed the log books, film canisters and charts in front of me, and I was asked to identify them, which I did.

"The general then nodded to the uniformed airman, who spent a few minutes confirming our route on a map, then asked me where the base we had flown from was located. I told him what I could, because I had only seen it from the air a couple of times, but that I knew it was close to Bergen, and gave him the approximate distance and direction to the base.

"Then he asked me about security arrangements at the airfield. I told him that although the area where we lived and worked was heavily guarded, the airfield itself was secured by a few German infantry troops, *Luftwaffe* personnel, and a number of Norwegian auxiliaries loyal to Vidkun Quisling, the Nazi-supported leader of Norway.

"Taking out a map of the Bergen area, he asked if I could locate the secret area where the planning took place. I tried to do so, and the American seemed satisfied.

"The fellow with the British accent was next. He told me my family's situation was unchanged and that Itter Castle, where they were being held with other prominent prisoners, was being closely watched by local anti-Nazis.

"The American lieutenant colonel then informed me that his people were in regular contact with the gendarme Rion, who had been decorated for his service with the resistance and promoted to a very high position in the French police.

"The man then told me that Rachel Liebeskind had still not recovered, but that the doctors were optimistic about her prognosis. He seemed evasive, unable to look me in the eye. I did not like that and began to worry even more about Rachel, on top of all the other things I was worried about.

"I asked about their progress in finding a suitable priest, and the general rather gruffly informed me that they were working on it.

"After that, the British fellow and the general began a whispered conversation with a third man in civilian clothes. The lieutenant colonel nudged the general and indicated me with a glance, whereupon the general ordered the young lieutenant to summon my guards, and I was driven back to my quarters.

"I went about my routine for the next few days and eventually was summoned to the commandant's office and introduced to a priest, Father Nicholas Weber, who shook my hand and immediately asked the commandant where we could meet privately for a few hours.

"The commandant reminded him of the sensitive nature of my information and the priest assured him briskly that he had been briefed and fully cleared, whereupon we were directed to the little room where I had been interviewed on my arrival.

"As we walked along behind a guard, I sized the man up. He wore the uniform of an American army chaplain, with a number of ribbons, of which I recognized only one, the Purple Heart, or US wound badge. He appeared to be older than me, about fifty.

"He was tall, about six feet, trim and well-built, with short-cut white hair. A large scar ran from his left ear onto his neck, disappearing beneath his shirt collar. The scar was well-healed, but still livid against his pale skin. As we went along he told me that he spoke German — in case I wished to use that language — that he had been born in New York of German parents and had been serving in Europe as a chaplain and interpreter for *Wehrmacht* PoWs. He told me he had been wounded in France and sent back to the United States to recover.

"I liked him at once, and was grateful to the American authorities for locating such a man to help me sort through my concerns. We settled in to the little room and Father Weber donned his priest's stole, gave me a blessing, then turned slightly to one side, shielding his face with one hand, and asked me if I wished to confess.

"For the next hour and a half, I poured out my heart to this man. I told him of my history and unburdened myself about my guilt over the deaths of my crewmen, anxiety about my family and Rachel, fear of what would happen to Germany and Austria when we lost the war, given the atrocities we had committed. I told him that I had not paid enough attention to all of the clues I had received about what was going on in the East, that I might have done something if I had looked into it more closely.

"I expressed concern for my own future if I was returned home after the war and it was discovered I had been a traitor. I kept coming back to Rachel, that I felt I didn't really know what was going on with her, and asked him to pray for her. After that, I sort of ran out of words, exhausted, feeling helpless and empty.

"I had been speaking with my head down, since it was tradition that during confession one did not directly address one's confessor, hence his raised hand between us and my averted gaze. When I looked up after I stopped talking, I found Weber staring at me, his head slightly tilted, as if in thought.

"'What?' I asked. He shifted in his chair and then told me that he had heard hundreds of men from our forces confess, first in England, then men recently captured in France, but had never heard such introspection or contrition.

"He continued that captured SS personnel in Paris, who were certainly responsible for shipments of women and children to the East under deplorable conditions, none of them had acknowledged remorse. *'Befehl ist befehl'* — orders are orders — they chanted, all of them, like some sort of Nazi mantra. 'Yet here you sit, Max,' he said, 'peripherally involved — if involved at all — feeling terribly responsible, feeling guilty, beating yourself up.' He said he was touched and impressed. I could only hang my head in shame.

"Weber placed his hand on my head, granted me absolution, prayed with me and told me to take heart. He said that the death of my crewmen may have been the price for the saving of thousands of lives at Detroit.

"He continued, and I remember what he said, 'For all you know, Max, those two slipped up trying to get out of the plane and drowned, and the rest of the crew are merrily bubbling their way back to the Fatherland.' Of course I knew those things, but hearing someone else say it helped. He also said that from what I had told him of Krause, I would probably have had to kill him to take control of the aircraft, and then I would have had a murder on my conscience.

"Weber asked me if I had confidence in what I had been told about my family. I answered that since their security seemed to be in the competent hands of Tomas Klaibisch and his group, I was confident that everything possible was being done. Then he asked how he might obtain information about Rachel, and I gave him Rion's name and his situation, but I wondered aloud how he would be able to find out more than the US Army.

"Weber laughed. 'Are you joking, Von Waldberg? I am a member of the Society of Jesus, a Jesuit, a soldier of the church. I am part of an enormous worldwide organisation, an organisation much more efficient than any army. When it comes to information-gathering, the US government doesn't stand a chance compared to us.' I had to laugh, despite my concerns, as we shook hands in farewell. Then, to my astonishment, he folded me into a huge muscular hug and whispered in my ear, 'Have faith, Max, and pray for me. I may be able to help.'"

CHAPTER 35

"The days passed uneventfully after my meeting with Weber. I felt better, my mood lightened by the experience of sharing my worries and fears and the routine of rotation through household assignments. The PoWs had started some classes in mathematics and engineering, taught by prisoner specialists.

"I was asked to help teach English, using textbooks and study guides provided each month by the American Red Cross. That experience not only helped me pass the time, but also improved my own language skills.

"It was early December before I saw Father Weber again. I was called to the small conference room, where he was waiting. We greeted each other warmly, and sat down across from one another.

"Weber started a prayer in a loud voice, then handed me a small folded piece of paper. He held a finger to his lips and pointed to a telephone on a small shelf in a corner of the room, which I had never noticed. He then cupped his hand over his ear, indicating that the phone was a listening device.

"I nodded. Then Weber scooted his chair back, as if preparing to kneel, and his chair leg squashed a little grey box attached to the wall near the floor. That box was connected to the telephone, and there was a short electrical hum and a puff of smoke from the thing after Weber's chair smashed its cover. 'What a terrible accident,' said Weber. 'I think I may have damaged something,' he continued, with a wink. 'If for any reason we are not allowed to meet again, follow the instruction on that card.' I nodded again, indicating I understood.

"Weber motioned for me to kneel, and I knelt next to him, our heads inches apart. He spoke very quickly. 'We only have a few minutes before they figure out what happened and come to fix it. First, Norwegian commandos got onto the airbase near Bergen and destroyed the remaining JU 390 and a number of other aircraft. The Quisling guards weren't very motivated, it seems, so there was little resistance at first.

"The commandos also stole that big lead box and whatever was in it. The thing was sitting there on a heavy truck, so they fought off the small group of Germans guarding it, drove the truck away and dumped it into a deep fjord, so that problem is taken care of.

"'Second,' he said, 'Rachel Liebeskind is quite ill, and not doing well in that French hospital. The French hospitals in Paris are overloaded with returning refugees, people coming back from forced labor in Germany and survivors of deportation. Many of those returnees are desperately sick, having been malnourished and abused. The hospitals are short of staff and supplies, so we have arranged to have Rachel transferred elsewhere, under a different identity, to a place where she can get better care.

"'Third, this whole building is bugged; there are microphones everywhere. Now put that card I gave you into your shoe, and assume an attitude of prayer with me. I hear someone coming.' I put my head down, murmuring the Lord's Prayer, and within seconds, the commandant and an MP burst into the room without knocking.

"I was reeling from the news about Rachel, dying to ask Weber a thousand questions, but the commandant stated brusquely that our session was ended, that the building was being put under lockdown due to a security breach. The commandant escorted us into the hallway, where another guard met me and took me to my room. Weber was asked to go to the commandant's office with him. As I climbed the stairs, I saw a man carrying a toolbox going into the little conference room.

"When I got back to my room, I quickly retrieved the folded paper from my shoe and stashed it in my special hiding place under a loose floorboard. I had slowly been building up a small collection of useful items, like some American currency and a couple of small tools, with a vague plan of escape if the authorities decided to send me back to Austria after the war was over.

"Shortly thereafter, a two-man team of guards arrived and thoroughly searched my room. They said it was part of a general shakedown of the entire facility, but I was convinced they suspected something going on between Weber and me. The guards confiscated my magazines and went through all of my books and what few belongings I possessed, but found nothing incriminating.

"Late that night, when everything had quietened down after the general search and a time-consuming roll call, I stealthily went over my tiny room inch by inch, checking everything in the moonlight as much by feel as by vision. The room where I lived had been a servant's quarters and was high up in the building's garret, very small, with sloping interior walls.

There was just enough room for my cot and a tiny cupboard, so it didn't take too long to search the whole space. I knew any listening device would require a source of power, so I examined the single overhead light fixture and old-fashioned electric outlet very carefully, and finally found what I was looking for.

"There it was! There were four tiny, carefully-drilled holes in the wall just above the electric outlet. I could feel the seam where plaster had been removed and then replaced. I moved carefully, wearing thick socks to muffle my movements, and recovered Weber's note from its hiding place. I huddled next to my small dormer window and read what Weber had given me by the rays of the moon.

"Peggy, that little piece of paper, when unfolded, proved to be a devotional card, the sort of thing that is displayed in racks at the back of Catholic churches. There was a picture of a saint on one side, and the other side was headed: 'Instructions for Lenten Worship'. Below that was a list of recommended practices. '1. Attend Mass whenever possible. 2. Take the Eucharist and pray for those in need. 3. Make sacrifices during the Lenten period. 4. Remember always the poor souls in Purgatory.' The card was signed in ink with a cross. The message seemed odd, but I noticed the first item — 'Attend Mass whenever possible' — was heavily underlined, also in ink. Clearly, Weber wanted me to start attending our PoW services.

"I started moving noisily about the room, grumbling in German to myself about an upset stomach, complaining about the baked beans we had been served for supper. I stalked off to the bathroom, where I remained for twenty minutes, groaning softly and flushing the torn-up card piece by piece down the toilet. I knew that if the guards found the card, they would know it was from Weber, and I didn't want him implicated in getting me a message. Then I went back to my cot, where I faked snoring for the benefit of the hidden microphone, while my mind raced.

"I was relieved that the dreadful radiation mission had been thwarted, and in a frenzy to learn more about Rachel. Where would she be sent? What was her new identity and how had she acquired it? How would I ever find her again if I didn't know her new name? I was still worried about my family, but incredibly grateful that it seemed I had gained a very powerful ally — 'Holy Mother, the Roman Catholic Church', as we called it back then."

Max started coughing. Then the recorder clicked, indicating a pause. When the voice came back, Max's speech was slurred, which, in addition to the low volume, made it even harder to understand what he was saying. Ian stopped the tape, went out to his truck and brought back a pair of headphones for Peggy. He kissed her, told her he would see her in the morning, and left for his hotel, saying he was tired from the unaccustomed fresh air and exercise.

Peggy was so preoccupied with Max's narrative, she started the playback again before Ian was out the door. There was a time when that would have irritated him, Peggy recalled, when he felt he should be the centre of attention in their relationship. Now, having more experience, he seemed content to support Peggy in telling this terrific story, and she was very grateful.

She hoped he would be warm on the drive back to his lonely rented bed. Tomorrow is another day, and another night, she mused.

CHAPTER 36

"I am Catholic, like many Austrians," Max said, as the tape began again. "I am what is called a 'cradle Catholic'; that is, I was born into the religion. I was educated in a Catholic school through what you call high school, attended church services regularly when I was young, and in all respects conformed to conventional Catholic norms and traditions. I was an altar boy for five years.

"However, after I became a pilot, I found that many of my old habits of worship fell away. I was too busy, I told myself. Sunday was really my only day to rest, I thought, and the effort of getting up, cleaned up and dressed was too much. In truth, though, part of the problem was that I didn't want to go to confession, and I also didn't want to take the sacrament while in what the priests called 'a state of sin'.

"I had been seeing more than a few women, especially when I was working for the Austrian airlines. I didn't want to confess what the women and I were doing, because to receive absolution I would have had to stop, to abstain, and I didn't want to do that.

"Of course, that put me in a tight corner. One couldn't attend Mass indefinitely without taking the sacrament, because the priest would notice and ask if you had some reason for not fully participating. On the other hand, I was taught that to deliberately receive the Eucharist in a state of sin was a sacrilege. Better to commit a sin by staying away from Mass than to risk the mortal sin of sacrilege, I thought. Meanwhile, I thought of the prayer of St Augustine — 'make me pure, Lord, but not yet.'

"Then, when my military flying started in Spain, I still didn't go to church regularly. I don't speak Spanish, so I couldn't understand the sermons, and I lost interest.

"In France, I started attending again during the Battle of Britain, but then got so busy and fatigued, I stopped again. There was no opportunity for Catholic services in Russia, so I became what is referred to as a lapsed Catholic.

"Now that I had confessed everything to Father Weber, I was happy to start attending Mass again, especially as Weber had recommended it. I found the practice comforting, and my steady presence was noted by our visiting priest, a semi-retired Boston monsignor named O'Brian, who asked one day if I had been an altar boy. I think he noticed me following the Latin of the Mass.

"Thereafter, I became his regular acolyte, and after a month he got me assigned as his assistant. He told me one morning that Father Weber had been reassigned, sent to a PoW facility at Fort Sheridan, Illinois. I was disappointed, but confident Weber would contact me somehow if something important happened.

"So, for the next three months, I busied myself maintaining the room designated as a chapel, rounding up prayer books, vestments, hymnals and other liturgical paraphernalia and making sure the organ was working. The room was also used by a Lutheran minister for Protestant services, and I helped him as well. All that and my English teaching job kept me quite busy.

"During that winter a new group of PoWs arrived, six of them. They told everyone they had been part of a huge counterattack that Hitler launched in Belgium. They were armor or communications specialists, and I got to know one of them, a Catholic teleprinter and code expert, very well. He told me Hitler had launched a 'do or die' assault, hoping to split the Allied armies and take the port of Antwerp.

"The man said that at first the attack had gone well because the area of the assault was thinly manned, either by inexperienced or worn-out troops. Also, he said that at first the weather was cloudy and foggy, which limited Allied air activity.

"Then the sun came out, the Allied aircraft pounced, and German vehicles that weren't blown up by aircraft began to run out of fuel. After that, he said, the thing turned into a disaster, a retreat, an utter defeat that cost Germany the last of her reserves of equipment and manpower. He was grateful to have escaped with his life and spent a lot of time in the chapel offering prayers of thanksgiving.

"If I had held any doubts that Germany would lose the war, that story absolutely dispelled them. All I had to do now was figure out what to do if they tried to send me back to Europe at the end, and as the months flew by I plotted, schemed and made my plans. I did *not* want to go back to the *Reich*, if I could help it.

"As the spring of 1945 arrived, I had my final contact with the people to whom I had given information about my flight. I was summoned to the commandant's office to meet with the American lieutenant colonel who had been at the earlier sessions. He was accompanied by the fellow in civilian clothes with the British accent.

"The uniformed American began, saying, 'The threat you brought to our attention has been eliminated, and we thank you for your help. As to Ms Liebeskind, I have some unfortunate news.' My heart sank and he said, 'No, no, Von Waldberg, she is not dead, as far as we know, but we cannot find her. She was checked in to a French hospital in August and never checked out, but she is simply not there. We are looking into it urgently, and we will keep you informed.'

"He then asked the man in civvies to continue. 'The group guarding your mother, grandmother and the French notables is beginning to suffer desertions. Some of them have sought shelter with local civilians. Their morale is cracking as American armoured forces approach. Klaibisch's people are standing by and will step in immediately at the first opportunity.' I thanked him.

"The American took over, saying, 'The last bit of news should make you happy. We are going to send you back to Europe very soon.'

"The American saw the look on my face and said, 'We have done a great deal for you, Von Waldberg, and while we are grateful for your information, Germany and Austria need men like you to rebuild. You have impeccable anti-Nazi credentials and you should do well at home after the war has ended.' I thought, *'Oh, yes, I'll be fine if the diehards don't kill me.'* I was then dismissed, to wait on pins and needles, as you Americans say, to find out what was next.

"Then, on 15 April 1945, the blow fell. It was clear from the newsreels we were shown that the European war was nearly over. The Red Army had unleashed a huge offensive on Berlin, and discovered another hideous extermination camp at Bergen-Belsen. Clearly, Germany had lost the war and retribution would be awful.

"I was informed that I was to be sent to nearby Fort Devens to await transport to Bremerhaven. My departure was scheduled for 8 May. I had to report to our small clinic for a number of injections, which made me ill for a day or so, but I had recovered enough to assist at Mass on Sunday, 22 April.

"As the men filed out after the service, Father O'Brian offered me a blessing for a safe voyage, and asked me to kneel. After the short Latin ritual, O'Brian leaned over, put his hand on my head and said, 'Father Weber sends his greetings. He is praying for your safety and told me to tell you that Pete and Celine have an illegitimate child at Owl's Head.' I must have looked confused, uncomprehending, because O'Brian then said something like, 'Wait, wait— um—Weber said— ah, Pete and Celine have a *love child* at Owl's Head. Yes, that's it, that's what he said.' I stammered out my thanks, shook his hand and fled to my room to try to figure out what that meant.

"I sat on my bed and pondered what O'Brian had told me. How could Pete and Celine have a 'love child'? They had been married for many years and had been unable to have any children, according to Pete.

"Then it hit me like a thunderbolt. *Ach, mein Gott!* Weber speaks German! 'Love child' in German is *Liebeskind*! I knew then I had to get to Owl's Head. I had to escape!"

At that point, the tape, having reached its thirty-minute, approximately six-thousand-word limit, ended.

CHAPTER 37

Peggy cursed, and fumbled for the final tape, which was still in the recorder she had given Max. When she tried to rewind it, nothing happened, even though she had changed the device's worn-out batteries. Then she tried to remove the tape from that machine so she could rewind and listen to it on her other, newer, recorder.

The "eject" button on the older machine did nothing, neither did the "record" or the "play" button. Peggy thought about simply forcing open the cover and taking the tape out. She had done that once when she worked in Boston, using a letter opener, and had ended up with a totally useless nest of thin brown tape, which nobody could restore.

She examined the machine, and noticed a large dent and cracked plastic at one end. It seemed the thing had been dropped or stepped on.

"Better not try to get that tape out by myself," she thought. *"This looks like it might be the last tape Max made, and I certainly don't want to destroy it. I'll ask Ian in the morning; maybe he knows a trick or two."*

Meanwhile, she needed to talk to Celine. Celine should know what the message about "love child" was all about. But Celine was at the church with Ed, and Peggy was tired, too tired to stay up and wait for her, because "the bingo" usually went on until eleven or later. Peggy went to bed, thinking she might puzzle out what Max had meant while she waited for sleep; but then other, more pleasant thoughts, mostly involving Ian, intruded and she drifted off within minutes.

The next morning, Peggy woke early and instantly remembered she needed to ask Celine about what Max had said. She threw on some clothes and went down to the bakery, where Celine was bustling about her usual morning routine, getting ready for the day's baking. Uncharacteristically, she was humming a popular tune.

Peggy made her stop and sit down, got them both coffee, then told her what the priest had said to Max, and about Max's strong reaction to the message. "What did the priest mean?" Peggy asked Celine.

When Celine didn't immediately respond, Peggy told Celine what she knew about Max's brief but passionate affair with a Jewish woman named Rachel Liebeskind in Paris, and asked how that was related to Celine and Pete at Owl's Head, as the priest had told Max.

Celine looked away, then stood. "I do not know everything, but the time, it has come for you to meet the man who does. I will call him at nine o'clock and ask him to come, but until then, *mon cher*, I am afraid you must wait."

Peggy flushed. She had seldom been angry with her mother, but now she was truly upset. "How long must I wait, mama? I have been working on this at full speed for months, and now you say I must wait? How long, please, mama, how long?"

"You have always been impatient, *ma petite*, but I think it will be no more than a week or ten days until the man, he comes, who knows everything. He will have to come from Europe. I do not wish you to hear only part of the story, and what I know I may not have correctly remembered, so please, please, be patient, Peggy."

"Ten days, ten *DAYS*?" Peggy cried, and was about to object more strenuously when there was a knock at the door. Peggy looked out the front window of the shop and saw an idling telephone company truck. A uniformed man stood on the porch steps, carrying tools and a pink princess telephone.

"Ah, he is early," said Celine. "The phone man, he is coming to put in the second phone."

"A second phone?" asked Peggy. "Why do you need a second phone?"

"I do not need such a phone, but you do," answered Celine. "He will also make a message, so that when someone calls for the bakery, they press the number 'one'; and when someone calls for Peggy Pederson, the famous news reporter, they press the number 'two'. That way I can run my business, and you can run yours, *non*?"

Celine showed the telephone installer where the phone lines were and went on with her work while the man got busy drilling and hammering. Then Celine's two helpers arrived, forestalling further discussion.

Peggy went back upstairs, furious and frustrated. She was barely able to control the urge to rip the lid off the recorder and yank the tape out.

By the time Ian arrived, she was steaming mad, not sure whether to cry or scream. She showed Ian the damaged recorder and asked him to take it to Rockland and see if he could get it fixed, or at least get the tape out in useable shape. She snapped at Ian when he reminded her that their plan had been to go out to Max's cabin. It was another beautiful day, he said, a great day for a ride.

"This is important! I am completely stymied without that tape! If it can't be recovered, I'm going to have to sit here for a week or ten days with no progress, waiting for a person to come and tell me what happened. I've got to wait here until the man puts in a phone up here, or I'd go with you, so please just do as I ask."

Ian did as she requested, but Peggy could see he was hurt. She felt a stab of regret at having treated Ian so roughly and was tempted to call to him, but then her determination to finish the task at hand overwhelmed her as always, so she let it pass.

The phone man came in and spent an hour or so installing an ordinary desk phone after Peggy told him she didn't want the pink one Celine had ordered. He tested the new phone and left, and it almost immediately rang. Thinking it was another test, Peggy was surprised to hear Ian's voice when she answered.

Ian told her the recorder couldn't be worked on in the small appliance shop in Rockland. It had to be sent to Boston or Portland. Repair or recovery might take as long as three days, according to the man at the Rockland shop, because the larger facilities always had a backlog of work.

"My God," said Peggy. "What else can go wrong? Can you please take the thing to Boston and bring the tape back as soon as they can get it?" Then Peggy had a thought. "Maybe you could look into where Max was held and how he got away from the FBI while you are waiting?"

"Oh, Peggy," Ian answered. "We just got back together, and now you want me to go back to Boston?"

"Please, Ian, please, otherwise I'm just *stuck*. I'd do it, but I can't drive, the train is too slow and I can't afford to fly or hire a driver. Please, Ian." There was a silence on the line for a bit.

"Well, OK then," Ian answered. "I'll see you soon, I guess", and he hung up. Peggy noticed there was no expression of affection at the end of the call. *"Doesn't he understand how urgent, how important this is?"* she thought.

CHAPTER 38

For the next four days, Peggy kept busy, trying to distract herself from her overwhelming desire to move ahead with her work and burning curiosity. She re-worked Celine's accounts and supply purchase schedule, set up Ed Williams as the bakery delivery man, and answered her phone, which rang at least five times a day.

Most of the calls were from reporters, from America and abroad, wanting more information about Max. She told them her work was exclusive to the *Rockland Courier*, and that they should watch that publication for any further news.

Other calls were from literary agents who had heard she was working on a book, and wanted to discuss representing her. Peggy told them the book was not yet finished, but that she would call them back in a couple of weeks or when the work was complete.

She had to be insistent with two of them who kept talking after being informed of her position. Maybe she wouldn't call those two back after all, she thought.

Then, on the afternoon of the fifth day, a package arrived from Boston by special courier. Peggy saw Ian had paid over eighty dollars to send it. She knew her own resources were being drained, having been out of work since her fracture. She wondered about Ian's funds, which might be getting exhausted as well.

Once again, she felt grateful to Ian, and regretted being so brusque with him. She ran up the stairs and ripped open the package, overwhelmed by curiosity and her desire to finish the project at hand.

Inside the package was an eight-page typed document, a note from Ian and the tape he had gotten recovered from Peggy's damaged recorder.

The note explained that Ian had decided to write-up Max's escape from the FBI in the style of a news story, because the tape was very hard to understand and a verbatim transcript seemed impossible due to pauses, coughing and long periods of blank tape.

Ian said he had interviewed retired and active FBI agents, an elderly retired bus driver, a retired Boston police lieutenant, and the owner of a tavern across from the main gate of Fort Devens, Massachusetts, for the story. He also noted that he had reviewed archived documents from Fort Devens, an autopsy report from the Middlesex County coroner, and police records of the town of Ayer, where Fort Devens is located.

He went on to say he would be back in a day or two, after he nailed down some details.

Peggy sat down and read Ian's article.

Edward "Fat Eddie" Kelly was the least FBI-looking FBI agent anyone ever saw. He wasn't just overweight; he was what people call "sloppy fat", with three chins and a prominent wobbly beer gut.

He was also sloppy in his personal habits, often poorly shaved, his suits were wrinkled and his ties stained with a couple of days of spilled food, mostly soup because, as Eddie put it, "I live on liquids," though most of those liquids were, it seemed, more alcoholic than nutritive.

How Eddie got to be an FBI agent in the first place was a story in itself.

In the late '30s, the director of the FBI became concerned about the number of foreign-born naturalized citizens living in the US, especially in areas with large ports, like Boston and New York.

Hoover knew a war was coming, and was worried that the Italians in New York — who might have tendencies to support Mussolini's fascist government — or the notoriously English-loathing IRA-affiliated Irish in Boston, might cause problems on the docks in the event of a war with the Axis powers.

And, of course, there were the German immigrants, and the Japanese on the West Coast.

Labour unrest, sabotage, espionage or large-scale theft were all concerns that troubled Hoover, so the word went out to find and recruit agents who were familiar with the targeted populations.

It was evident that Hoover's elite college-educated accountant and lawyer-type agents hadn't the vaguest idea of how to even speak to, let alone infiltrate, such groups.

Ergo, enter Eddie Kelly, an experienced forty-year-old Boston police detective with deep roots and contacts in South Boston (called "Southie" by everybody who lived there), Dorchester and Roxbury, the primary Irish working-class communities in Boston.

Kelly was hired hastily in the rush to staff-up after the war began for America near the end of 1941. During the next two years, the FBI had been forced to expand, almost doubling its employees between 1941 and 1943.

Nobody in the FBI knew that Kelly was on the verge of being fired by the Boston Police when he was signed on to the Bureau. He was in trouble for chronic alcoholism and repeated episodes of corruption.

This was remarkable, as the Boston PD was known for routine alcoholism and corruption among its members in those days, but Kelly's conduct had exceeded even that undistinguished standard. However, when the FBI checked with Kelly's supervisor on the Boston PD, the lieutenant gave Kelly a favorable recommendation. "Hell," the lieutenant told his sergeant, "if the G-men want Fat Eddie, I say 'Go with God, Brother Edward.' Saves us the trouble of firing him, and telling everybody why."

Kelly straightened himself out for two weeks — quit drinking, spruced up, and got through an interview with an overworked FBI personnel manager. The fellow was impressed by Kelly's truly encyclopedic knowledge of the Boston clans and gangs, so he recommended Eddie for a covert position in the Bureau.

After Eddie was secretly hired by the Feds, he did good work, providing intelligence to the Boston FBI office, working undercover. His "back story" as an undercover agent stated he *had*, in fact, been fired by the Boston PD. The Police Department was more than happy to back up that story, and it made Kelly acceptable in the underworld.

His undercover efforts stymied several attempts by Irish nationalists to buy or steal arms from shipments bound for Britain, and he was able to tip off the Bureau about a couple of attempts to organize work stoppages linked to waterfront gangs and the Boston mob.

That, however, was the peak of Ed Kelly's FBI career.

Eddie had started to revert to his old habits, and when the director himself travelled to Boston to congratulate the division for its work, Hoover saw Kelly in person for the first time.

Kelly had shown up severely hung-over and red-eyed. He reeked of stale alcohol and cigars, and had lapsed to his previous stained, poorly-shaven and rumpled appearance.

The puritanical, image-conscious Hoover was stunned, and quickly ordered the Boston Agent-in-

Charge to "get rid of that slob, or at the very least, hide him".

And so they buried Kelly in a basement office, where he provided intelligence to more presentable agents, and advised them on relationships among the gangs and other criminal elements.

Kelly also routinely berated the agents he dealt with, calling them "college-boy pussies" and "a bunch of clerks, not a real cop in the bunch". This resulted in calls for Kelly's dismissal from some of the department heads.

"I can't fire him, he knows too much," the Agent-in-Charge told his assistant. "I certainly don't want him working for the other side, so he's ours 'for the duration', and after that we'll dump him. Nobody else is going to hire him, so he'll hang on here as long as we provide booze money.

"Meanwhile, we'll get him out of the office as often as we can. Send Kelly on every out-of-town bullshit detail that comes up; and, above all, keep him out of sight. Got it?"

"Okay, boss," the assistant responded.

That was why, when the sheriff from Rockland, Maine, reported the discovery of bodies in German uniforms near Owl's Head, the FBI sent Ed Kelly to handle it.

"Ever since those Germans landed on Long Island, every corpse that washes up from the ocean is a Nazi spy," the AIC said. "This thing in Maine is probably a couple of dead fishermen, so send Kelly up there, and tell him to take his time getting back, er, I mean... to perform a long and careful investigation."

For the same reason, when the sheriff called again and said a game warden had captured a German aviator in the Maine woods, it was Ed Kelly they sent to look into it. "Why not just have the MPs from the Naval Air Station up there pick him up?" groused Ed, looking at the nasty weather outside.

"Sheriff says he's got top secret information and he'll only talk to us," the AIC told Ed. "The trip will do you good."

The trip hadn't done Eddie any good, because he got stranded on a train going to Rockland. The weather was too bad to fly or drive, and it took Ed two days to get up there, and another two to get back. The train didn't have a bar car, and Ed was in a foul mood and all too glad to be rid of Max when they eventually got back to Boston.

Finally, eight months later, it was Ed Kelly who was assigned to pick up Max at an FBI safe house and transport him to Fort Devens for custody as a PoW. "Jaysus, you again," Kelly growled when he saw Max.

"Nice to see you, too, Agent Kelly," was Max's reply, as another agent helped the manacled aviator into the back seat of an FBI sedan. The second agent started around the car to sit next to Max, but Kelly waved him away, saying, "I don't want to bring you all the way back up here when I'm done. This fella won't be any trouble, we're old pals, and I can just drop the car downtown afterwards," and he drove away.

Max was very happy to be out of the safe house, even if he had to enjoy his relative freedom in the back of a car driven by the cigar-smoke-reeking Kelly. The streets of Boston were crowded with healthy-looking, busy people, and hundreds of trucks and buses rumbled along, belching exhaust fumes.

No buildings showed any signs of damage, and nobody looked demoralized. The contrast with the pictures he had seen of a devastated Germany was stark. They passed a harbor teeming with ships of all sorts, and a factory where rows of airplane engines were lined up next to a railroad track. *"How did anybody ever think we could win?"* Max wondered.

As they rode through the sunny streets, Max thought about the past months.

His confinement had been comfortable but restrictive. After the first two months he was only interviewed every two weeks or so, by a number of different agencies.

The meals had been very good, and astoundingly plentiful compared to those available on the continent. Luxuries like ice cream were always available, as was fresh fruit and red meat. Real coffee was available every Sunday, with rich cream.

There was another item that Max at first could not figure out, a suspicious brown substance that frankly looked fecal, but which Max grew to crave. "It's called peanut butter," one of the guards told him.

"*Erdnussbutter*," Max had muttered, and spread a bit more on a slice of awful porous soft white bread. The bread was the only thing Max hadn't liked from the generous American menu. The bread, and that ghastly bright yellow stuff they called mustard.

One of the other detainees, a German ordnance colonel, said to Max, "This must be a propaganda trick. Surely average Americans cannot be fed this well. They are trying to fool us." But Max had seen what American maintenance workers carried in their lunch pails, and he wasn't so sure.

Max was snapped out of his reverie by another blast of cigar smoke, and Kelly loudly asking, "Bet yer gonna be glad to get back to the Fatherland, right, Heinie?"

"*Ja*, I miss my mother," Max answered. But he was lying. He did not want to go back to Germany or Austria. If he returned, there would be questions. How had he survived? What had happened to the rest of his crew? Had he been a traitor? Furthermore, he had reason to believe he might locate Rachel if he could get back to Pete and Celine.

For these and other compelling reasons, if at all possible, Max wanted to stay in America. He had told that to the FBI, the OSS, the State Department, US Army, and every other agency he spoke to, but they all said they had done enough for Max. He was to be transferred to a PoW facility and returned to Europe along with other prisoners, they told him.

Max figured that now that the European war was over, security in PoW facilities would be relaxed. He had heard that parties of PoWs were sent out from the main camps to work in the countryside. If that happened, Max was going to try to escape. He had gathered things for his escape kit.

He had sold his decorations to a souvenir-seeking MP for fifty American dollars and some pocket change. The bills were now tucked into his underwear.

During one of his stints as a kitchen helper, he had pocketed a multi-purpose tool which contained a small sharp blade, a corkscrew and a can opener. That was now stashed in his sock. He also had three heavy paperclips taken from his own file during a break in an interview.

His most valuable escape item was an ID badge he had stolen from a coat left in the front hallway. It was a badge identifying a government clerk who had come to the safe house only once to deliver some documents. The photo looked only vaguely like Max, but an official approval stamp obscured much of the picture, and Max thought it would suffice if flashed quickly in low light. *"Just good enough to get through a gate if the guard is tired and bored,"* Max thought.

While he was considering these things, the car pulled up at the entrance to Fort Devens. Max noticed a number of men dressed in floppy green fatigue uniforms with a giant letter "P" painted on the back of the jacket and another on the trouser leg. They were cutting grass and raking up clippings or painting stones that lined the pathways between buildings. Guards stood around with shotguns.

Obviously, these men were PoWs. Max's heart sank. *"I'll never get away wearing something like that."* Max had been given clean khakis for his trip to the PoW camp, but now he realized that once inside he would have to change to the prisoners' distinctive garb. *"Verdammt!"* he cursed mentally.

Kelly flapped his wallet at the MP gate guards, and after recording the licence tag, they waved the car through, automatically saluting the khaki-clad figure in the back seat, which made Max smile. He couldn't return the salute.

When they reached the PoW compound within the base, Kelly was required to step out of the car and sign-in, as well as show his ID, which irritated him. While Kelly was at the guard shack, Max quickly reached into the front seat and grabbed a crumpled map that was lying on the dashboard.

Kelly got even more irritated when the guard told him that he could not drop off a prisoner at that time, because all of the clerks and officers were at lunch and would not be back for an hour. An argument ensued, ending when Kelly exploded. "What the fuck am I supposed to do for an hour?" he roared, blowing cigar smoke in the NCO's face. "Sit here and look at holy pictures?"

"I don't give a rat's ass what you do for an hour, sir, but you can't leave this car here. Why don't you go across the street and get some lunch? The joint across from the gate has great sandwiches."

"You assholes, act like the war is over. We still gotta beat the Japs, ya know!"

"Move along, sir," the MP sergeant said. "We've got to keep the gate clear."

Kelly turned the sedan around and went back through the main gate, pausing again to show his badge and expressing impatience when the gate MP again wrote down the plate. "Jackasses already got the number, fah Chrissake!" he muttered as they pulled out. The guards saluted again. "They still got the old rule," Kelly added, "if it moves, salute it. Whadda buncha maroons."

The restaurant across from the gate did look inviting. Kelly sized it up, noticed a sign announcing a special on corned beef, and said to Max, "I'm gonna get something to eat, and I'll bring ya something when I'm done." He got out of the car and opened the back door, removed one of Max's handcuffs and secured it to the armrest. "That oughta hold ya, Heinie. I'll be back in a jiffy," Kelly said, and trotted heavily across the street, dodging traffic.

Kelly blinked when he entered the dimly-lit room, his eyes adjusting to the gloom. A rich smell permeated the place, a tantalising mixture of fried onions, stale tobacco smoke, and the pungent bouquet of decades of spilled beer.

Kelly ordered a sandwich, which he finished quickly, washed down with two bottles of beer. He ordered a second sandwich and slowly ate half of that, with another beer. Then, for dessert, he had a shot of Old Fitzgerald. He wrapped up the remaining half sandwich for Max, slid off the stool, paid his bill and stepped out the door onto the bright street.

Max, alone in the car, had immediately gone to work on the handcuffs. After forty-five minutes, using first the paperclips, then the corkscrew, nothing had worked, so he simply tore the armrest loose from the door. It had only been held on by two small sheet-metal screws and came free fairly easily, though he bruised his wrist in the process. Then he worked the broken armrest through the handcuffs and stuck it back where it belonged. It would only stay there until someone touched it, but that might be a day or two, he thought. He opened the map and quickly located the railroad station.

Max considered what to do next. *He could kill Kelly fairly quickly, either strangling him with the handcuffs' chain or cutting his fat throat with his little blade, but that seemed very risky in broad daylight on a crowded street. Max decided he wasn't that cold-blooded. He was also certain the Americans would look for him much harder, and execute him if they caught him after he murdered an FBI agent. Better, perhaps, to simply walk away and disappear into the crowd, hoping to get some distance away before Kelly raised the alarm.*

Max took Kelly's fedora from the front seat, put it on, and clipped the ID badge to his pocket. He tucked the handcuffs up under his sleeve, took his file from the front seat, put it under his arm, and stepped out of the car. He thought he looked like any worker on his way to the factory, and his hopes rose.

At that instant, he saw Kelly emerge from the restaurant, and they locked eyes.

"Hey!" Kelly bellowed. He was dazzled by the sudden transition from the dim restaurant to a blast of midday sunlight, and he stumbled a bit as he stepped off the curb, his eyes blearily focused on Max across the street. He took a step or two into the street to recover his balance.

"Hey, you!" he yelled again, just before a crosstown bus hit him squarely at twenty-five miles per hour. Kelly might have survived the impact, had he not been thrown against a steel lamp post. He stumbled backwards, arms windmilling, desperately trying to regain his balance, but he slammed against the lamp post and his head snapped back, striking the metal pole with a distinct gong-like sound.

The blow threw Ed Kelly's brain against the hard interior surface of his skull, tearing a large cerebral blood vessel. Momentarily stunned, he crumpled to the street.

Kelly was struggling to get back to his feet when bleeding from that torn artery massively increased the pressure on his brain stem, which in turn stopped his heart, causing his death.

Max walked away, ignored by the growing crowd gathering around Ed, and headed for the train.

CHAPTER 39

After she finished the article, Peggy listened to the first part of Max's final tape, the part that seemed to cover his escape. Max's voice was even more difficult to understand than before, and there were long pauses, during which Max seemed to be asleep. The tape would keep running, but Max remained silent, and once Peggy thought she heard him snoring.

She really had to strain to hear it, but the story Max told tallied with what Ian had written. Peggy switched off the playback and thought for a few minutes.

Peggy decided to use Ian's story for the book, after she was able to talk with him about a few details and have a look at his documentation. She was amazed Ian had gotten so much information so quickly.

Ian's writing style was different from hers, but he told the story so well she decided to use it without alteration rather than try to rewrite it. She also realized she should give Ian credit as a contributor or even co-author.

Peggy turned back to the recorder and started the playback again. Max's weak voice came back on, interrupted frequently by coughing spasms and long periods of silence.

Peggy decided to create a transcript omitting the interruptions and retaining Max's voice by using quotation marks and trying to duplicate his speech pattern. She would continue to write as much of the story as possible either as narration or as an ordinary conversation, as if some person had listened in and transcribed it.

The rest she would document as an observer, simply writing down what happened but staying within the facts as she could gather them from Max's fragmented recording. When she inserted the material in the novel, she would simply add an explanatory note.

Because of the cast on her arm, it was difficult for Peggy to write long-hand, but after trying several different pens and pencils, she found one that she could hold fairly well. She first listened to a segment of the tape, then turned off the playback and laboriously put down what she had heard. Then she went on to the next part.

This is what she wrote.

"I got to the railroad station without having to ask for directions and picked up a timetable from a rack near the ticket counter. I located the proper train for Rockland, Maine, which was scheduled to leave in one hour. I went into a stall in the restroom and worked on the handcuffs with the small corkscrew tool and a bent paperclip until, finally, the lock snapped open. I hid the handcuffs behind the toilet. What a relief!

"Then came the largest hurdle. I had to buy a ticket, and that meant I had to speak to a ticket agent.

"In those days, my accent was more obvious than it is now, so I decided to simply point to the train number and say as little as possible. The ticket agent asked if I wanted a one-way or round-trip ticket, and I managed to answer 'one' by holding up one finger. The agent looked at me curiously, and then asked me for a certain amount of money.

"That threw me. I wasn't familiar with American currency denominations, so I fumbled a bit and finally decided to give the man the largest bill I had, a twenty-dollar note, and hoped for the best. The agent counted out some change and handed me a ticket. He looked at me again, and asked where I was from. My stomach lurched.

"'Me Norway,' I said. 'Work Rockland. Fish boat.'

"The man smiled and said, 'I knew you were a foreigner. You want track three,' he continued, holding up three fingers. 'Takk,' I said, which I had learned from Pete was Norwegian for 'thank you'. I breathed a huge sigh as I turned towards the proper gate.

"'Wait!' the clerk called out, and I froze. 'You forgot your change, Norway.' I faked an embarrassed laugh, picked up the money, and thanked him again. I walked away in a cold sweat.

"After that, the trip was uneventful. The only problem I had was hunger. I hadn't had any lunch and I did not have a ration book. I wasn't sure what was needed to buy a sandwich, so I was famished by the time

I got to Rockland and damn near fainting by the time I had walked the four-and-a-half miles to Owl's Head and found Pete's cabin. Months without exercise had made me weak, and I was panting as I walked.

"Celine opened the door when I knocked and her face went pale. 'Oh, *mon Dieu!* It is you, Max. Pete! Marie! Come quick, it is our *cher* Max!'

Pete came from another room, shook my hand and pounded me on the back. Then someone else appeared. It was a woman, who looked familiar.

"She was very thin, had short dark hair and huge luminous eyes contrasting with sharp, emaciated features and very white skin.

"'*Guten Tag*, Max,' the woman said. I instantly recognized her voice.

"I realized it was my own Rachel! I rushed to embrace her, babbling a thousand questions as I hugged her and realized how fragile she seemed. It was Rachel. Rachel, who had either been quite ill, or malnourished, maybe both. I held her to me and wept for joy. She was crying, too, and we stood there for a while. Then I had to ask why Celine had called her 'Marie'.

"'That is my name now, Max. I am Marie Durand, an Alsatian Catholic refugee girl from France, and I have papers to prove it.'

"We could not stop looking at each other, touching each other. She told me I had gained weight and I asked what had happened to her, that she was so thin. Celine made us sit at her table, poured coffee and put out lovely fresh *croissants* with some ham, of which I ate three very quickly, then settled down to hear Rachel's story.

"After leaving my apartment, Rachel had been shuttled towards Spain on an escape line she had helped set up while working at the American hospital. The group, called '*Goulette*', was one of the networks which got downed Allied airmen out of France and into neutral Spain, from whence they could be returned to England.

"Rachel's group sent aviators from one point to another, where they were sheltered and fed while awaiting a chance to get across the Spanish border by crossing the Pyrenees. Priests, ordinary French people, Basque separatists, shepherds and mountain guides all participated in moving the young fliers.

"I told Rachel I remembered the officers in Paris interrogating me about that name, '*Goulette*'. I asked if the policeman Rion had been involved with that operation.

"'Involved? Oh, Max, Rion was *deeply* involved. He was the heart and soul of many operations in and around Paris. He was up to his neck in sabotage, espionage, forgery, theft, assassination and any other skullduggery that annoyed the Germans. Rion saved many of us, like he saved me, when the Gestapo closed in after the American Hospital was betrayed. Many escaped, but many others were caught, tortured or executed, and others were sent to places like Buchenwald and Auschwitz, where most of them died or were murdered.'

"I shuddered, thinking what might have happened to Rachel if she had been caught, as she went on. 'I ended up living in a tiny village near the Spanish border. My job was to help take care of any injured men before they attempted the difficult crossing, and to help those who had been forced to turn back because of injuries from falls or things like frostbite. I also served as an interpreter, because I speak English and most of our young "passengers" didn't speak any French. Then the network collapsed.'"

"'Why, Marie... I mean Rachel?' This from Pete.

"'Someone was careless, got caught and talked. We had to scatter. We took to the "*maquis*", as it is called. The word is used in Corsica to mean "brush or bushes" — that is, somewhere to hide. We simply took off, with inadequate clothing or food and little shelter. I got sick from drinking contaminated water from a stream, and two of my friends died of dysentery and exposure. We could do nothing for them.' Rachel started to cry and Celine comforted her until she could continue.

"'How did you get away?' I asked.

"'Actually, I didn't get away. A group of French collaborationist militia caught me and another woman, a twenty-year-old from the provinces named Lily, living in a damp cave. The other girl was even sicker than I was. We were both very weak. The Vichyite militiamen beat us up and were taking us to a prison camp, when we were liberated by a group of young *résistants*, just kids, from the French Forces of the Interior, the FFI. They shot up the cars in our convoy, killed all of our

341

captors and turned us over to an advancing American army unit. I gave the Americans Rion's name and we were sent to Paris on the train.'"

"'Is that when you went to the hospital?' I asked.

"'Well, first there was a bit of a *"contretemps"*, or as you say here, a fuss.'

"'What happened?'

"'As I said, while our little group was hiding, I became quite ill, with a high fever. One of the old home remedies for fever is to cut the patient's hair, thinking that heat would then be lost through the scalp, lowering the temperature. Lily had already had her hair cut off, and we joked about it, about how odd she looked. I didn't protest when my colleagues cut my hair, since we had no other remedies and I was miserable.' Rachel smiled briefly and then said, 'It turned out to be a good idea, not because my fever went away, which it didn't, but because I had acquired lice, and at least getting rid of my hair stopped the terrible itching.'

"I cried, 'Oh, my poor Rachel, your lovely hair!'

"'Well, that was not the worst of it. When our train arrived in Paris, there was a lot of confusion on the platform. People were trying to find relatives, children were crying, and there was a group of surly-looking armed civilians wearing FFI armbands, who were presumably supposed to be maintaining order. It looked to me like they were just lounging around, smoking and looking important. One of them spotted me helping my friend down from the carriage. He shouted to the others, "There's two of them! Two *collabos* — get them!"

"'You see, they had noticed our shorn heads and assumed we were what they called "horizontal collaborators".'

"'What is that?' asked Pete, who had been quietly listening.

"'Right after the Liberation, a lot of women who had slept with German soldiers were rounded up and abused by crowds of so-called *résistants.* Sometimes these were genuine FFI fighters, but often they were just thugs who had managed to get their hands on a gun, bent on revenge, trying to recover their lost masculine pride, and somehow erase the shame of France's defeat. These unfortunate women were beaten and humiliated by having their hair cut off in public. The men at the railroad station thought we were such women.

"'My friend and I were quickly surrounded and the armed men began to close in, shouting at us and calling us vile names. Members of the crowd joined the men and soon we were cowering against the rail car while they taunted and threatened us. I actually feared for my life. Then a shot was fired, and everyone turned to see the source of the sound. There stood Rion, in full uniform, a smoking revolver in his hand. "Get back, you dogs!" Rion snarled. "You brave men, you! You Johnny-come-lately *résistants*. You are great at beating up women and shooting Germans in the back now that they are on the run. Where were you in 1940, 1941? I don't remember seeing any of you then. These women are heroines of France, *résistants* from the first hour, and I'll plug the first person that takes another step!"

"'You can't kill all of us!" one of the women in the mob screamed.

"'Perhaps not, but I can kill five of you. Who wants to be first?"

"It was quite dramatic," Rachel said, "and it worked. The crowd dispersed, the thugs skulked away grumbling, and blessed Chief Inspector Rion got us both to a hospital."

CHAPTER 40

"'Lily, much younger than I, recovered quickly and was discharged. I did not do so well because the fever held on and I kept losing weight and couldn't keep anything down. The hospital was crowded with sick people returning from being prisoners. Overworked doctors and nurses couldn't help much and I kept falling asleep.

"'I knew I was in trouble when they moved me to a ward where there seemed to be very few staff. It was whispered that the people in this ward were being left to perish, and I began to lose hope.

"'Then one day a miracle happened. Two French nuns and an American military priest showed up at my bedside with a wheelchair and whisked me outside to a large luxurious automobile, which bore the pennant of the Bishop of Paris. I fell asleep on the lovely leather upholstery, covered with a beautiful fluffy blanket.

"'When I woke hours later, we were passing through Bayeux, and shortly thereafter I found myself at the enormous artificial harbor the Allies had constructed on the English Channel, at Arromanche. I was taken aboard a hospital ship bound for England.

"'One of the nuns handed me a set of identification papers, work permits, travel orders, a ration book and a significant sum of money in English pounds and

American dollars. She told me to memorize the name and other information on the papers, wished me luck and kissed me goodbye. I was led to a small cabin, given a new set of pyjamas and put to bed on marvellous clean sheets.

"'I was absolutely astonished to discover that I had supposedly been employed as a translator for the US Army Chaplains' Service since August, and that I had official travel orders to report to a Catholic hospital in Boston.

"'I was taken from England to America, arriving in Boston Harbor in November 1944. I was transported to a large hospital, where I was received by motherly nuns in spotless white habits, some of whom spoke French. I stayed there for over a month, and the good sisters or their assistants fed me something every time I woke up, whether I wanted it or not.

"'The hospital was lavishly equipped, with many intravenous units, and I was given dextrose infusions every day. My weight began to go up. A doctor came to see me each week, and once or twice he gave me an injection of a yellow-brown fluid. I asked what it was and he told me it was a new drug, called penicillin, which he said was produced from cheese mold and that it killed bacteria. He told me the new drug was not routinely available in Europe, and that he was glad I was in America so I could benefit from it.

"Cheese mold?" I said. "I hope it is Camembert, that's my favorite"; and for the first time in years, I laughed heartily, and so did the doctor.

"'Soon, my fever went away. I began to be able to take care of myself, even help out a bit. Then I was told that a couple in Maine wanted me to come and live with them. That seemed mysterious, until one of the nuns handed me a note that said the couple were *"amis de Max"*, friends of Max. A few days later, Pete showed up and brought me here; so, *mon cher* Max, *"nous voilà"*, here we are.'

"Celine, who had mostly been listening, now asked me, 'How did all of this happen, Max? How could Rachel come all the way from France to Boston, in the middle of a war? How did she get a different name, new papers?'

"'I find it hard to believe myself, Celine, but I'm pretty well certain this is all the work of a network of Roman Catholic priests, the almighty Jesuits.'

"I told them the story of my meeting Father Weber, the secret message from him telling me to start attending church services. I went on to relate what Father O'Brian had told me, about the 'love child/Liebeskind' clue and how I got away from the FBI.

"'As for the new name,' I continued, 'I'm betting on Chief Inspector Rion, our old friend from Paris. He would have access to any necessary papers, official stamps and so forth. It would be easy for him to find Rachel a new identity.'

"'But why would Rachel need a new identity?' asked Celine. 'Couldn't she still be Rachel Liebeskind instead of Marie Durand? What is the difference?'

"'Ah, Celine,' Rachel answered, 'I figured that one out myself. The difference is that Rachel Liebeskind is one of those scary Germans, from Berlin. She is Jewish, and has a Jewish name. Marie Durand is a Catholic girl from Alsace. America still has immigration quotas, and a French Catholic girl from Alsace is a more attractive prospect than a German or a Jew. Particularly since Marie was employed by the US Army Chaplains' Corps and brought over by Catholic charities, so let's leave it at that.'

"And so they did. Pete and Celine had set up a little place in the basement for Rachel, and I simply moved in with her until Pete could arrange other quarters.

"The basement had a small alcove at one end, and that had been converted to a bedroom and sitting area. There was a square of carpet on the floor, a cot and a bedside table with a pretty, pink-shaded lamp and a radio. One window, high on the wall, admitted some ambient light. Along one wall was an upholstered couch.

"The rear wall held a set of wooden shelves, where a lot of preserved fruit and pickles were kept in glass jars. A few pipes ran along the ceiling.

"'It's not the *Crillon*, but it's cozy enough,' said Rachel. 'I help Celine with the baking and cleaning, and those American dollars the nun gave me in Arromanche have been useful for groceries and supplies. I have lived in worse places, Max. I have been happy to be here, especially now that you are with me.'

"We had both decided not to have what we primly called 'relations' until Rachel was stronger. I proposed to sleep on the couch near Rachel's cot, but in the middle of the night Rachel joined me, and we snuggled peacefully together on the sofa, murmuring to one another and dozing until morning.

"Our resolve lasted all of two days. On the third day, Pete announced that he thought he had found a place for me to hide: an abandoned fire-watcher shelter deep in the woods nearby. He said he would take me there in the morning. Rachel asked if she could stay with me, but Pete sadly told her that for now it was just too rough for a woman recovering from serious illness.

"There was no electricity, telephone or running water, Pete said, and the little shelter was just barely habitable. There was only an old moss-covered outhouse for a toilet, and no proper bed; just a small wooden bunk.

"The rundown cabin could only be reached by a four-wheel-drive vehicle because the trail that led to it from the highway was badly eroded after years of neglect. Pete had heard that the state intended to auction the place off in 1946 and he was prepared to bid on it.

"He had chopped and stacked wood for the little iron stove that heated the place, and stocked some non-perishable food items that I could heat up. He asked me if I thought I was up to it. I told him I had camped and hunted a lot when I was a boy, and thought I would be all right for a while. Pete told me he would stop by at least once a week to bring supplies.

"I asked why I needed to move so soon, and Pete told me that he was afraid the FBI would soon show up looking for me. Pete said that if that happened, the sheriff would probably give him a courtesy call, but there still might not be enough time to get me away before agents arrived.

"That evening after supper, Celine and Pete went to a function at the church, saying they would be back about eleven.

"Me and Rachel washed the dishes and put them away, meaning to spend the evening listening to the radio; but then," Max said, his voice very weak and hesitant, "nature took its course."

Peggy could hear Max walking away, then the sound of water running. It was a full five minutes before he started speaking again, and then he seemed sedated, his speech slurred and sometimes garbled. Max seemed to be in a reverie, talking to himself. His mind seemed to wander.

Peggy stopped writing, her wrist and hand aching, and concentrated on deciphering what Max was saying.

"We dealt with the dishes, the washing, drying, our fingers touched. We brushed against one another. Warmth of her through her dress, soft in all the right...

"We were downstairs, kissing, touching, undressing gently. 'Gently, gently,' I said. She hissed, her teeth flashing white, rolled me over, pinned me down. Her skin was pale blue in the moonlight... Only that one small window high up... She was so thin, ribs showing. Her legs were strong, gripping...

"At the end, she threw her head back and cried a sharp stabbing howl. Was she injured? Had I hurt her? She cried out again, louder, and this time… *Could it be?* From somewhere very close, a wolf answered. Long, quavering musical tone. Rachel collapsed on top of me. She was sweaty… So was I."

His voice faded, even weaker than before, mumbling inaudibly. Then, suddenly, Max seemed to rally.

"*Ach*, I forgot that thing was turned on. I have made a mistake. I didn't mean for you to hear that." There was much clicking, a thud, and after that only buzzing for a moment, then nothing.

CHAPTER 41

Peggy slumped in her chair, afraid she had just heard Max's voice for the last time. There was so much more she wanted to know, things she might never discover. She realized that Max had probably tried to reverse the tape and erase what had embarrassed him. In his impaired state, he probably knocked the recorder off the table and perhaps stepped on the thing when trying to retrieve it. She felt sad, realizing that some time after the machine was damaged, Max took the poison that killed him.

She was also very tired. It was one-thirty in the morning, she realized, and she had been up since five. She crawled into bed, missing Max, but also keenly missing Ian in a way she never had before. How could she have treated him so shabbily, sending him off to Boston like an errand boy when he had been so kind to her? She mulled this over as she drifted off, and the germ of an idea began to form.

By late morning the next day, she had contacted one of Celine's innumerable cousins and arranged a ride to Rockland. She visited her bank, then the Grocery King, where she spoke to Bob's dad and told him what the doctor had said when he set her arm, about the great job Bob had done immobilizing it. The man thanked her and said he would tell his son about it soon. He said Bob was doing much better, but wouldn't be home from the VA for a while. Then Peggy bought what she needed and went on to the next task.

At the clinic, the doctor removed the hated cast and examined her arm. It felt wonderful to be able to rub her arm, and heavenly when the nurse washed it with alcohol. The swelling had gone down, the doctor said, and he wanted to fit her with a new, smaller, cast. Peggy pleaded with him, noting that a cast was a terrific handicap for her, asking if there was any alternative.

After an X-ray, the man said he could fit her with a lightweight brace, so that she could write and even type, as long as it didn't cause pain. She still could not drive her stick-shift automobile, he said. That would take at least another fifteen days.

Peggy decided half a loaf was better than none, and left the clinic elated, feeling ten pounds lighter, and headed for the Forest Service office, where she talked with the ranger, one of the men who had transported Max's body.

He agreed to take her out to the cabin and wait for a while as she looked around.

Peggy rearranged a few things, tidied up and put some things away in the cabinets and fridge. She did a quick search to see if there were any more tapes. Finding none, she got a ride home from the ranger on his snowmobile. She returned to the bakery very happy with her day.

The next day, Peggy was working on the account books in the bakery when she saw a black chauffeured limousine pull up in front. Two well-dressed men got out and one of them knocked on the door. Celine hurried to let them in. They stood in the entryway, stomping snow from their well-polished shoes, obviously enjoying the fragrance of the place.

Celine greeted one of them, an older man, calling him 'Ernst', as he introduced her to the other person, a severe-looking young gentleman wearing an elegant bowler hat and an extremely well-cut black suit. She called to Peggy, saying, "The man I said would arrive, he has come!" Celine quickly cleared her worktable and produced a plate of cookies. Her helpers brought in some chairs, and Celine, Peggy and the two visitors sat down with fresh coffee.

Celine sent one of her helpers to fetch the chauffeur some coffee and cookies. Then she asked the two young women to work in another part of the shop while the group talked.

The older man, munching on a cookie, introduced himself as an old friend of Max from the war and gave his name as Ernst Ludwig, intending to continue, until Peggy interrupted him.

"Ernst Ludwig?" she said. "Are you the same Ernst Ludwig that flew with Max at Stalingrad?"

"I am that person. I did not know Max had told you about our work together," he answered. "Presently I am retired, but I worked for many years as a Senior Pilot for *Lufthansa*, flying between Germany and Boston. In that capacity I was able to assist Max with a number of arrangements that made his life here in America more comfortable and, ah, secure."

"But I thought after your injuries in Russia you couldn't fly any more."

"Oh, my, Max *did* tell you about me. After the war I had a number of surgeries to repair the damage to my sinuses. Also, airliners were soon routinely pressurized, so I had no severe discomfort when I started flying again. I requested the Boston assignment after Max was able to contact me through intermediaries, and communicate his location and requirements."

Peggy obviously wanted to ask more questions, but Ernst held up his hand. "I will tell you more as we proceed, but first let me introduce my colleague. This is Heinz Lindeman."

The younger man stood, bowed slightly, and shook hands with Peggy, handing her an elaborate engraved business card. "*Herr* Lindeman represents the *Schweitzerdeutsche Commerzbank*, which is based in Basel, Switzerland, but has a branch in New York, where he works. He will explain the role of his bank in managing Max's assets, and ask you, Peggy, to sign certain documents."

"Documents? What documents?" Peggy asked.

Lindeman spoke up after glancing at Ernst, who nodded slightly. "The documents in question are related to an immediate partial distribution of Baron von Waldberg's estate and will establish your responsibilities in the ongoing management of the assets

355

not dealt with today." Lindeman had a nearly undetectable accent, but that made his speech seem very precise.

"I am totally confused," Peggy said. "I don't know what you are talking about. What 'assets'? What 'responsibilities'?"

Ernst put his hand on Lindeman's arm, causing him to pause, before answering Peggy. Ernst then turned to Celine and gave her a long look. "She does not know? She hasn't been told?"

Celine averted her eyes, studying her hands in her lap. "No," she answered. "Max told me to wait for you to come. He wanted you to do it."

Ernst sighed, nudged the younger man and pointed to one of the documents he had arranged on the table. Lindeman handed it to him, and Ernst placed it in front of Peggy. "My dear Peggy, if I may call you that, please look at this document while I explain your position.

"This is a certificate of marriage, recorded in summer of 1947 here in Owl's Head, Maine, at St Joan's Church. It memorializes the marriage of Maximillian, Baron von Waldberg and *Fräulein* Rachel Liebeskind. The small private ceremony was performed by a Father Nicholas Weber and the witnesses were Piet and Celine Pederson. This certificate has been verified with the diocese of Portland and it is in all respects authentic and legally incontestable."

Peggy felt a lump in her throat, she was dizzy and slightly nauseated as Ernst Ludwig continued, sliding a second document across the table.

"This second sheet is a Certificate of Live Birth prepared at Knox County Medical Centre in January of 1948. It attests the birth of a female child named Margarethe Celine Wald at 0800 on 15 January. The father is given as Max Wald and the mother as Marie Durand, and the certificate is signed by the attending physician, a Doctor Harris. This document was officially corrected in 1949, changing the father's name to Max von Waldberg, and the name of the mother to Rachel von Waldberg born Liebeskind.

"The last name of the baby girl is also amended, to Von Waldberg. This document is also genuine, properly recorded and legally valid.

"There is also a Certificate of Death for Marie Durand, dated 18 January 1948, duly recorded by the Knox County coroner."

Ernst stood up facing Peggy and said slowly, "To summarize, my dear young lady, as you may have guessed by now, *you* are Margarethe Celine von Waldberg, only child of the union of our friend and comrade Baron Max von Waldberg and his deceased wife Rachel Liebeskind. You are therefore the sole legal heir to the estate of Maximillian, Baron von Waldberg, which includes some Von Waldberg assets and all of the Von Kesselstein properties.

"All liquid assets are handled by *Herr* Lindeman's bank, and are invested in solid companies. The Von Kesselstein estates are supervised by a competent estate manager, a man named Goetz, who succeeded his father and is thus the second generation of his family to manage the Von Kesselstein holdings.

"Those properties and enterprises produce tidy profits each year. You are not what the media would call 'fabulously' wealthy, my dear *fräulein*, but annual revenues, dividends from prudent investments and interest on banked funds can provide you with a reasonably comfortable income for the foreseeable future. I congratulate you." Ernst bowed slightly from the waist, sat down, folded his hands and nodded to Lindeman.

Before Lindeman could begin, Peggy turned to Celine. Her voice shaking, she cried out, "Why didn't you tell me in all these years? My biological father was just up the road and I never met him until a few months ago. Why was that?" Peggy was angry, overwhelmed, suddenly terribly tired. All she wanted to do was crawl into bed, but she knew that feeling was the result of stress, so she resisted it, for now.

"Max made me promise," said Celine, wiping her eyes. "He was afraid that if I revealed your identity, he would have to reveal his own. He feared that if he did that, the US Government would find him and imprison or deport him. He was afraid that Pete and I would get into trouble for helping him hide after he escaped. He also worried they might go after Father Weber or even Ernst here. Max was slightly what we might call... ah... para-something?"

"Paranoid," interjected Ernst.

"Ah, *oui*, paranoid."

Ernst spoke, his eyes locked on Peggy's. "You must understand, Peggy. Many of us who survived Nazi Germany and the war are 'slightly paranoid'. We are always looking over our shoulders, always a bit worried, often afraid of the government.

"We lived in a state where people could simply be snatched up on the street and thrown into a miserable camp to be murdered. We assume our mail is opened and our phones are tapped. No wonder Max was cautious and secretive. He thought the government was after him because, at least at first, it seemed it *was* after him. *Nein*?

"That was why Max had to use clandestine means to communicate with Germany and Austria. That is why Pete and Celine acted as middlemen, sending Max's letters to a secretarial service that forwarded them to me.

"That was why I acted as a courier and why discreet Swiss bankers like *Herr* Lindeman here devised ways of providing Max with funds that were deposited monthly to Max's account in Rockland Bank.

"Max first designated Pete, then Bob, the brain-injured Vietnam soldier, to withdraw money from that account and bring it to him when he needed cash. All of his monthly bills were paid by cheque, except for incidentals like groceries, for which he paid cash.

"Perhaps it might be well now for you to listen to *Herr* Lindeman, evaluate what he has to say and save your questions until later. Agreed?"

Peggy nodded, shook her head to try to clear her mind, took a deep breath, and turned her attention to Lindeman.

The dapper young man cleared his throat, shuffled his papers and began. "The *Herr* Baron recorded a Last Will and Testament with our lawyers last year. He had discovered that he had a lung disease caused by asbestos.

"It seems many aircraft in the 1940s contained significant amounts of that material for insulation. The baron wrote that he remembered a grey powder floating around his aircraft during his last flight, and realized that was probably asbestos. He knew the illness was incurable, and that soon his condition would be terminal.

"In the Will he made a bequest to Celine Pederson..." — he handed Celine an envelope — "of a significant sum of money. For you, *Fraulein*, he arranged for his Rockland Bank account to be transferred to you.

"You will need to complete signature cards I will give you, and I will arrange for them to be sent to the bank, along with affidavits, the baron's Death Certificate and so forth."

Lindeman showed Peggy Max's bank book, pointing out the balance on hand. After that, everything was a blur. Lindeman droned on about monthly income, arrangements for income taxes, and seemingly endless other details. She signed whatever he put in front of her, utterly numb.

Finally, when it was over and the men had left, Peggy dragged herself upstairs and crawled into bed, initially intending to stay there and sleep indefinitely, as she had after the twin shocks of breaking her arm and learning of Max's death. She was furious with Celine for keeping all of this secret, and terribly sad that Max was gone.

After an hour, she sat up abruptly.

Peggy suddenly realized she didn't want to withdraw, to sleep forever. What she truly wanted was to see Ian, to be with *him* forever, if she could. Then her practical, determined side asserted itself and she spent the next hour preparing a list of questions for Ian.

CHAPTER 42

When Ian arrived at the bakery a day and a half later, Peggy was more than delighted to see him. She was calm, her mind free of anger or anxiety. She had had a long talk with Celine, and finally accepted Celine's rationale for keeping Peggy's origins to herself. That, and the fact that she knew any financial worries she ever had were now moot.

She noticed Ian wasn't driving the rented pick-up, but his own car, an elderly Volvo that burned oil but was reliable. She was glad she had made her arrangements while Ian was gone. She ran to meet him as he got out of the car, threw her arms around his neck and kissed him long and hard. Ian was a little taken aback, but was even more surprised when Peggy led him around the back of the bakery.

There, on a small trailer hooked up to Peggy's little Toyota, was a nice-looking snowmobile. "It's used, but the guy I bought it from gave me a one-year guarantee. Do you like it?"

Ian only then noticed the brace on Peggy's arm. "Can you drive it?"

"Alas, not yet, but it's not for me, it's for you, to help you get to Max's cabin and back."

"Um, I'm confused. Can we go inside? It's a little chilly." He seemed a bit cool, and not entirely from the weather. Once they got inside, he greeted Celine warmly and Peggy led him upstairs.

In Peggy's sitting room, she explained that she had talked with Celine, and they both thought Ian might like to stay at the cabin, rent-free, of course, until he made the next decision about his career. "We would like someone to be there, just for security, and… I could, well, come out with you sometimes and, uh, if it's all right with you… sleep over?" Peggy blushed, then put her head down, a bit anxious, as Ian hesitated.

"Oh, Peggy, that's a lovely offer, but I'm not sure about that last part. Is that just a sort of 'thank-you' thing? If it is, then no. I'll be moving along after we nail down some details for the story. I don't want to get hurt again," he said, looking her in the eye.

Peggy looked away, tears coming to her eyes. "Oh, Ian, it's not a 'thank-you' thing. Maybe it's partly an 'I'm sorry' thing. Maybe it's partly an 'I feel bad I treated you like an errand boy' thing — but mostly it's an 'I've had time to think and I want to be with you thing'. Is that a good enough answer? Please, let's go to the cabin and we can talk about it more." Her voice broke a little. She cleared her throat, then said, "I've got a nice supper ready, if you're hungry."

Ian looked out of the window. "It's going to be dark soon. We won't be able to get back before morning because I don't trust myself to drive the snowmobile in the dark."

"That's OK. Tonight is 'the bingo', and I've talked to Celine. I told her we had work to do, that we'd be back in the morning." She took Ian's hand and he could see the wetness on her cheeks. Then he got a lump in his throat, and felt his heart beating faster.

Within an hour they were on the trail. The ride was even more beautiful in the light-fading dusk, and by the time they reached Max's home the moon had risen and everything was bathed in blue-white light.

They went in and Peggy warmed the things she had bought and put away in the fridge a few days before. Lovely roast chicken, crunchy French bread she brought warm from the bakery oven, accompanied by freshly-made *pommes frites* and a really elegant, expensive white wine. Cheese and grapes served as the dessert.

While they ate slowly, Peggy asked Ian some of the questions she had written down, the first being why the FBI hadn't come to Owl's Head looking for Max. "After all," she said, "Owl's Head was the only place in America that Max knew anyone, right?"

"Yeah, I wondered that myself," said Ian, taking a deep drink of the lovely wine. "I interviewed the retired assistant to the Boston agent-in-charge. He said that after Kelly was killed, nobody was sure Max was even missing. Kelly's FBI sedan had entered the main gate of Fort Devens at twelve noon or a few minutes later.

"Then Kelly signed in to the PoW compound ten minutes after that. He left the PoW compound twenty minutes later and went out the main gate at twelve forty-five. I've confirmed all of this with old archives at the fort. The FBI guy that looked in to it concluded that Max had probably been dropped off in that period."

Peggy gave him a beaming smile, leaned across the table and planted a chicken-flavored kiss on his lips. "Ian MacDonald, world's greatest investigative reporter. Did the FBI follow-up with the army at Fort Devens?"

"They did. Devens said they didn't have any Max von Waldberg as far as they knew, but the MP officer they spoke with said that there was a great deal of confusion, what with the influx of PoWs from smaller camps in New England and the rush to get them back to Germany and Italy once the European war was over.

"After that, the assistant told me, the agent-in-charge ordered the matter be dropped. He told the investigating agent that as far as the FBI was concerned, Von Waldberg got checked in, and if the army lost him, that was not the FBI's concern. The fellow I interviewed also told me that by then Kelly's autopsy report was on the boss's desk, showing just how loaded Kelly had been at the time of death.

"According to my source, the agent-in-charge said, 'God help us if Hoover ever finds out anything went wrong after we let Kelly escort a prisoner alone!' — so the assistant buried the whole thing. How could the FBI search for a PoW that wasn't missing?" Ian said.

"What about Max's mother and grandmother? The women being held by the SS?" Peggy asked, pouring Ian another glass of wine.

"Well," Ian began, "that is one hell of a story. I found it by looking up sources about Kufstein, Austria — Max's home. It seems that as American armor approached Kufstein, the SS guarding Max's folks and the others simply took off after their commander fled. The prisoners, which included some high-ranking French generals, armed themselves with weapons abandoned by their former guards and awaited the arrival of the US Army.

"Another local SS commander, a real last-ditch diehard, decided to grab the prisoners and use them as hostages to obtain good surrender terms for him and his men. Well, then a real old-fashioned gun battle ensued, with the prisoners trying to fight off the SS long enough to allow Allied forces to arrive. Just in the nick of time, an American task force with a few tanks made it to the castle and joined the defence, but it was still touch and go.

"Finally, a large American unit with a lot of tanks arrived and the diehards fled. The rescue force was guided by members of the Austrian Resistance and assisted, believe it or not, by a group of regular German Army troops.

"This seems to have been the only time during the war when *Wehrmacht* troops joined with Allied forces to attack the SS. It's called the Battle of Castle Itter, a very obscure event in the history of the war."

"Wow, that is a great story!" Peggy said.

"Well, there was one sad occurrence. During the gunfight, Max's grandmother, Margarethe von

Kesselstein, died of a stroke or heart attack while firing at the SS. A witness said she looked like a Valkyrie, grey-blonde hair and ferocious blue eyes, toting a 98k rifle. It seems she picked off one of the enemy, a clean shot from over two hundred yards, then turned with a bright smile and collapsed."

"Oh, my," Peggy said, on the verge of tears. "Did Max ever know of this?"

"He must have, Peggy. His mother visited him after the war and she was present during the fighting, so she would have told him."

"My God," Peggy said. "This is going to be one hell of a book if I can fit it all in. I am so grateful to you for uncovering all of this."

Ian, a bit tipsy by now, said, "I've got one more titbit for you, if you want to hear it."

"Oh, please, Ian, don't tease."

"When I was at Fort Devens, I decided to visit the PoW cemetery on a hunch. Turns out PoWs who died in captivity from all over New England are buried there. Some remains were sent back to Europe after the war, but many were not.

"I found two *Luftwaffe* graves, with dates of death that seem to confirm Max's story. They were named, according to their grave markers, Gerhard Nordland and, wait for it, Hans Notke."

Ian sat back and sipped his wine.

"Oh, gosh, Ian. This is wonderful. The letters on the hat Ed Williams gave me were 'NOTK' and maybe two more. I'll bet it read 'Notke H'. I could have those names checked at the *Bundesarchiv*, I'm sure. All of this is powerful proof of Max's story. Thank you so much again, Ian. Now," Peggy said, moving her chair next to his, "I have a few things to tell you."

Forty minutes later, after she had told him everything, Ian sat at the table, utterly dumbfounded. Peggy giggled, kissed his cheek and said, "If you will put the dishes in the sink, I will meet you in the other room and we can talk some more, okay?"

Ian, shaking his head, was stacking the dishes and putting away leftovers when Peggy called out to him, "Ian, come quick, we've been robbed!"

Ian hurried to the bedroom to find Peggy, wearing a silky white bathrobe, pointing to the floor. The room was lit only by a small pink-shaded lamp and moonlight, so at first, he had trouble understanding what she meant.

"The rug, *our* rug, Max's bear, it's gone! Someone must have gotten in here and stolen it."

"Oh, no. Who could it have been?" he said. "Maybe the guy that gave you a ride here, the Forest Service guy. I'll go see him in the morning. I know what that rug meant to you, to both of us."

"Oh, wait, Ian, I think I found it." Peggy pulled back the quilt on Max's large bed, and there was the rug, draped over the sheets in all its furry, ferocious splendor. Simultaneously, she shrugged off the robe.

Peggy stood naked for a moment, gorgeous in the soft pink lamplight.

Then she snapped off the lamp and climbed onto the bed, her skin now blue-white in the moonlight. She lay on her back and patted the black fur next to her. "I didn't want to sleep in the bed because I was worried that Max died here, but the Forest Ranger told me they found him in that big chair in front of the VHS player. Care to join me?"

Ian obliged, shedding clothes in seconds, and began tickling Peggy. "That's what you get for tricking me," he said, pinching her bottom so hard she yipped.

Tickles led to caresses and kisses, kisses everywhere, until Peggy moaned and pulled him to her, babbling apologies to him as they rocked together, telling him over and over she loved him, a chant in rhythm with their movement. Their lovemaking reached its crescendo and Peggy cried out sharply. Ian stopped, listening intently. "What?" asked Peggy, breathing hard, wanting him to continue.

"Didn't you hear that?" Ian answered, moving with her again. "I thought I heard a wolf."

THE END